HELLO

You got my book!? That's awesome! I'm ecstatic that you want to read Creations! All I ask, is that you leave a review of how you felt about the book on Amazon, IBooks, Goodreads, Kobo, or any retailer that sells Creations. If you have the time all of these places would be amazing, but I know you're busy! But below, I've added a code for you to download my ebook, Creations, onto any e-reader device you own! I look forward to reading your reviews!

– Crystal C. John...

Go to smashwords.com and use the code BM32W for your free Creations ebook.

Creations
Copyright © 2017 by Crystal C. Johnson
Books In Bed Publishing
First print edition published 2017
Edited by Polished It
Alberta, Canada

ISBN-13: 978-1544144405
ISBN-10: 1544144407

CREATIONS

BOOK II

CRYSTAL C. JOHNSON

To DJ

I want to thank you. If it weren't for you asking me
when my books would be finished, who knows
when I would have finished them. I can't wait to
see what you create one day!

PROLOGUE

"Henly."

"Dad?" I stretch my tired limbs.

"How do you feel?" he asks, eyeing me.

"Good." I smile at him with confusion. "Why do you ask?"

He smiles back. "No reason."

He pulls something free from his pocket. "I brought you something." He hands me a tattered and torn book.

"*The Prince*? Really, Dad? You've read this to me a million times."

He shrugs his shoulders. "It is time you had your own copy. Get dressed. I have someone in the study I want you to meet."

I smile as he kisses my forehead and get out of bed. I walk to my dresser and place the book on my dresser. I turn to the mirror and stare. Letting my hair fall past my shoulders, I rub my eyes. Small flecks of emerald dance around my irises. I pull off my nightshirt and examine the white scars that cover most of my torso. The surgeries have gotten worse, and my memory hasn't gotten any better. The accident that took Davis is a blur of graphic photos my father has shown me. I throw on a pair of jeans and a white, long-sleeved T-shirt and meet my dad outside of my door.

We walk into his office, and I sit at his desk. As my father walks out to greet someone, I look across the room and spot a book that lies open on the shelf. I grab the book and flip through the pages. For some reason, I feel short of breath as I read the title: *The Alchemist*. I set down the book as my father walks back in. A tall man with dirty blond hair dressed in military clothes accompanies him. The strips of valor pinned to his shoulder, gives me the impression that he's someone important.

"Kiddo, I want you to meet the senator." He looks to the man. "Senator Renner, this is my daughter, Henly."

My body flinches when I hear the senator's name, like I've heard it somewhere before.

I extend my hand to the senator. "It is nice to meet you.

PART I

CHAPTER 1

HENLY

I trace the scar on my forearm with my fingers as the images burn into my memory. They gave me magazine clippings and newspaper cutouts to remind me of the cause. They all say the same thing: the mutations, the deviations, creatures transformed from the very vaccine that was supposed to save them, are attacking everything in sight. The violent images pour across the pages, each one more vivid than the last. They confuse me. The people in the photos look so normal, so ordinary. My father tells me it is something the Militaris has done, that they've engineered the perfect killing machines from the safety of their quarantines. We're trying to fix it, but they say I'm the only one who can. I'm different. I'm infected, but it didn't affect me like it did the others. It changed me, made me better. I'm stronger, more rational. I can analyze and think without emotion. My muscles and wounds heal quickly, and I have yet to find anything I can't do without ease. With all of these so-called "improvements," I have a hard time remembering who I used to be. The articles on the desk in front of me depict a different story.

"Sawyer!"

"Rathe?" I inch the papers into my desk and turn toward the door, waiting for her to burst through it.

"Hey! We have work to do." Her voice is excited.

This is the part I hate the most, the part where I'm forced to do my job. We capture those aligned with the Militaris, torture them, and if they don't respond, we're ordered to go as far as possible until they break. We need to know what they know. I'm told this is the only way, but I can't be sure it is. With every new captive, I'm reminded I'm Ana's daughter, especially when the research becomes more important than the person. The simple reminder that some part of her is still with me disturbs me more than it should. I don't remember much about her anymore, but her betrayal still stings.

"When do you go back under?" she asks, eyeing the clock above me.

"Tomorrow morning," I say as I trace the raised line on my collarbone.

The aches of my last surgery linger, but this is routine. I go in, they look at what the virus has perfected, and then they stitch me up. Then, they wait and see how fast I'll heal. Since I'm the only one who has adapted this way, there aren't very many people to test.

"Let's go."

"Thatta girl! We're going to Level Four." The elation in her voice is unwavering.

"Level Four?" *Did I just hear her right?*

Level Four is the final process; it's when we inject the captives with a configured version of the virus. Then, we chart them to see if and when they change. Lately, most of them have been dying, so there is not much to report.

"Yeah, Kellan had the girl you're about to work on in Level One, but she hasn't cracked. Doc's orders." She smiles. She knows I can't disobey my father's orders.

My dad went from being head surgeon to leading the cause. Well, he actually does both now. He and the senator have made it their mission to find a solution to what the Militaris has unleashed. We ride the elevator down in silence as I prepare myself for this. My dad trained Rathe and I specifically for this purpose. It is not their deaths that bother me so much, but rather the fact that their deaths produce no results. It is such a waste.

"Ladies."

"Kellan." I raise my brow in distaste.

"She is a spitfire," he says as his face lights up.

I force a smile, but don't cover my disdain.

"Sawyer, let's go." Rathe walks through the doorway.

When I walk in, the girl is barely conscious and overly exposed. The process up to this point is so brutal that, by the end, most of them are barely recognizable. I shake my head, letting out a small disapproving *tsk* while I pull up a white sheet to cover the majority of her exposed body. The brutality of the bruises that trail down her arms, torso, and legs are distracting. *Kellan has done his job too well.* She shifts her body and pulls at the straps that keep her tied down to the table. Opening her chart, I scan the list and see what they have exposed her to.

"I'll wire her," Rathe says.

Looking up from the chart, my eyes follow the wires to the case where all of the different colored vials sit, each one more potent than the last. Handing the chart to Rathe, I make my way to the shelf and grab a vial gun. On the shelf below it, a green vial sits next to several other different colored ones. My dad has been creating similar anecdotes that mirror the effects of the virus; we're trying to work out the kinks. So far, our attempts have been unsuccessful, but we're so close to finding the right strand. I feel it in my bones we're close. I walk over and place the needle of the gun against the girl's arm.

"Henly?" Her eyes barely open.

Something in my stomach clings to my spine. I jerk away, staring with a dumbfounded look. The distraction of her bruises have evaded and now she's a person again—not just flesh to experiment on.

Her breaths are shallow and uneven. "What are you doing here?" She winces as she sucks in another breath. "Get out of here. You need to go now!" she chokes out. Her voice barely rises above a loud whisper, but the veins that strain from her neck tell me she's trying to yell.

"What? How do you know my name?" I keep a steady eye on Rathe, who is across the room entering meaningless data.

"What?" she scoffs. "You can't be serious!"

My eyes narrow in confusion.

"You've got to be kidding me!" She flinches when she sucks in a breath. "If they didn't send you for me, then what the hell are you still doing here?"

"Who would send me for you?" My voice inches toward disgust.

I search my thoughts for her face and find similar ones, but all the images are contorted and blurry.

"Rathe, I need a minute," I say, staring at the girl who claims to know me.

"What? Now?" she replies with annoyance.

"Yes." My voice is loud as my head begins to throb.

She rolls her eyes and says with a deep exhale, "Fine, but make it quick."

There is a tradition only Rathe participates in—one that is gruesome and cruel and brings out the worst of mankind. When she is fed up with a prisoner who refuses to break, she goes the extra mile by cutting off extremities that are important to said prisoner. Male or female, she relishes in their screams. It gives her a sense of satisfaction when they break. My research ends when her abuse begins, and I refuse to be a part of it— there is no science to it, just cruelty. Anyone can beat a dog when it is down. So, when her vile traditions begin,

I excuse myself to the farthest room possible to drown out the screams.

Out of the corner of my eye, I see her shadow lingering. "I'm glad you're finally getting into the spirit of things. Enjoy!" she finishes in a high pitch singsong voice.

As soon as the door clicks shut, I rush to the door and slide the lock into place.

"You can't honestly tell me you're on their side?" The woman mutters.

I turn back to her she's the sick kind of frail. Even if I hadn't come she wouldn't last long. "Who are you, and how do you know my name?"

"Reina!" she yells, but I'm not sure if it is due to her pain or frustration.

Staring blankly at her, I wait for more.

"You're Henly Sawyer! We found you and brought you back to our compound!" She looks at me as if I should know what she's talking about. "Me, you, and Dex left to find your sister, Davis!"

I flinch a little when she mentions Davis. "You knew my sister?"

She shakes her head. "I *know* your sister. Think! Aurora, Renner, Dex, Ellie!"

"How do you know Davis?" I yell, feeling the harshness back in my tone.

Her eyes fall silent of accusations. "They really did it, didn't they? There were rumors they did this to people, but I can't believe he would do this to you..." she trails off as the door pounds, matching the same frantic rhythm of my heart.

I shake my head and feel the room blur. "Who did what? Spit it out! Fast!"

"He took them, took your memories!" she yells.

I try to think of who this girl could be, but I can't recall her. *I have all of my memories. I know who I am. Don't I?*

"Henly, open the door!" I hear the echoing thumps at the door, keeping pace with the thumps in my head.

The last thud forces me back to reality. "Stop saying you know me. If she, if *they* find out, it'll be a lot worse."

She scoffs. "For you, or for me?"

I raise my hand and thrust it into her already sore body. She lets out a tearful howl, and I swing my fists into her a few more times and cringe at the screams. It has to look believable.

I walk to the door in a haze, and everything seems so unreal. *Why don't I remember this girl who clearly remembers me?* With a click, the door unlocks.

"What's going on?"

"Doctor Royce?" *What is she doing here? She should be with my father in surgery at least for the next thirty minutes. She may be a friend, but I'm not sure how much I can trust her.* At this point anyone would be better than having Rathe here. "What are you doing here?" I ask, looking around behind her for Rathe.

"Rathe got called up to assist Dr. Sawyer. It'll be me and you."

She lingers in the hallway when I finally look up at the girl again. *I need to find a way to make sure no one knows she knows me.* "Let's start then."

"You want me to inject?" she asks as she walks through the doorway.

"Yes, I'll run the monitors." I hesitate, looking at the vial gun sitting next to her. "Give me a second to get ready," I say as I walk to the machines.

I set my hearing piece in place and wait for Royce to do the same to the girl named Reina. The more I try to think about who she is, the thicker the cloud becomes. *If she dies, I'll never know who she is, but if she lives, what will she expose?*

CHAPTER 2

RENNER

Henly's face appears to me like a ghost in a dream. She breaks through the crowd, and every time I try to fight my way to her. I stand, watching as her face contorts into pain when Andrew Sawyer digs his fingers deep into her torso, dangling her in front of the bullet that was meant for him. Steady streams of tears race down her checks as he drags her into the darkness. I fight harder, but my limbs turn sluggish, and I know that it is futile. I know how it ends. The nightmare always ends the same: I wake, and she is gone. With each day that passes, my paranoia of never seeing her again only fuels my desire to find her. I rise from the tangled sheets and see the exhaustion from sleepless nights of patrol and rescue missions in the dark circles underneath my eyes. When the steam of the shower fills the room, I close my eyes and let her drift from my mind to the edge of my memories.

After getting dressed, I leave my room. The faded gray brick walls of Aurora keep out the cold November air. I head down the hall to meet Hill in the medic unit. Honestly, nothing has been the same after Havre. Every time I walk into the medic unit, Ellie's absence is noticeable. It is different now with Hill taking charge and Quinn following behind. After my parents passed away, she took me in and, in her words, made sure I didn't become bitter. Even though I was old enough to take care of myself, I'm grateful she did. She and Quinn were the only family I had.

"You wanted to see me?" I ask Hill.

Hill looks up as I enter. He wears a heavy look of exhaustion. "Yes—" he coughs to clear his throat "—I found something." He grabs a folder and passes it across the table to me. "I know you don't want to involve Ana, but she could help move the process along a lot quicker."

"No." I shake my head.

When Hill was released from quarantine, he chose to be a medic. He spends most of his time looking through the files from Havre. Hill met Ana a year and a half ago. Since her return, Ana shares the same title, but under some restrictions. The only way she was allowed to live was by helping the quarantines find a cure. She said she would do whatever was in her power to change what she had done. At her trial, Davis's testimony helped. She had testified her father had done all of this and her mother was trying to keep her safe. I'm not sure I believe it, but the majority of the Board did, so she was allowed to live.

Hill rubs his face. His voice is distant when he says, "We're running out of time."

"Is it Tucker?"

I look over my shoulder to find Dex followed by Davis standing at the entrance.

Nodding a hello to Dex, I turn back to Hill and ask, "How's he doing?"

Hill shrugs. "He is getting better, but his blood is different than Henly's." He pushes away from his desk. "Renner, I don't want to run out of time, and I know that if Ana helps—"

"No," I say, cutting him off.

"Renner, my mom can help," Davis says softly.

Turning to Davis, I see Henly's necklace loosely draped around her neck. Dex had told me that when they were stuck in Havre, Henly had given the necklace to Davis to show her she was real. Somehow, they've all forgotten how Ana's involvement placed both of their lives in danger. When I turn, I find Ana leaning against the door with one eyebrow arched.

"I see you've inherited your stubbornness."

She talks about me like she knows me. My eyes narrow as I turn from Davis to Dex and then back to Hill. "You've already asked for her help?" When I look back to Dex, his face is confused and angered.

Without another word, I leave, but not before I glance at the pearl pendant—a gift returned to its original owner. It is a cruel reminder she is gone.

"Wait." Davis's voice is soft as it barely reaches me down the hall.

I turn to face her and ask, "Is there something else?"

"Here—" her fingers slip to her neck "—you should keep this."

"No, she would want you to keep it." I stare at her extended hand, the pearl hanging from it. I won't be softened by this gesture, not so they can have their way.

She reaches for my hand and places the necklace inside of it. "No, I don't think so. Dex tells me stories about you two, how you kept her safe, how you took care of her." Closing my fingers, she finishes, "I know that you're still trying to keep her safe, but Ana can help. I promise she can."

For a second, I narrow my eyes. I drop my arm to my side, feeling a piece of the chain fall away from me. My fist tightens around the pendant as if in some way it will protect Henly from her mom. The irony is she doesn't need protection from Ana—not anymore.

"How can you trust her after everything she has done?" I ask this more to myself than to Davis.

Davis shrugs her shoulders. "Renner, my mother's only fault is being weak to her ambition."

Though the two look nothing alike, I find Henly in those words. Henly often spoke of her father that way, as if she had to defend him, protect him. Davis does the same with Ana. It must be a Sawyer thing. In some way, their parents leaving them alone has made them stronger, better. Though, I would never say it aloud; their parents don't deserve credit for their strength.

"Fine, but don't corner me like that ever again," I respond.

"Dex didn't know either." She looks away.

Looking past her, I see Dex talking to Hill. The two of them have grown close. "Okay."

I watch as she turns away and walks toward Dex. The pendant burns against my palm. Unable to look at it again, I push the pendant in my pocket and continue down the hall.

* * *

It is just before dawn when I meet Dex outside of the training center. In the middle of the night, Dex got word that there was activity in Bowden. Some of Drew's people were seen gathering those who are not infected. It is strange to see their efforts be so successful. I don't know if they are being brave or reckless. Their odds of surviving against the deviations are low, and now faced with Andrew, the odds don't seem to be getting any better. Andrew needs more of them each day, and if we don't find them first, I have no doubt in my mind that he will eradicate the whole human population.

We make our way down to Ave 5. The Nevada quarters are filled with the overflow from California.

"Quinn?"

"Yeah, one sec!" she responds.

Dex slings his pack onto his back, and he seems surprised when he looks up. I turn to see what has caught his attention.

"Where the hell are you off to?" Zoe points to the three of us.

"What do you want?" I rub my forehead in agitation.

"Are you authorized?" She glares back at me.

"Yes," I say, my patience wearing thin. "Look, I don't have time for this."

Zoe is one of the only childhood friends I have left. We grew up down the street from each other, and it was always easy with her, which is why we stayed friends. We shared the same loss of our best friend Kenton and leaned on each other when we needed it, but things change. Now, she wants more, and I can't give her that. Without validating her, I turn away.

"Renner, she's dead!" Zoe shouts. "You brought her body back!"

I stop cold in my tracks, my back straightens, and my jaw hardens. It has been more than a year since I saw the body of what was supposed to be her. Dex and I went out every chance we got. It didn't matter the time or the day, we were out searching for Henly. When we weren't searching, we were here planning and mapping out all of the places that she could be.

One day, we had decided to go back to Havre—the place where she had last been. When we landed, there weren't any signs of life, just bodies sprawled across the grounds of the hospital from the last time we were there. When we went inside, we split up and searched every single room, but there was no sign of her anywhere. As I was walking out of the hospital, Dex's voice blared across the radio. He kept telling me to run, to hurry. I wish I would have taken my time, but I didn't. I ran as fast as I could, and by the time I got there, Dex had pulled out a black body bag. Fear coursed through me as I pushed past him.

"Don't," he said.

But I ignored his warnings and unzipped it, and there she was. Her face was bruised and blue, and her eyes lay open, staring straight up into the sky. The same vibrant, green eyes that once had so much fight were now lifeless. I took her face in my hands and felt the coldness of the soil move through her and into me. In that moment, I was cold as she was. I forced my eyes to stay open and stared at the grave her father had created for her. I memorized it. I had to, so that when I saw Andrew again he would pay for what he did to Henly. She didn't deserve this ending. I zipped the bag closed and turned away from her. She died alone, and they left her here for the worms to keep her company. I stood there for a while, not knowing what would come next.

All I knew was that my year and a half journey to find Henly had been in vain. I didn't get to her before Andrew did.

We flew her body back to Aurora. Quinn started her tests to see what had been done to her. The days that followed were dark. I blamed myself for her death. I left her behind to save lives, but it didn't turn out that way. I never would have guessed that Andrew would blow up the hospital in Havre. The guilt of leaving her alone never left, but when her body surfaced, and I saw the bruises along her face, along her body, it was crippling. I swore in those dark hours if she were really dead, I would make her father pay for everything he had done to her and Davis. I would make it right, no matter what lengths I would have to go to. After hours and days of destroying everything in my path, I met with Dex and Quinn. The ache in my chest only subsided when Quinn told us the bodies had similarities, but they weren't exactly the same. Quinn's mom, Ellie, had done Henly's examination when she first was admitted into Aurora, and luckily, Quinn knew where her mother had placed the original charts.

"They made a double," she had said. "They want us to think she is dead."

"Why?" I had asked in disbelief. The possibility of her being alive was something I had only imagined in my dreams.

"So we would stop looking for her," Quinn had said.

"Are you sure?" I had asked as I stared at the pictures that looked unmistakably like Henly.

"Not one hundred percent…"

"How certain are you?" I had demanded. On the outside, I tried to remain composed, but on the inside I felt lighter. This new revelation was what I needed to feel less guilty, and my hope was like a drug that kept me going.

"Ninety percent."

"Good enough," Dex had said, speaking quicker than the words could leave my mouth.

The memory of that day still stings, and I hate that Zoe uses it to get a reaction out of me. She was present when we brought her body back, and she damn well knows how it hurts me. What she doesn't know—what no one else, except for Davis, knows—is what Quinn found. We figured that there would be too much to explain that we couldn't. There is no time to argue with her, so I simply walk past her and feel Dex and

Quinn follow.

We get to the helicopter pad in a matter of minutes. As we board, I signal the pilot to start the engine, and then we are off.

"You all right?" Dex asks as he looks out the window.

I nod my head and stay silent. A part of me clings to the idea she is still alive, but the other part of me knows that the ten percent might be more realistic than I want it to be. The thought is heavy.

"How's Davis doing?" I hear Quinn ask Dex.

"Good. She likes working in the labs. Adam says she is a great researcher."

"And Ana?" she asks hesitantly, her eyes briefly locking with mine.

"I don't know." Dex shrugs with distaste.

Ever since Dex found them in the hospital, he makes an effort to make Ana's life hell, except for when Davis is around. He and Davis have found comfort in each other. They both lost family, and they find it easy to distract one another with whatever task they put together.

"Davis knows Henly is alive," Dex responds. He knows how deeply her confirmation hits me. "She knows her dad would never let anything bad happen to her."

"I know," I say.

"We'll find her," Quinn reassures us.

"Where are we headed?" I ask them. I hope changing the subject will relieve the nagging feeling that has started to form in the back of my mind. I fear that another body like hers will surface; though this time, it will actually be her. I also worry that we will never find her unless her dad wants her to be found.

Dex untangles the map from his pack. "Here—" he points north toward the quarantine in Calgary "—there was some activity there last week. We'll scout it out and see what we can find. We'll stay there tonight and head back out tomorrow afternoon."

CHAPTER 3

HENLY

I watch from the gallery above the operating room as her shoulders tense and her eyes search the blank air for someone. Doctor Royce looks up at me and flashes me the signal to go ahead and start. A deep shudder runs through my body before I begin. Her eyes flutter, and I see them search the darkness of her eyelids as the serum begins to work through her system.

"Can you hear me?" I ask as I focus on her vitals on the screen.

"Henly?" she murmurs.

"How do you feel?"

"Tired," she responds. "What are you doing to me?" She screams as her body distorts and seizes against her restraints.

"I'm testing a new strand of the virus on your body...to see how your ailments are affected when the strand is engaged. How do you feel now?" I say through the mouthpiece as I gesture to Royce to inject the strand.

"Henly! What are you doing to me? Stop!" she yells as she pulls against her restraints. "No, you can't,

Henly! Stop! You're not like this!" she shouts. Her voice is frantic. "Henly, you and Renner—ah!"

My eyes widen when Royce looks away from the girl named Reina to stare at me. "Her pain levels are increasing. If we're going to continue—"

"No," I say, knowing that we need her make it through the rest of the injections. "Wait."

Doctor Royce sets down the vial.

"How do you know me?" I ask, even though I have heard the story.

"We found you!" she screams. "Henly, stop! Please, it is burning." Her body quakes and thrashes against the straps.

"I will soon if you hurry and tell me how," I lie. I know she won't make it much longer, but this is what I am good for—giving false hope to those who have no chance of surviving. Rathe tortures them, and I make them trust me, but only to kill them. What weighs on my conscience is how satisfied I am with every experiment. Each one takes us another step closer to our desired outcome: perfection.

"Ah! I'm Reina. I met you when we found you and Renner in Great Falls!"

"Renner? Why would the senator be there with

me?" I respond, and my eyes lock on Royce's. Her expressions are carefully masked, except for one flinch at the senator's name.

"I don't know! He loved—loves you! You loved him! And Dex...they were your family!" she screams. "You don't belong here! You belong—"

I pull off the headset and, without hesitation, head toward the stairs. I make the dissent quickly, flinging open the operating room door, and grab the needle from Royce. I stick it into the girl's body.

"I won't listen to your lies, traitor," I whisper in her ear. "You're one of the reasons why I'm not where I belong! You took them away, and now, I'm going to take everything from you."

She tenses beneath me. "Do me a favor...ah...when you see Vi...if you see her again, don't tell her how this ended. Don't tell her you killed me...ah! She doesn't deserve to know!"

I turn away from her, but her words echo, ringing in my ears. Squeezing my eyes shut, I burry my face into my hands. Confusion pulls at my sanity as I try to make sense of what just happened and of how I just killed her. After the ringing stops, Royce authorizes me to take her off the ventilator and watch as her vitals stop jumping and flatten into a straight line. Leaning against the wall, I take out my earpiece and sit back. Royce leans beside me. She has been my confidant since I woke up here, someone I can talk to. She is my dad's age. Her short blond hair is cropped and smoothed nicely. Her eyes are as blue as the huckleberries back home, and most days, she is the only person I can trust.

"You all right?"

I nod my head. "Are you going to tell my dad?"

She shakes her head no. "Did you know her?"

Suddenly, it becomes hard to swallow. I didn't know her. I have never seen her, but still something eats at me.

"What are you thinking?" Royce asks, interrupting my thoughts.

"Nothing," I finally say, trying to mask the insecurity I feel inside.

"Henly, that wasn't nothing. Who was she?" she replies as she stares at the data on the screen above us.

"I don't know." I rub my forehead against the inside of my hand. "Everything is so confusing. The more I try to remember who she was or the stories she was telling me, the harder it becomes for me to remember anything."

"So, you don't know who she was?"

"No…" There is something in Royce's expression that gives me the feeling I should know who she was. "Do you? Am I supposed to know who she was?"

"I don't know her. They brought her in from our facility in Havre." She stares at me, still trying to read my expression.

"So, she was no one? Just another traitor spouting their lies?" I stare at her body on the slab a few feet away from me.

After my first experiment, I told my dad there were other ways. I wasn't even able to finish the session. Rationally torturing someone to death didn't seem like the right way, but I was wrong. My father convinced me this was the only way. At the beginning, he forced me to watch it, to watch what he did to the boy who was aligned with the wrong side. It was my lesson. It was a lesson I had learned fairly quickly: don't attach yourself to the experiment. They're here for one purpose alone and that is to test them to see what we can learn from them—nothing more.

I print the results of the session and lay them on the counter. I watch Royce submit a false report, stating the girl died from the virus.

"He won't find out, right?" I ask, remembering the boy who was used as my lesson.

"Not by me, and not by this report," she responds.

She heads for the door, and I watch her leave. I stare at the lifeless body again. *I killed her.* Her face will swim among the others who drown me in my sleep. They all haunt me, but there is one face that serves as peace when my fear is stifling. He keeps me afloat, from becoming a blur in all of the commotion of war. Every time we are out on patrol or at a rally, I look for his face among the sea of people, but no one ever comes close. His features are so jarring that every time I see him in my dreams, it takes me a minute to regain my composure.

"Sawyer!" I turn to see Vaughn, Royce's son. "Let's go."

I take one last glance at the girl and then turn away. I feel an odd sting in my throat. I swallow the lump and leave her to Kellan. If he does his job correctly, he will dispose of her quickly, and that will be the end of it.

I follow Vaughn out of the makeshift hospital and into the yard where we were ordered to take over patrol for two other soldiers. We climb the stairs to the roof, and I take in the vastness of the mountains, the way they peak and fall into each other. A fresh layer of snow covers the ground, and the cold Alaskan air burns as it makes its way into my lungs. The cold makes me miss Denver. I try to picture what it would look like this time of year, but my absence has made remembering hard. It feels like some distant place that I saw once in a movie. I wonder what became of my friends when everything hit.

"Hey, you all right?" Vaughn asks me.

"Yeah," I reply hesitantly.

"Are you still thinking about what the girl said?"

"The girl?" I whisper.

"My mom told me what happened."

Dr. Lily Royce, Vaughn's mom, rarely keeps anything from her son. Vaughn said after they lost his father, they became closer than ever. I guess that's what happens when you lose someone or something you love: you cling to whatever you have left.

"Oh…no. I don't know. Yes." I feel as confused as I sound.

He stands across from me. His short, disheveled hair is lightly kissed with the same blond as his mother's. Their blond hair is the only way someone would know they were mother and son since they don't even share the same last name; taking someone else's last name is not something Dr. Royce would do.

"What are you doing tomorrow?" he asks. The stubble around his jaw and cheekbones makes him look rugged and brawny. His blue eyes stare up at the splotches of white in the sky that seem to be moving with the breeze.

"Surgery," I say with dread. Surgery means I will be out of commission and stuck in my room for days doing tedious research and recovery, waiting for my wounds to heal.

"What if I could get you out of it?" he teases.

"Why would you do that?" I smile.

"You need a break, Sawyer. Look at you. Some girl strolls in and now you're confused."

"I know what happened, Vaughn." I pause before I continue, "I know she's lying."

"But you have doubts?" his gaze studies me.

"Sometimes I do when I can't remember anything, and then today…" I trail off and think about the names she kept repeating—Dex, Renner, and Davis. I've told Royce that some nights I have dreams of people with these names, but they're strangers. This girl Reina sounded so confident, so determined, that for a brief moment, all of those people came bounding out of my dreams and made sense, yet they didn't.

"If I am who my dad says I am, then why is everything so confusing?" I ask.

"If she wasn't lying and she knew something, then why did you kill her?" he asks as he approaches me.

I stare past him toward the mountains. *I killed her. I killed the girl who could have been the only person who could have answered all of my riddles.* The worst part is regretting something so definite it cannot be changed or undone.

"I had to." I keep my eyes locked on the snowflakes that fall around us. At the time, the fear of what I didn't know outweighed any curiosity about what she was saying.

"No, you didn't. You had a choice, and you made it. Why?" His voice isn't angry or accusing, it is probing.

"She made me doubt my dad. She put everything he has said into question."

His eyes narrow as if trying to understand, but then he gives up. He closes the distance and wraps his arms around me. He tries to make the embrace comforting, but it falls short. "I'll help you figure it out."

"You'll be in more trouble than I will if my dad finds out," I whisper.

He lifts my chin and lightly brushes his lips to mine. "Eh, it'll be fun."

He smiles as he retreats back to his post, and I wonder if he ever takes anything seriously.

* * *

"Hey."

I wake with a jolt when I notice Vaughn standing at the edge of my bed.

"You talk in your sleep," he says.

I throw my pillow at him and rollover. "Go away!"

I feel the pillow crash back into my head. "Get up. We're leaving."

"No, go away. I have surgery soon," I

grumble.

"Not today. Hurry up," he responds.

I sit up without a second thought and change into my clothes. With one foot out of the door, he stands as a lookout while I pack everything.

"Ready," I say.

He glances over his shoulder to one of the photographs that was taken of my father and me. "When did you take this?"

"A few weeks ago at the Anchorage facility."

"It's a good picture of you." He unsticks it from the wall and slides it into my pocket. "You should always have a memento when you leave home. It's good luck," he says, his smile mischievous.

"What are you up to?" I ask, knowing that when he smiles *that* smile it never amounts to anything good.

"Why would I be up to anything?" he asks sarcastically and then disappears around the corner.

He is definitely up to something.

Once, he convinced me it would cheer me up if we went hiking. I had been in and out of surgery that month more than I had actually been healthy. On our dissent, my latest stitches tore open, and I almost bled to death. Luckily for us, we had parked the car nearby. My father was furious when we made it into the clinic. Vaughn made up a lie that I had fallen down a flight of stairs due to the lingering side effects of my painkillers. He painted such a vivid picture of me falling that my father decided to lower my dosage, which backfired. The original dosage was barely keeping the pain away.

His lies are always convincing, unlike mine that require a lot more foresight and detail. He always has an idiotic plan with the potential for catatonic results, but I can never help myself. He is a fresh breath of recklessness, and it is intriguing.

He gets so close to me that I can feel the heat of his body radiate against mine, and then, he kisses me. Before I have a chance to question his motives, we are walking down the corridor and out into the open where the helicopters are roaring to life. I see my dad a few yards away talking to the senator.

"Dad!" I call out.

"Kiddo!" he yells back as he excuses himself from the senator.

"You postponed surgery?" I ask.

"Your friends have convinced me it would be good for you to get a little break."

I follow his gaze to Vaughn, who is in a deep

conversation with Rathe.

"Right…"

Vaughn looks away from Rathe and flashes me a grin.

"He likes you, you know," my dad teases.

"Really? We're going to do this now?" I reply as I stare at the ground.

My dad laughs. "I'm just saying. I see the two of you. I've got ears and eyes in this place." He shrugs his shoulders. "He gets what's important. He knows what we're trying to do, and he gets it."

"Which is?" I ask.

"You." He smiles as he gently rubs my shoulders. "You're important, Hen, and we're going to change the world." He pauses to take a breath. "I approve if that matters any."

My cheeks burn as I exhale. "Where am I heading?" My dad wouldn't send me anywhere unless he knew he could, in some sense, control the situation.

"A rally."

I press my lips together, letting it sink in. "We're collecting more for research?"

"Yes, we need a small collection of deviations as well. Kellan is in charge of that."

"Is that it?" I ask, knowing that my father's way of collecting specimens is less than honorable.

"The senator will be there. Just put on a good face, okay?"

"A rally? That's how you disguised it this time?" I ask slightly disgusted.

"Henly, we've talked about this," he responds.

"I know. We do what is necessary."

"Good. Make sure to try out the modifications on the deviations, but don't get too close."

"I'll try," I whisper.

"Love you, kiddo." He kisses my forehead.

"Love you too." I turn to the helicopter.

I feel irritated thinking about his notion of what is *necessary*. I've been to a rally before, and it is the way we gather the uninfected that should haunt me. A few weeks before we go in, we send someone to spread the word that we are coming with water and food. When we finally arrive, we stand around and make sure the crowd stays under control. When a substantial group gathers, we unleash the deviations and promise the people a safe place, safer than the quarantines of the Militaris. Then, we take them to different facilities. They never know what's going to happen to them, but I do. I know what happens to each and every one of them.

CHAPTER 4

RENNER

We land in Bowden late, and through the illuminated sky, the earth is tinted white in a thin layer of snow. Bowden is just how I remembered it, except the greenery from the summer has evolved into frozen thorns that shield a majority of the quarantine. The frosted vines tangle up the walls and blend into the marbled mixture of snow and dirt. If you didn't know what you were looking for, you would miss it. We enter through the hatch that leads us underground to the heart of Bowden. We are led to our over night quarters and spend the rest of the evening discussing tomorrow's tactics.

Sleep has evaded me; my mind is too focused on everything that has happened. From the world going to shit, to Henly's disappearance, and now searching for Andrew to kill him consumes me. I walk around the quarantine. I feel like I'm in an ant colony, the hallways constructing an intricate maze. The walls have some distant feeling of familiarity. Before my parents died, we traveled to all ten of the quarantines in North America. Bowden was the last place I had been with both parents, the last time the Renner's were a family. As I walk through these halls, the memory seems so different, like something I have read or seen. I have done well on my own for so long that it feels like this is how it has always been—but it wasn't. After their deaths, I would wake and think they were in the next room, but in reality, I was alone in a huge apartment that was made for a member of the Board of Governors and his family. The space was too much for a teenager who rarely used it, so I opted for a smaller one in Ave 3. The small space suits me more. I have thought about going back to the apartment, but always decide against it. There is no point rummaging through the past.

I take a quick right, which leads me to a door that takes me outside of the quarantine across from the bridge that connects to a train station. Pulling up my coat, I walk over to the bridge. Below me, a train is parked, while another approaches from the north. When it pulls to a quiet halt, Militaris soldiers file in and out of the train before it jets off to a new location. From where I stand, if you pay attention, you can hear the shuffle and cries of the deviations. They have found a way to communicate. It is strange how they have adapted. They are alive, full of rage and a strange desire to kill, and now they can communicate with one another. I don't know if it was the Sawyers' original plan to keep the deviations somewhat human. Ana denies any allegation that this is what they wanted, but Hill and Adam believe otherwise. My feelings about Ana aside, I believe her. She went out with the gatherers once, and on their report, they had written about her fascination with the way the deviations have evolved. She too wrote about her fascination.

"Renner."

I turn to find Dex a few feet behind me. "Hey," I say to him.

"Creepy, isn't it?" He points to the city ahead of us.

I nod in agreement. "Yeah."

Turning his attention toward the incoming train, he asks, "What are they doing?"

"They go into the city at night to set the traps. At daybreak, they go in and collect them."

"Traps?"

"The deviations. When they're finished securing the deviations, they go around and deliver supplies to ensure everyone who opted out of coming to the quarantine is taken care of."

"Crazy," he responds.

"What? The traps?"

"No, that people opt out of being in a quarantine."

"Some people think the quarantines are trying to control them. It always depends on the facility. Some make them stay, while others give them the choice. Bowden is one that lets the people choose whether they stay out there or come in."

Quinn approaches us, accompanied by a Militaris soldier.

"We found someone who knows something. We're holding them in the interrogation room," the squad leader says.

"Ready?" Quinn asks, looking back and forth between Dex and me.

We turn and follow Quinn back into the quarantine. When we arrive, a Militaris soldier is standing outside of the room.

"He fought us, so we had to knock him out."

The boy with ashy skin is sprawled across the floor. His black hair covers the top of his face; the rest is covered with dirt. He looks young, not much older than fourteen or fifteen.

"Okay, we'll wait," I say as I walk into the room and sit on the other side of the two-way mirror.

Dex elbows me. "Zoe is here. She wants to talk to you. She is waiting outside." He stares at the door.

Quinn takes a seat next to me. "Go. We'll keep an eye on him," she says.

She can't take a hint, or in her case, a loud message. My hands grip each side of the chair as I force myself up and then into the hallway. When Zoe sees me, she stops pacing.

"What are you doing here?" I challenge.

Her face pinches together. "What do you think, Renner?" She hands me the paper in her hand. "The mission is unauthorized!"

I crumple the paper in my hands. "Zoe, I'm a member of the Board, the head actually. I don't need to have the Council authorize anything." I hand her back the crumpled paper. "Go home."

Before I can hear another word, I walk back into the room.

"Perfect timing," Dex greets. "Our friend is awake."

Without a second's hesitation, I go into the room. The boy rubs his eyes and looks around the small room. He realizes quickly he isn't home, but rather in an interrogation room. I watch as this all sets in.

"Where am I?" he asks.

"Doesn't matter," I reply. "What's the doctor up to?"

He shakes his head in confusion. "What?" A hint of fear is in his voice.

"Are you with them?" I ask the question already knowing he is, but I want him to confirm that for myself. *He doesn't look older than sixteen, and they have him out here doing...what?*

"I was with them, but I'm not anymore. What do you want from me?" he asks, his voice shaky and uneven.

"I want to know what Drew Sawyer is up to," I demand.

"Who?"

"Andrew Sawyer!" I yell, losing what was left of my control.

He shakes his head back and forth. "You want to know about the doc?"

"And his daughter."

"His daughter?" He looks around the room with confusion.

"Yes."

"The girl that died?"

"What?" I snap, suddenly caught off guard.

"His daughter...she is dead...she died a while ago," he says as he looks nervously at the camera above me.

"No, she didn't! She is still alive! Where is she?" I know I am yelling, but I can't help it.

There is a knock at the door. When it opens, Dex steps through, a grim look on his face.

"What?" I shout.

"Can I see you in the hallway?" he asks.

"No."

"Hallway, please." His eyes narrow at me.

Briefly, I close my eyes, and with a sigh, I follow him out. "What?" I ask with irritation.

"You're losing it. He isn't going to tell you anything. The more that you need to know, the more he has to bargain with," Dex prompts.

"He is lying. I know he is," I reply.

"I agree." Dex looks at the door when he says, "Let me finish. I'll get the information we need."

I am reluctant to let him finish, but if this is how I find Andrew, I'll do it. I walk into the adjacent room and see Zoe standing next to Quinn, staring into the interrogation room. When I stand next to her, she stays silent, and we watch Dex interrogate the boy.

"Sorry about that," Dex says to the boy.

The boy shakes his head and shrugs his shoulder. "Who is she to him?"

"A friend," Dex replies.

"She *is* dead. I-I-I saw it with my own eyes," he stutters.

"Did you see her or a picture of her?" Dex asks as he tries to catch the boy in a lie. He pulls out a chair across from the boy and takes a seat.

"A picture. It was proof she was dead," he responds quickly.

Dex becomes skeptical. "I thought you aren't with them?"

"Not anymore. They sent me here to spread the word."

"Spread the word about what?"

He looks back and forth and then straight at Dex. "I'll tell you whatever you want to know, but you have to guarantee I can stay here—" he swallows hard "—that you won't make me go back."

"Why?" Dex asks. "Why don't you want to go

back?"

"They do things to you. Experiments." His hands tremble against the table.

"What do you mean?" Dex asks hesitantly. "He experiments on the deviations?"

The boy shakes his head. "No, not until I know I'm safe here away from them."

Dex looks at us through the mirror then back to the boy. "You can stay for as long as you want."

"I need it in writing," he insists.

"It doesn't work like that. You can stay, or you can go. It is your choice," Dex responds.

"You won't force me to go?"

"No."

The boy exhales before he begins, "They're coming for more people. I don't know when, but soon. They do this every time they need people. They go to cities and rally all the people who have refused the help from the quarantines and promise to help them. They round them up into a small location, unleash the deviations, and then make them choose. They either go with them, or stay and get ripped apart."

Dex leans back in his chair. "How do you know this?" he asks.

"That's how they got me and my family." He looks like he is about to cry. He is just a child.

"When? Where?"

"About a year ago outside of Havre. They separated us, and I ended up in a facility in Alaska."

"If we gave you a map, could you point out the location?" Dex asks calmly, but quickly.

The boy nods.

Is that where he could have taken her? After all of these months spent in turmoil searching for her, I finally feel like I'm close. I know she is not dead. But even with the notion she is alive, there is still something that tugs at me that I can't explain. It is a mixture of desperation and angst.

"They separate them?" Quinn whispers to me. "How many facilities do they have?"

Looking at Quinn, I realize I need to think beyond Henly at the moment. "Drew can't be doing this alone. Someone has to be helping him."

"But who? Ana is with us," Quinn concedes.

"Yeah, but that doesn't mean she wouldn't know who could be helping him," I say.

"Your friend is gone," the boy talking to Dex blurts out.

When I look up, the boy is staring at the glass.

Gone?

"What do you mean?" Dex asks, capturing his attention again.

"You never really know what to believe when you're in there. The doc made this huge scene. He told everyone she was a traitor and all those who betray him will suffer. It is his way of keeping the rest of us in line. They make you guys look like the bad ones, blame you for the deviations and all of the deaths. He promises safety, but for a price. Though, we're all expendable, even she was. But there were rumors he didn't kill her and that he changed who she was, wiped away her memories. If she is alive, she isn't the same person anymore."

"What else?" Dex coaxes.

The boy shakes his head as if he doesn't really remember either. "Some say she helps him, that she is in charge of the experiments. Others say she is perfect, and he experiments on her. Most say she is dead." He pauses, looking at the glass. "I haven't ever seen her, only her body."

"That's why he needs more people," Dex says almost inaudibly. "He is experimenting."

"I guess so," the boy says barely above a whisper.

I look at Quinn and suddenly feel sick. *Henly wouldn't—she couldn't—be capable of the same monstrosities as her parents. Or could she?* The distant memory of our time at the compound in Montana reminds me of her own fears. She was afraid she would turn out like her mother, and though I would never tell her, I saw how, at times, she could be just as cold and calculated as Ana. *If her father has found a way to strip her of who she was, could she be capable of helping him?* A thought hits me: *Could she be staying there on her own free will?*

"We have activity downtown," Ferruli, one of our fellow Militaris soldiers, says to Dex as he opens the interrogation room door.

"They said they would be here in a few days," the boy says, and the way his voice trembles makes him sound scared.

"When did they drop you off?" Dex asks.

"Four days ago. They're here," he says, his eyes frantic.

Without hesitation, I walk into the interrogation room and ask, "Is she there?"

Ferruli shrugs his shoulders. "I don't know, but if we want to catch them in time, we have to go now."

I look up at the kid who is terrified and say, "Zoe, take him down to quarantine and have him vetted. Make sure we know everything he knows and then set him up in a room." I don't wait for her response.

When I turn, Quinn and Ferruli are running down the hallway to meet up with the rest of the soldiers from my unit, Johnson and Riddle. Solie, our pilot, comes from behind me and tosses Dex and me our packs with our weapons.

"Ready?" Dex asks.

"Let's go," I reply.

CHAPTER 5

HENLY

The ground is frozen into a thick pile of ice and snow. My boots sink with every step I take toward the makeshift stage setup. Looking around, I see a crowd is gathering and my collar suddenly seems too tight. If only I could warn them, tell them to run while they still have a chance. But, if I do, we won't be able to further the process of finding a cure. There is a loud echo to my right, and I catch the senator in the corner going over his lines, trying to invoke action. Every little noise has me on edge.

"Is this really a good idea?" I ask. "We're in the middle of a Militaris area."

Vaughn nods. "There is more of an incentive to do it here."

"It's suicide," I say.

"I thought you wanted to have fun," he replies playfully.

"How did you get my dad to agree to this anyway?" I ask quizzically.

"I have my ways." He smiles mischievously.

"He likes you. He gave me the 'okay' today," I

say.

He laughs. "Oh, I feel so honored," he says sarcastically. "I could not care less about your dad's approval. Just yours."

I force a smile. I'm not sure what I feel, nonetheless what to say.

He pushes me playfully. "Relax, Sawyer. I don't need to know it now. C'mon, let's get out of the cold."

He pulls me into a red brick building where people pass around weapons and food. Some faces are familiar, but most of them are strangers.

"The senator is giving the speech today?" I ask, looking around the room.

"Yeah." He rolls his eyes.

"Wow. You? Questioning authority?" I respond to his eye roll.

"History," he says and turns his gaze out the window to the stage.

History? I don't press it, letting it go, I ask, "What time is this starting?"

He motions to the poorly built stage. "Now. You ready?" he asks more seriously.

I look past him and see the people gathering

around the stage. As it begins, the crowd watches and cheers as Senator Renner takes the stage. They know him, probably from the messenger we sent a few days ago. Whoever has been spreading the rumors has done a good job; they adore him. The soldiers stand and keep watch. My father is not even here to prove with science—actual facts what is happening, and they consume every word the senator says as if he were their last hope. I am astonished by how far their adoration stretches for him.

"Idiots," I say under my breath.

"Watch your tongue, little Sawyer. We may be friends, but I won't hesitate to keep you in line." Rathe turns and flashes me a warning glance.

"Lighten up, Rathe," Vaughn says.

I scoff at her loose interpretation of our relationship. We are as close of friends as a lamb is with a lion. My father has Rathe under his thumb, which, through association, is another way for him to watch after me. His orders alone are the only ones she follows.

"Heard what you did to the girl in training the other day." She throws a left hook to the invisible body in front of her. "It's about time."

I don't respond. Even the slightest inclination

that she thinks I enjoyed it as much as she does makes me sick. I leave her behind and walk away with Vaughn.

"Idiots, huh?" Vaughn says to me as if questioning my statement.

"No." I shake my head, realizing I may have voiced my opinion too loudly. *I just don't understand why anyone would follow my dad so blindly. Why do I follow him so blindly?*

"Sawyer, if you could change things, would you?" Vaughn asks.

I look at him perplexedly. "Of course, that's what this is all for."

"No, I mean, if you could end the surgeries and live a normal life, would you?"

Living a normal life will never be a part of my story. I will always be this creature, perfected for the purpose to save humanity. Before I can answer, there is a whipping noise in the distance that sounds like blades slicing through the air. Turning my head, I look in the direction of the noise, but nothing is visible until it's too late. "What is that?" I ask.

He looks up when the crash shakes the earth. His playful demeanor shifts to something more serious. I follow his gaze to the helicopters in the distance. They're here. I turn to Vaughn, who has already taken off toward the stage and hear a clear loud voice.

"The militaris, they're here! Sawyer, get a move on it!" I hear Rathe yell over the crowd. "Get to the chopper."

I search the crowd for Vaughn, but know I'm better off without him. I run at a full sprint and dive at the last minute to take cover. A mixture of bullets and snow shower down on the people around me. In the distance, I see Vaughn and Rathe protecting the senator when, out of nowhere, the senator falls. He doesn't move. My eyes widen in horror when Vaughn shakes his head and tries to make Rathe move away and leave The Senator, but Rathe won't. She grabs onto the senator and drags him to the chopper. Between glances to the helicopter and Rathe, I catch Vaughn shake his head no. I turn in time to see the Militaris file off the helicopters that quickly come into focus one by one. Suddenly, my throat feels hoarse when I see them. The hazel eyes that torment me in my dreams. He stands tall, like a ray of sun in the midst of a gloomy snowstorm. Blinking, I notice the boy next to him, and he looks familiar too. I try to focus, but every time I try to make sense of them, my mind blurs. It's happening again. I turn away and shrink against the wooden stage. I look up when Vaughn pulls on my arm.

"Sawyer, let's go."

They're real...he's real? No, he can't be real.

"Henly!" Vaughn shouts a few feet away.

I shake my head to make some sense of what he is saying. I'm too distracted by the people that shouldn't exist. They aren't real. I blink my eyes until Vaughn's voice is too loud to ignore. He starts to make sense; he keeps repeating himself, over and over again. He wants me to follow him out into the chaos. He grabs my shoulder and pulls me out. People are running in every direction, trying to escape, when suddenly the fence behind the stage breaks, and the deviations flood the grounds. Searching for the nearest chopper, I spot one to my right and take off into a sprint. I feel Vaughn right behind me and am caught by surprise when he throws me into a boarded up store.

"No," he says out of breath.

I follow his gaze to where the chopper is getting overrun by those trying to escape. I turn back in the other direction and see another chopper in the distance. I look to the sky and see the one Rathe had dragged the senator to flying in circles above us. I squint trying to use on my enhancements to see who is onboard, but the plane is too far. *Did the senator make it out alive?*

"Look." I point to the chopper in the distance "We can make it. All we have to do is make a clear run to those trees, and they can land over there." I point to a clearing a few miles up.

Vaughn looks at me. His familiar smirk tugs at the corner of his mouth. He must see the determination in my eyes. "You're on." He pauses to ready his gear. "Let's see your dad's work. First one there gives—"

I don't wait to hear him out. I race, duck, and dive from the people and the bullets. I'm almost there when my foot slips on a thick slab of ice. I roll onto my back and take in the brightness of the white sky above me. The white sheet messes with my eyes, and I start to watch as the sky falls to the ground. The snow hasn't stopped, and at this rate, it shows no sign of quitting. The snow is good. It will cover everything that has happened here. No one will know.

"Sawyer!"

Vaughn's voice breaks me from the clouds. Rolling over on my stomach, I see him a few yards away. He is searching for me. Quickly, I stand and curse at myself for being so easily distracted by the snow. I'm almost to Vaughn when I hear it, the voice that soothes my nightmares. No matter how much I will my body to move, it freezes.

"Stop!" the voice shouts. "Turn around. Drop your weapons. Hands above your head."

My throat constricts as the smooth voice demands me to turn around. When I don't, he shoots off a warning. I let the gun slip through my fingers to the ground, letting him think he has won. Slowly raising my hands in the air, I reach for the pistol that lingers on the nape of my neck. That is when I see him, the one who appears so vividly in my dreams, the very same one who frees me from the torments of what I have done. I'm startled by how real he is. But, if he is real, then I can no longer run from what I have done. My arms shake and my body tenses at the sight of him. All in one motion, I press the gun into my shoulder and aim. The trigger ceases easily under my finger. The bullet escapes the chamber, and while I wait for it to hit its target, my eyes fixate on him. *He's here.* At the last second, I turn away and run.

PART II

CHAPTER 6

RENNER

"Henly?" My aim waivers.

I stare at the ghost who has materialized in front of me. Her hand is steady on the trigger, and there is an unfamiliar look in her eyes. A sense of validation runs through me. For months, I have been looking for her and seeing her proves that my search wasn't in vain. I was right. She is alive. She focuses on me for a half-second before her finger squeezes down on the trigger, releasing the bullet into my shoulder and knocking me to the ground.

She shot me? It takes a few seconds for the pain to register before I act. Gripping tightly to my radio I call out for the only person who can help me now. "Dex!" I yell in my radio. The pain from the bullet begins to drum as if it were pumping adrenaline through me that I have to yell the rest of my orders, "She's here! Don't let her get away!"

"What!" he shouts in reply. "Renner, who?" Dex's voice is muffled through the radio.

"Get Henly!" I respond, partially in shock, partially in doubt.

Out of the corner of my eye, I spot Dex. He lowers his gun and sets out into a full sprint after her. My fingers trace my shoulder until they find a bullet hole no bigger than a dime right below my shoulder. At first, the pain seems shallow enough to pull the bullet out myself. I trace the small hole and press my fingers further into it. A sharp taste fills my mouth, and the world seems to stop when I feel the edge of the bullet with the tips of my fingers. *I can pull it out.* On the count of three, I ready myself to pull it free, but a familiar face breaks through the snow.

"Need a hand, friend?"

"Kenton?" I say with disbelief. His demeanor carries the same cockiness he used to wear when we were kids. *How could Kenton Vaughn, my childhood friend, be here—alive?*

"You were never good at leaving things alone," he says as his fingers dig into my shoulder. I let out a deep growl, my jaw clamping shut to keep me from shouting. When he finally pulls the bullet free, he looks at me and shrugs. "You're lucky," he adds, extending his hand.

"She's a poor shot," I reply as I take his hand and remember how Henly used to hesitate before every shot. As the throb from the wound moves down my arm, I'm incredibly aware of how true the boy's words were. Andrew has changed her.

He shakes his head and smiles. "She may have been, but she isn't anymore. If she wanted you dead, you'd be dead."

The throb in my shoulder is a steady pulse now, making it hard to think. "And you know this how?" I reply with a heavy breath.

He smiles. "All in good time, friend." He takes some of my weight as we jog back to Quinn, who stands near the chopper helping all those who are injured.

"What happened?" Quinn barely glances at my arm.

When I turn to introduce her to Kenton, he is gone. I let my arm fall and look back at the carnage, which has now slowed to a small fight. It is clear that we are losing. I look at the scattered field and see the mixed bodies of those that are deviations and many that aren't. Some wear the same gray uniform that Henly and Kenton are wearing, but most are just civilians who came here looking for hope, but found death. Quinn comes to my aid.

"Hurry up. She's out there," I say to the chaos

in front of me. For every second that passes is another second of being unsure.

Quinn forces me into a chair while she finishes with another Militaris soldier who is wounded.

"She shot me," I say in disbelief. "Actually shot me." I laugh.

"Did she recognize you?" Quinn asks.

The way she looked at me, there is no way she didn't know who I was. I nod and wince as Quinn finally looks at my wound. After a few minutes of probing and prodding, she sees that the entire bullet is gone and pours a dry substance into the hole, temporarily sealing it.

"Renner!" the voice blares from my radio.

I stand as Quinn ties a few pieces of shredded fabric around my shoulder. I wince as she ties the last one into a tight knot. "Dex," I answer.

"We got her," his voice sounds heavy and tired.

She is alive. The small ember of hope I had been holding onto has now ignited into a full flame. *She is not the same, but she is alive.* I reach for my radio to order an immediate evacuation, but a voice beats mine.

"Renner, perimeter is secure. Over," Romero

reports.

"Good. Kill any remaining deviations. Let's round up everyone and get out of here," I respond.

With my good arm, I do my best to help Quinn load all of the injured onto the helicopter and wait for our convoy to the train.

Dex's voice breaks through the static on the radio to report his status. "On my way to convoy, loading, and heading back to base. I won't let her out of my sight. Over."

I don't radio back. He gave me his word that he would take care of her last time, but he failed to do so. If it were up to me, I would have escorted her there myself, but it's not, so I'll concentrate my efforts on helping Quinn load the injured.

The thirty-minute ride to the station feels like three hours. Words fail me when I see Dex waiting for me at the edge of the platform. I rush past everyone to where he is standing and hope he didn't lose her again. I try to keep it together as my mind races back to a different day when I found all of them in Havre. Dex had been shot and had told me Henly was right behind him, but there was a look on his face that made me doubt his words. I remember the way Henly looked months ago, her pale complexion making her almost unrecognizable as Andrew pulled her back into the hospital. That day still haunts me.

Just as I had outside of the hospital that day, I demand to know where she is, "Where is she?" I'm no longer able to hide my angst.

"Inside," Dex replies hesitantly. Before I can walk past him, he stops me and adds, "Renner, she is a little...different."

"What do you mean *different*?" My shoulder begins to feel heavier and with it comes a pounding inside my head. The exhaustion and fatigue are catching up to me and the ache of my shoulder reminds me to stay alert when it comes to Henly.

"How is she?" I hear Quinn ask as she approaches.

"I just—she's just not the same person." His eyes shift back and forth between Quinn and me. "The boy was right. Davis was right." His voice is low.

I feel my frustration rise. "Where is she?"

"Dex," Quinn prompts when he doesn't respond.

He turns, and we follow him. "She is in I-N-T thirty-seven."

"Why is she in an interrogation room?" Quinn asks. "She's one of us."

"No, not anymore," Dex says, keeping his eyes focused on me. "She's one of them…"

I don't want an explanation. I don't care for it. My shoulder experienced this Henly first hand. "Where's Kenton?" I ask, suddenly remembering my old friend.

"Who?" Dex asks with confusion.

"Kenton Vaughn." I gesture as I say, "Six-foot, blond hair, blue eyes."

"A real smart-ass," Quinn adds.

Dex's brows pull together. "Yeah, I-N-T thirty-eight."

We reach Henly's room, but something stops me from going in. I don't think and force myself in. I open the door to the observation room, and there she is. Instantly, I can see what Dex meant earlier. She *is* different. Her hair is longer; it is tied into a braid that goes down to the small of her back. She looks stronger. Her runner's build is back. Her eyes trace the lines of the room as if her mind was analyzing every detail. Her eyes are darker, as if in some way Andrew has changed that about her too. Nowhere can I find the girl I left almost two years ago. This Henly is different. I stare, not knowing who she is anymore. When she turns toward the glass, I feel anxious not knowing who she is. My whole purpose this last few months was to find her to make sure she was okay, but now that she is a glass panel away, I'm not sure I have succeeded. She is not okay. She is not *Henly*.

"Maybe I should go in. Try to talk to her?" Quinn suggests.

Dex shrugs his shoulders. He doesn't know what to do anymore than I do. Quinn walks out of the room and reappears on the other side of the glass with a bottle of water in hand.

"Thirsty?" Quinn asks as she sets the bottle of water on the table in front of Henly.

Henly sits, arms crossed over her chest, defiant of any and all authority. *It's nice to see some things haven't changed.* Her silent demeanor echoes the same determination she had the first time she was locked in an interrogation room.

"Where am I?" Henly's eyes narrow at Quinn.

"You're in a quarantine." She coughs to clear her throat. "You're safe here."

"Where's Vaughn?" Henly questions, her voice

rising in contempt.

"In the next the room." Quinn hesitates before she asks, "Do you know who I am?"

She looks at the glass and then back to Quinn. "No." Her hands ball into fists, and it seems like she is fighting to keep control.

"I'm Quinn."

"I don't care who you are! Why am I here?"

"Henly, you're sa—" Quinn tries to say, but Henly interrupts.

"How do you know my name?" Henly nearly yells as she stands from her chair.

Quinn rises slowly, and after a few failed reassurances, she leaves the room and meets us in the hallway.

"He did it." Dex is the first one to say what the rest of us are thinking.

"Ana told me he might do this, but I didn't know how efficient he would be," Quinn says.

A sharp exhale leaves my lungs. I had hoped that this would go better. It hits me that the only other person who knows anything about Henly is in the next room. I leave without a word and walk into Kenton's interrogation room.

"What do you know?" I demand, skipping past the pleasantries.

"It's nice to see you too," Kenton replies

He crosses his arms and relaxes back into the chair. "What? No, 'where you've been? How is it going? I heard you might have died...'"

"Damn it, Kenton. I'm serious!" I reply as I take the seat across from him.

He scoffs through a smile and shakes his head. "So am I."

I lean back in my chair and remember how annoying my old friend is. "We—I went back for you, but you were gone." I pause and then continue, "Your house was empty."

He keeps his face clean of any emotion. "We got out right as it hit."

"So, you've been with them." It is not a question.

"They found us and took us in." His arms untangle from his body as he leans forward. "Where have you been?"

"Aurora—California. I took my father's place on the Board after he died," I say, feeling distant from my friend who used to be inseparable from Zoe and me. He was our third piece.

His face turns serious, more serious than I think I have ever seen before. His eyes flicker back and forth as if he is struggling with his inner demons. "She won't remember you—any of you."

"He took away her memories?" I ask, though I already know the answer.

"Kind of," he says. "Remember when we were kids playing in your backyard and we thought we could fly—"

I laugh a little at the memory. "When you *convinced* me we *could* fly."

"Yeah, do you remember when you woke up? You couldn't remember anything, but you were mad at me, and you couldn't figure out why."

I nod. I have a faint memory of waking up in the hospital to a ten-year-old version of my friend. His eyes were bloodshot from crying. The whole incident had been wiped away like it never happened. I couldn't remember anything until after my father had told me what had happened. It was then that I had finally understood the anger that was already there. It wasn't until I saw my best friend's leg in a cast that I had learned he broke his leg trying to save me by jumping off after me. After that, I forgave him. That was how he and I used to be. If one jumped, we both would jump. That had become our unspoken motto when one of us was hesitant to do something risky.

Before I have a chance to press the matter further, there's a knock at the door. It is Dex.

"She wants to see him," he announces. "She refuses to cooperate until she knows he's okay."

Of course she does. She has a way of making everything so damn complicated sometimes. I let out a sigh, and for the first time in months, I feel defeated. "Let's go."

"Anson, about your dad..." Kenton catches my arm.

"What?" I respond. "What about my dad?"

"Nothing. Let's go."

Kenton shakes his head and leads us out of the room.

CHAPTER 7

HENLY

I shot him. My heel taps uncontrollably against the cold tile surface. *Her name is Quinn. His name is Renner—like the senator's? And then there is Dex.* I look up when I hear the door scratching against the floor. It is Vaughn. I think of rising to hug him, to see if he is okay, but stop when I see the glass that shines our reflection, reminding me of the people who watch us from the other side. So, instead of showing any emotion, I raise my brow. He sits across from me at the small table in the even smaller room.

"How's your head?" he asks.

I touch the welt on the nape of my neck. It throbs at an unsteady pace. After I shot him—the boy from my dreams—one of the militaris lackeys came after me. We tussled on the ground for a few minutes before I had him pinned to the ground with my gun. I was about to pull the trigger when Vaughn showed up, and then everything went black.

"I'm fine. What's going on?" I nod to the door.

He leans over his shoulder and speaks to the glass wall, "She shouldn't find out this way, and it shouldn't be me who tells her, Anson."

The buzz from the door sliding open quickens my heartbeat.

"Let's go." Vaughn nods for me to follow him.

I follow him out into the hallway where I find the redheaded girl in conversation with the one I had shot. The other one who wrestled me to the ground is there, lurking in silence. My fingers instinctively flinch for a gun that is no longer on my hip.

"We can't fly out until morning, so we'll set the two of you up in a room here in Bowden for tonight."

"Together?" Quinn responds to the man that suddenly resembles the Senator.

"No, Anson and I have a lot to catch up on. We'll room together," Vaughn replies casually.

"Wait?" I say, taken aback by Vaughn's sudden compliance with the Militaris's offerings. "You know them?" I ask, suddenly feeling defensive.

"No, just Anson Renner. He's an old friend," Vaughn replies as he points to him. "Go with Quinn— the red head. She'll get you situated for the night."

"What?" I look at Vaughn unable to tell if he is being serious. "I won't go anywhere with anyone," I say, feeling uneasy about the situation.

"I'll take her," Vaughn volunteers with a sudden annoyance in his voice.

"No." I'm disturbed by his compliance with the Militaris. "I won't go anywhere with any of you until I know what's going on."

Hazel eyes answers for him, "Your sister and your mom can explain it better than we can."

I take a step back. "My sister? No, she's dead."

"No, they made it out of Havre," he says. He takes a step toward me, but then two steps back, his eyes piercing, stay with mine. *He has my attention now.*

The confusion whirls through my mind like a dust storm, making it hard to decipher truth from dream. "Where are they?" I ask.

"Aurora," the redheaded girl answers. "I'll take you to a room for tonight," she offers.

"No, I'll stay here until we leave," I respond defiantly.

I walk back into the room and shut the door behind me. The glass across from me flickers as I pace back and forth. I know they're on the other side watching my every move. I kick my feet up onto the table in front of me and fold my arms. I close my eyes, trying to remember what my dad had told me about

Ana's and Davis's deaths, but everything is foggy. Panic overwhelms me when I think about everything that has been said. *I wish Royce were here. She would be able to help me navigate through all of this mess. I do know one thing though: I won't believe them until I have proof that my sister is alive.* I open my eyes when I hear a buzz. I look up and find him idly standing by the door.

"Need something?" I ask with annoyance.

Hazel eyes smirks, and I avert my gaze before I'm unable to control it.

"I need to debrief you," he says as he pulls out the chair across from me.

I shake my head and press my lips together.

"Look, I don't want to do this anymore than you do—"

"You'll get nothing from me until I see my sister," I spit.

His exhale is deep like he is already annoyed, but we have just begun. He sets a bottle of water on the table followed by two small aspirins. "For your head. Quinn should really take a look at that."

"I'm fine." I'm not, but I can't decide whether the pain is from the blow to my head or being told my sister is alive.

"Henly—"

"Is that it?"

"Yeah." His scoff is heavy when it leaves his chest.

"You can go," I say harshly.

He stares at me with confusion. "You really don't know who I am."

I scoff. "No, but clearly by the devastation on your face I should," I say as maliciously as possible, except I don't know why I am being so harsh. Here he is, materialized in front of me from the countless dreams he has appeared in, and I am treating him like a villainous nightmare. *What is wrong with me? Why do I feel so betrayed by a stranger who I thought was a figment of my imagination?* His eyes searched mine desperately, begging me to try. "Please, enlighten me then. Who are you?" I say, my words dripping with sarcasm.

"Forget it." His shoulders sag as he leans back in his chair.

"It is Renner, right?" I say, leaning forward, inches from his face.

He nods.

"Please. Evidently there's something I've forgotten that only *you* can remind me of. What lies do you have for me today?"

"They're not lies."

"Okay." I patronize him.

His jaw tightens and his eyes close for a moment, the frustration building into his muscles as they flex. "Listen, Dex, who's outside, and Quinn, they're your friends from Aurora," he says, eyes pleading.

"And just by throwing out a few names I'm supposed to know who they are?" My brows furrow and my tone mocks him. "You listen! I remember everything, and I don't know them! But do you want to know what *is* familiar? Being dragged and told lies by people whom you've never even met, having to stare at people who know only chaos and murder."

"What happened to you?" he asks, his voice low.

"People like *you* happened to me!" My fists smack against the cold table. "People like you who take what they want and destroy everything!" My voice is louder and echoes in the small room. "Your friend over there—my supposed friend—" I look at the two-way mirror "—knocks me out and brings me here, and suddenly I'm supposed to trust you? You've told me nothing, yet you expect some sort of appreciation from me—like you're saving me." I let out a mocking laugh. "If you're waiting for me to jump into your arms and exclaim joy, then you're wasting your time. So you can go," I finish with a tone that shows how much I hate them.

His jaw sets hard, and without a word, he stands and walks out.

***

I awake when the door creaks open. My heart floods with annoyance when I think Renner has come back to argue more, but instead I find Vaughn with a steaming cup in his hand.

"Rough night?"

"Shut up." I take the cup from him and taste the chocolate that has been mixed with coffee. "Thanks," I say after I swallow.

"Why do you have to make things so difficult? You could have stayed in a room…with a bed." He takes a sip from his mug.

"Sorry, betrayal isn't all that high in my book." I take another drink and feel the steam warm my body.

"Ouch." He laughs, clearly unaffected by my insult. "How often do you speak before thinking?" He laughs again.

I scoff and glare. *He's one to criticize me about my words. He's the one who told my dad that he was on the verge of crazy once*—my *dad, who I'm sure, by now, has probably discovered my absence.*

"Why did you help them bring me here?" I ask.

"Who says I did?"

I look up to his devious smirk I have seen too many times. "I know you, or at least I think I do, and you would never give up that easily," I say.

He avoids my gaze. "And you? If you didn't want to be here, you wouldn't be. They don't know about your modifications."

I don't say anything because he is right. I should be fighting their every move and decision. Instead, I'm curious. I want to know if what they are saying about my sister is true. If she is alive, then I will get her out of here. My stomach drops, and for the first time, it occurs to me that they could find out what I am. I rub my forehead and feel the room shake.

"Are you okay? How's your head?"

I swat away his hand. "I'm fine."

"Time to go," a voice says.

We both look up and see Dex at the door. I turn back to Vaughn, feeling unsure. "Are you sure this is a good idea?"

He grins. "Eh, why not? We have nothing better to do. Well, you have surgery to get back to"—he says as he nods toward the door—"but I suggest we do this instead."

It wouldn't be hard to break out of here and run. Really, it would be as easy as scratching an itch, but I'm more curious to see what they have to show me. If I don't leave now, I can leave when I get to where they are taking me, to where my sister is.

"Hey—" I look up to Vaughn "—this is all your choice. You want to break out and go, then let's go. This is all up to you."

He reaches out for my hand, and I take it. We walk out the door. At the surface, the helicopter waits for us. The blades whisk the cool air that burns against my face. I let go of his hand to swat at the falling snow to get a clearer look at where I am. If I hadn't been downtown, I would have thought I was in a forest. The frost-covered vines conceal most of what I can see, forming a large wall in front of me. I look back to the helicopter and know it is time go when I see Vaughn take his seat. When I see Renner, my back instantly straightens, and I force myself into the helicopter. Without looking at me, Renner sits across from me.

The flight to Aurora is relatively smooth. From time to time, I glance away from the window and catch Renner watching me. I'm not sure what he is looking at. I'm not going to spontaneously combust. Honestly, his attention makes me wary. Every time he looks away, I feel the walls close in. It is as if, in some way, his glances are comforting, but what drives me crazy is my inability to understand why. When I look at Quinn, she too stares at me with a curious look.

"What?" I ask defensively.

"Nothing." She smiles. She looks at Renner, and they exchange some kind of secret conversation.

There it is again: a pang of envy, a feeling I can only discern as longing. He looks so familiar to the dreams that flooded me on the nights when I was strung out on morphine. For a while, all I did was crave those morphine nights when he visited me in my dreams, always reminding me to wake up. Except, in the small enclosure of the helicopter, I don't know what to think. *If he's been real all along, what could have happened for me to forget everything? To forget these people I'm supposed to know? What has happened to me?* Then it dawns on me—the girl. It takes me a minute to recall her name, but these are the people she went on about over and over again. They are the people she was referring to. I swallow hard and wish the images away, but they linger behind the back of my eyelids—her pleas for me to save her, the pain she felt as the final serum ran through her body. *Did I make a mistake?*

"You all right?"

I open my eyes and stare, transfixed on Renner's gaze. His eyes give it away. He looks at me with such saddened curiosity, as if he were waiting for the girl he used to know to do something to comfort his growing fear. After my cruelty toward him last night, the last thing I should expect is kindness.

"Sawyer," Vaughn shouts, breaking me from Renner's gaze.

"Yeah," I respond to the ground instead of Vaughn. I turn to look out the window and see Dex smile before his gaze follows mine out.

"That's Aurora," Dex says, pointing to the mountain.

I focus my gaze and feel something click in my brain. I try to decipher what it means. I squeeze my eyes shut again and see images come in and out of focus, but nothing sticks. I don't open my eyes again until I feel the shake of the chopper as we land on a helipad that sits atop a mountain peak. The doors open, and I see a small elevator hatch across the way. Through the lit up elevator door, I see a familiar face.

"Dr. Royce?" Suddenly, I'm filled with the hope that she is here to take me home. As I walk past Vaughn, he abruptly puts his arm around me and whispers.

"Everything is going to change, but I promise no more surgeries."

"What?" I whisper as we approach Royce.

"Anson. Kenton." Royce smiles past me to the boys who linger not too far behind me.

"Mom," Vaughn replies.

"Mrs. Royce," Renner says stiffly, but he looks confused.

She motions to the guards behind her. "Detain her, and take her down to quarantine."

CHAPTER 8

RENNER

Henly fights the men well, better trained than I've ever seen her, but Kenton filled us in on this much. If it hadn't been for the five of us, she would have killed the Militaris soldiers trying to contain her. In the end, it was me who injected her and made taking her down possible. They quickly took her to the medics unit to be examined, three rooms down from me.

Her sedation must have kicked in because I can no longer hear her fighting or yelling. I pull my shirt over my head and examine the worn bandages around my shoulder. Now that we are back in Aurora, Quinn has forced me in to tend to my gunshot wound. Quinn comes around the table with a threaded needle and scissors and slowly cuts away the gauze around my shoulder. I jerk when the first thread weaves through my flesh. Quinn tells me that I'm lucky that it should be infected, but I don't feel lucky. Yesterday's events keep playing in my mind like some drug-induced dream. Whatever happened to Henly in her father's facility has forever changed her. Even though I brought her back, she isn't the same, and I highly doubt that what's been done to her can be undone. No one can come back from that kind of hell. I've been defeated.

I exhale as Quinn finishes the last line of stitches. "Thank you," I say, even though the words are forced.

Her smile is vacant, almost forced, as she places a square cotton bandage on my lower shoulder, pressing it hard into my flesh. My shoulder hangs as the pain reverberate through me—it's cold and aches in a way that makes me feel hallow. Quinn retreats to the far corner of the room and places each item in their exact spot on the metal shelf, the glass exposing her reflection. *I wonder if she sees her mother in herself as easily as I do.* She has effortlessly picked up Ellie's mannerisms, her determination, and her strength. I'm transfixed by how much she echoes Ellie. In some strange way, I want to confide in her like I once did with Ellie.

"Quinn," I say, walking to her.

"I thought it'd be easier," she says, catching me off guard.

I stop short next to her, leaning against the wall. "What'd be easier?"

"I thought it'd be easy not to blame her for my mom's death, but seeing her reminds me of what was taken from me." Tears roll down her cheeks and onto the floor. "Where do we go from here? How do we justify my mom's death now?"

"I don't know what you mean?"

"We found her, but now…all of this…is she even still in there? Everything my mom did to protect her…she died for her, and now it's all pointless."

"No." My answer catches me off guard. "She's not." I reach for Quinn's hand and grab onto it. I'm not sure why, but it makes me feel better to know that someone else feels the way I do. *Useless. Disappointed.*

Quinn turns to me. "I'm sorry. You tried so hard…"

"Stop," I whisper, my voice hoarse. I don't need to hear what I already know.

She nods. "I'm going to go check on Dex."

"Do you know where Kenton is?" I ask before she leaves.

She shakes her head no and then turns and leaves me to the silence. I sit idly, waiting for any amount of energy to pass through me to make me move—to make me give a damn. Finally, when the ringing in my ears becomes too much to ignore, I stand and make my way back to my room.

I fumble with the door and push it open the door and find Zoe pacing back and forth. Her eyes catch mine before I have time to tell her to leave.

"Are you all right? I heard you were shot!" she says, throwing her arms around me in a tight embrace.

"I'm fine." I wince.

She gives me a quick look and then shakes her head. "No, you're not."

My smile is forced. "Just some stitches. Nothing I haven't dealt with before."

"I was worried sick."

"I'm okay," I reassure her.

"I heard about Henly."

My eyes drop to the floor. "Not now, Zoe. I don't want to hear it."

"You need to hear it." She takes a few steps away. "She is not who she was—"

"Zoe," I plead, trying to keep the desperation out of my voice.

"No, let me finish. She's not there anymore, and you have to let her go." She pauses as she sits next to me. "You brought her back to her family. There's nothing more you can do. You *have* to let her go."

My shoulders sag in defeat. "I can't," my voice cowers as if too afraid to realize the truth.

"Renner, you barely even knew her." Her voice is low, almost irritated. "You were only with her for a few weeks," she finishes.

I was with her a lot longer than two weeks. Zoe doesn't know about the time in quarantine. When I found Henly, all matted hair and bleeding, she was a mess. At first, when my team brought her in, I didn't think much of her, but as the days progressed, she surprised me. The life she knew was gone, yet she was so determined to survive. That is what she does: she survives. As they studied her, they tried to break her, make her talk, but every time they asked her a question or tried anything, she would fight. I respected her for her resilience. She was brave. I rooted for her. I wanted her to survive and live a good life. After everything she had been through, I thought that she deserved to, but it doesn't always work out that way—we don't always get what we deserve. I never could have guessed the impact that she would eventually have on my life.

"Renner." Zoe pulls my face toward hers. "Did you hear me?" she asks as she stares hard into my eyes. "I can help you move on."

Before I have time to pull away, her lips are on mine, but there's no rush, no lightening, just a dull pull of what I should feel. A cold shiver runs through my spine, but it is not the same eager desire I had felt with someone else. This feeling is brittle and empty. I know I should push her away and tell her to leave, but the sudden inclination of Henly never remembering me has me clinging to her. It is as if kissing Zoe will ease the pain that lingers in my bones. In a moment of weakness, I give in to her. Not because I want her, I'll accept any easy distraction handed to me. At this point, to feel anything would be better than feeling nothing. I know that it's not a good idea, and I try to resist the seduction of her lips, but I lose the fight. When I close my eyes, I let her distract me.

It's late when I wake to find Zoe curled into me on my bed. Slowly, I ease my way out of her embrace, this shouldn't have happened. I pull my shirt over my head and grab my shoes. I quietly make it to the door and escape into the hallway to lace up my shoes. I have never crossed that line with Zoe, no matter how bad she wanted to be more. I never did, and I still don't want to. Last night's mistake has filled me with even more guilt, and like all things, my problems have not been eased by her distraction. If anything, they are worse. I know I have things to do, but I want to see how Henly is doing.

When I get down to quarantine, I find Adam carrying small vials full of deviation blood. Adam is Aurora's youngest and brightest scientist. He has an apartment in Ave 1, but he mostly stays here. He says, "it shows his commitment to the cause." He smiles as he passes me.

"Adam, which cells is—"

"Renner! Where have you been?" Dex asks almost out of breath.

"Around. What's up?" I say. *I'd rather not confess to where I was exactly.* A small pool sweat has gathered around his temple that streams down his neck. He sticks his finger in the air gesturing for a minute. "What?" I ask again hoping he'll quite panting like a dog and just spit it out.

"Ana and that doctor friend of yours have Henly. They're going to try to reverse her memories," Dex says.

What is Kenton's mom doing with Henly and Ana? "Is that even possible?" I ask. Suddenly a flash of Zoe at my lips takes me back to last night, but I try to push it away. *Had I been here, last night never would have happened, and Henly wouldn't be with Ana.*

"I don't know," Dex says, venting his frustration, his breath finally back to normal

"Adam!" I shout down the hall. "Where did they take Henly?"

Adam looks down at papers in front of him and then back to me. "The simulation room."

"Do you think they can really return her memories?" Dex asks Adam.

If anyone would know the answer, Adam would. He practically runs the science wing, and he is no older than I am.

"It's possible, but dangerous."

"Dangerous how?"

"Ana and Drew created a treatment to take—or alter—some of her memories. It took precision and an in-depth mapping of Henly's brain. If they don't use the same modifications to return the taken memories, she could very well end up incapacitated."

"Brain dead?" Dex asks, and for a moment, I think I see him shake.

"Yes."

Dex looks at me, and I don't wait. We take off down the hall and up the stairs.

CHAPTER 9

HENLY

The darkness is consumed by the very people whom I have broken for my father; their faces swim through the serum. The burden of their deaths has committed me to my own purgatory, one I am doomed to relive every time I sleep. My father wanted it that way. He knew I would be more willing to go into surgery. The morphine would quiet the dreams that bring back the hazel eyes that kept my purgatory at bay. But darkness like this, the one that can't be helped by morphine, brings my worst sins to life, especially what I did to *her*—the one who tried to warn me, the one who knew the truth.

I told you, didn't I? I can hear her taunting me. *Get ready because it is their turn to break you!* Her hysterics echo through the small room. The memory of her laugh propels goose bumps down my body. *This is how it ends.*

I shudder awake. Slowly, my eyes open and expose me to a room filled with people.

"How are you feeling?" Royce asks.

I try to lift my hand to rub the sleep from my

eyes, but find the restraints stop me. The room is small and warm. My body is strung up to chords, and the beeps seem far too loud to be normal machines. My eyes narrow at the woman I thought I could trust.

"What are you going to do to me?" I shout. My fists close, and I try with all my power to break from the table. I know I can—I have done it before—but this time the restraints just dig into my flesh, almost to the point of drawing blood. Confused, I look up to Royce.

"Your enhancements are sedated."

"What? How? Why are you doing this?" I demand, but she doesn't answer.

My breathing becomes shallow as the sweat dribbles down my head. The images of all those who have haunted me resurface with a vengeance. I have traded places with them, and this is my penance. This is where they seek their retribution. Instead of screaming, I set my jaw and accept my guilt for everything I have done.

"It'll be over soon," Royce whispers.

I squeeze my eyes shut. Everything is so vibrant, so bright, it forces me to squeeze them even tighter. I'm taken to a place in my mind that has been kept hidden. Like being awakened from the dead, I'm enlightened to things I used to remember—a memory that was once forgotten.

It feels like a dream, but it is real. It happened, and I can finally remember it.

I sit across from a woman with dirty blond hair that is cropped short to her head. Blue embers burn in her eyes. They look so familiar, so honest. The room around me is shallow and dark. Some of the wood inside of the cabin splinters in different directions, casting shadows from the moonlight on the woman's face. It is Royce.

My attention snaps to Royce as she pleads, "Will you do this?"

"Do you know what you're asking of me?"

She nods. "If you stay, you will save many lives."

I sit across from Royce and contemplate her offer to stay in Alaska. It has been months—ten to be exact—since I have seen my friends, or even remembered them, their faces. I sift through the faces of people I have missed, through the faces and memories I now know my father took from me. Although, I wish some would have stayed away, Ana for instance, I'll bear her memories if the others get to stay. But now this woman is telling me *I* need to stay, that they need me in order to stop my father. She told me stories about my father's cruelty, but it was unnecessary. I remember now. I have lived these stories. They are the scars that stitch me together.

I stare at the desk in front of me and search its wood for an answer, but come up empty. When I close my eyes, I see Renner within my grasp, and my veins pulse with hope. All I would have to say is no, and I could go back to him. I could go back to Davis, to Dex, to my old life. But when I open my mouth, that is not the answer I give.

"How long? How long will I have to stay?" My finger traces a scar on my arm.

"Until we have enough information to find a cure…or to eliminate Drew."

When I exhale, my breath is shaky. "How do I know you're not with them and this isn't a test?"

"A test of what?" She looks at me confusedly.

"Loyalty. My father has a way of finding out who is loyal to him." The shudder that spreads through my body is involuntary.

She pulls a piece of paper out of a bag and

slides it across the table to me. "The Board just voted a few days ago. It was a unanimous decision to request your stay."

My eyes glide down the list of signatures. It is as if his black ink were stained red: *Anson Renner*. He agreed. A mixture of confusion and anger consumes me. *Why didn't he come?* Staring at his signature, *why is he making me do this?* I remember the Renner I know always does the right thing, regardless of who it hurts.

"I'll stay," I say, staring at the ink that has signed my fate. If he believes I should stay, then fine, I will.

"Good."

"How do I get a hold of you?" I ask. "To feed you information?" My voice is no louder than a whisper.

"You don't. I'll be on the inside with you." She grabs the paper and neatly tucks it back into the folder.

I swallow hard. "Okay, so how does this work?"

"We're going to take back some of your memories."

"What? No! You can't!"

"You're father is already a suspicious man. If he even thinks you're up to something, you know what he'll do," she responds calmly.

Of course I know what he will do. I've seen him do it to others. My palm rubs against my face.

"How will I know what is real?" I ask.

"We'll distort the stories you're father has fed you and make them fuzzy. We'll make the truth prominent in your doubts. I'll program memories between you and me so that you will trust me enough to tell me whatever your father tells you. You won't know I'm on your side until we're finished. When the assignment is over, we'll reverse it all."

"If you're in, then why make me stay?" I ask.

"Your father confides in you. Your modifications have made you loyal to him. He tells you things no one else knows, but we'll make it so you trust me more," she replies.

She stands and motions for me to follow her. We walk into a small room where she points to a table.

As I sit down, I ask, "Are you going to take everyone away again?"

She stops what she is doing and turns to face me. "I'll try my hardest not to."

Tears fall from my eyes. "Please try."

I'm afraid he will go as easily as he came. Closing my eyes, I feel the needle pinch into my arm. My lips tremble uncontrollably.

"Is Davis safe? Is she okay?"

"She is very safe. Your friend Dex makes sure she doesn't want for anything."

"Good," I whisper.

"When you wake, you'll be in your room. Make sure to write down every detail in a journal. If your father finds out and tries to wipe you clean, you'll be able to read the truth."

A quivered exhale escapes my lips as I nod, and then everything changes.

Suddenly, all of the pieces fit and everything has been answered. Eighteen and a half months ago they asked me to stay. The flashback hurts more as more memories settle into place. They crash into me, trying to fight each other for space, while I'm left feeling like my head might explode. I'm about to suffocate—it is too much. Droplets of water trickle down my cheeks, and there is no stopping them. My eyes fly open, and Davis's name escapes my lips.

"She's alive," a familiar voice says.

I turn to find my mother at a pair of monitors. Glancing above me, I see the room is filled with others watching. I rub my face and feel the wires tug at my flesh.

"Where is she?" I ask as I rip away the needles.

My mother doesn't respond.

Kicking my legs off the operating table, I shout, "Where is she?" Without restraint, I walk over to my mother and pin her throat against the wall with both hands. Pinching away at her life, I yell, "You left me there! You let him take me! You wanted me dead!" My memories of her consume me, filling me with anger.

"Henly!" Royce exclaims. "Let her go!"

"No! She wanted me dead! Didn't you?" My anger is misdirected, but I can't stop. I can't let go.

A strange satisfaction fills me when her complexion pales against my grasp. I hate her. Her nails claw at my grip. I fight the urge to let her go, and like a vise, my grip tightens. Her lips fade to a blue color, and her eyes stare into mine. I can see it in her pupils—she is afraid. If I don't let go, I will kill her. *I've killed enough, so what's one more?* In an instant, they are all here, all of the lives I was ordered to take; they come alive before me. Their pleas ring in my ears, *"No! Please, stop!" But, what's one more?* It feels like I have already lost my sanity. A renewed strength flows through me. She will die, and what better irony than to be killed by me—a monster she helped create. My grip loosens, but not by my doing. I find a Militaris soldier tugging at my arms. He is strong—I'll give him that. With one arm, I keep Ana pinned to the wall and throw the soldier across the room. They can't stop me. I turn back to face Ana. Everything she has put me through may have not been done single handedly, but she helped my father. She helped him and not once thought of standing up for her child. The fear in my mother's eyes reflects the monster that I have become.

"Stop!"

Renner stands ready to act, his expression a mixture of awe and confusion. His narrowed eyes meet mine and the room begins to shake. Ana's nails claw at my hands until I finally let go. She slides to the floor and takes in as much air as her lungs will allow. She'll live—*that's disappointing.* My fists clench so that I won't hurt anyone else.

Losing my balance, I cling to the wall next to

me. He runs to my side, helping me sit down. The people in the room above us are rushing out as quickly as their feet will take them; they are scared of me too. Renner's calloused hands softly pull my face to his. He is saying something to me, but I can't understand the slur of words. *What is happening to me?* I really look at him, take in the furrow of his brows, the golden fire in his eyes, the way his skin feels against mine, and I'm consumed with rage all over again.

"No! Get away from me. You forced me to stay! You knew what he would do to me, yet you asked me to stay!" I yell, throwing him across the room.

He rolls onto his stomach and then slowly puts his hands in the air. "Look at me." His voice echoes, "Henly, look at me."

I find his eyes and they study me. The sparks of ember entrance me, his lips move as if saying something, but it doesn't matter because everything else is a blur. He continues to speak, but the ringing in my ears won't go away. I cover my ears in hopes that the incessant ringing will stop.

"Her pupils are dilated, and her heart is beating too fast. If she doesn't calm down, she'll have a heart attack." Royce's voice slowly replaces the ringing in my ears.

I follow Royce's eyes to a pair of Militaris soldiers standing to the side of me. I can't calm down. The rage continues to course through me, giving me strength I have never felt before.

"No!" Renner shouts, but it is too late.

They are heading for me. I take a step toward them, and it is easy. As one tries to detain me, I grab his arm and twist it until I am using him to block the other's attack. The man's arm snaps, causing him to yell. As I let him fall to the ground, the one remaining comes after me with an elongated Taser. He jabs it into my side, but its nothing more than a small prick. Grabbing the device, I turn it back on him and ram it into his neck, rendering him unconscious. As the second man falls, I stare at my hands and feel the anger slowly drain and with it my energy.

"Hey! Henly! Henly, look at me!" Renner yells, forcing my eyes to his.

His eyes burn into me like hot sand. My breathing is uneven and shaky. I'm afraid of what I'm becoming, and with all of the memories that crash into each other, I can't distinguish in which order they go.

"Help me…" I plead.

CHAPTER 10

RENNER

"I will, Henly. I will," I say, but my words fall on deaf ears.

She collapses, my arms barely catching her as she falls. Quickly, I survey the room. I see Ana. Her hands are clasped around her neck. Her eyes, wide with fear, stare intently at Henly, who stirs in my arms.

Henly's accusations ring in my mind. *I didn't make her stay.* "What did she mean when she said I made her stay?" I ask Royce.

Royce and Ana exchange a look before Royce answers me, "It is…complicated."

"What did you do?" I demand.

"We—" Ana begins, but her coughs interrupt her.

"What she wants to say is that Henly needed to stay," Royce says. "There was no other option. She *had* to stay. We had to know what Andrew was going to do next. Anson, I'm sorry, but it was voted to keep you in the dark." She glances back to Ana and then to me, and I know something is kept hidden in the silence of their glances.

I look to Ana. "You knew where she was this whole time and still you said nothing?" I yell through gritted teeth. I pick up Henly, if they won't do what's best for her, I will. "You knew exactly what would happen to her—what he'd do to her…" I can't finish. I don't know how to rationalize with the kind of monster who would submit her child to that kind of torture.

"You can't take her," Royce says sternly.

"Try me."

"Renner, we need to make sure she is okay."

Hill walks in, blocking my exit. The fatigue looks noticeable on his face.

"I can't just leave her," I say to Hill. "Not with them."

"Then stay." Hill rubs his forehead unsure if of what he's just allowed.

He motions for me to put Henly down. Slowly, I lower her body onto the table and that is when I notice something—a rough edge of what looks like a scar. I pull up her shirt to find more rough, jagged edges that crisscross over intentional spots: her spleen, her kidneys, her lungs, and another across her heart. When I look up, I find Royce tending to Ana's neck.

"You left her there for this?" I point at the scars. "What have you done?" My accusations seem to ring loudly in the silent room.

"She's back—alive." Ana glares at me, motioning to Henly, her voice barely audible.

"At what cost?" I shout at her.

"We did what we had to," Royce interjects, and when she does, Ana's back straightens as if it had been the right thing to do.

"How do you use people as your pawns and justify it as the right thing to do?" I spit out. "And feel no remorse."

"Sometimes you have to do bad things for a good reason," Royce says, but she doesn't look at me.

Their ideas of nobility and honor are distorted far beyond anything I can comprehend. *How is it possible that this was ever the right thing to do?* I stroke Henly's hair as Hill connects her back to the wires that she had pulled free from.

Royce calls in a pair of transporters. "Take her down to the quarantine and secure her in the cell we made for her."

"Absolutely not!" I shout. The guards stop and wait for further orders, but at this point, I'm not sure whose orders they're waiting for.

"Out of your jurisdiction," Royce says. "She is a danger to everyone in Aurora."

"Out of my jurisdiction? Since when? I am a member of the Board and you are a guest! You have no say here!" I shout.

Hill places his arm on my shoulder. "Renner, she is not stable. If she can't control her enhancements, she could cause a lot of damage. Hurt a lot of people."

I don't refute with Hill. On some level, I know he is right. "I'm not leaving her," I say to him.

He nods, and I turn to the transporters and give the order. I help transfer Henly to the gurney the transporters brought. For a moment she almost looks dead—not peaceful, but vacant. Alone in some far world left to fend for herself.

Never again, I won't let them, I think to myself.

The thought pricks at my eyes and I feel sad for her. All of this time to have been alone, then to only be told that you have been forgotten. It's not right.

"Tucker is awake," Hill says to Royce. "When you patch her up, you should finish your tests. I'll keep an eye on Henly."

I look up to see Royce nod, but her eyes avoid Henly.

"Royce," I start before she leaves the room, "don't think for a second that my loyalty to Kenton extends to you. Mess with her or Kenton again and you'll be down there too, adjoined cells for both you and Ana. And if you think it's out of my jurisdiction, I'll make it a point to show you that it's not. I'll have you transferred and your status stripped. I'll send a message to Andrew and let the both of *you* fend for yourselves. " I look between Ana and Royce. "Do I make myself clear?"

Royce takes a few steps toward me. "Your mother would be proud."

I'm not sure how to take her remark, and for a moment, I wait to see if there is more, but there isn't. She turns to leave, and soon after, so do we. As we leave, I see Ana stare at Henly in such a way I can't discern if it is in pity, love, or disgust. Whatever she feels is quickly masked by a scowl, and without a single word, she disappears from my line of sight. With Hill, I follow the transporters down to the cell that was specifically designed for Henly.

"What is she?" I ask Hill.

He shrugs his shoulders. "Essentially—" Hill exhales "—a test tube. Andrew has packed so much crap into her it is hard to determine exactly what she is—or what he has done to her. He is looking for something, and he almost found it."

Almost? Before I can ask anything further, we make it to the quarantines. I follow him to a back cell that has been reinforced with steel. Apparently, she won't be able to break through the bars, but after witnessing her rage today, I'm not sure it will keep her contained.

* * *

Six hours have passed. Every now and again, Henly stirs in her sleep as if she is fighting something, and right when I think she will wake, she becomes deathly still—vacant. Hill assures me she will be okay, but I'm not naïve. A person can only handle so much before they break, but there is no way to know the details of what she has experienced. The only person who could know is Kenton, and I haven't seen him since she cracked his ribs.

Staring at her, I wonder if it was all in my head—something I had built up to be more than it actually was. *Have I in some way made her into something she isn't? Are a few weeks really worth all of this*? I look around her cell until my gaze settles on Henly. She fought against everything and, up until this point, managed to stay sane. I want to make the right choice for the both of us, but everything is so clouded that I don't know what the right choice is. I have never doubted myself this much. *But if this was all in my head, why do I feel so alive when I'm with her?*

"How is she?" My thoughts are silenced when I look over my shoulder to find Dex. He walks in and takes a seat next to me. One cup in each hand he extends one to me and I gratefully take it.

I slowly take a sip, tasting the coffee before I answer, "I don't know. She attacked Ana and then badly injured the two Militaris soldiers who tried to sedate her."

Dex laughs. "Sounds like Henly."

A small smile creeps into the corner of my mouth. *Maybe I haven't imagined everything about her.* "Yeah." After a few minutes, I ask, "Does Davis know she is here?"

"No, I didn't know what to tell her. I didn't exactly want to say, 'Hey, your sister is here, and she was okay, but then she went a little crazy when they gave her back her memories, and then she tried to kill your mom, and oh, she is back in quarantine.' Yeah, that's not a conversation I want to have."

"Makes sense," I offer.

"Yeah, it'd be nice to go to her with something good to say."

"She blames me." I blurt out my thoughts without control.

"No, she doesn't. She knows you kept looking for her."

His reassurances fail me. I shake my head. "No, I couldn't get there soon enough."

He doesn't say anything, which makes me think he agrees.

"Renner, you should get some rest," Hill says as he walks in. He comes in every few hours to check up on Henly.

"I'm fine," I lie. I'm not. I'm exhausted, and I haven't slept in days. I know there are things to get done, information to find out, but I can't bring myself to leave her alone.

"I'll stay," Dex offers. "You need rest. I'll come find you if anything changes."

If there is one person I still slightly trust, it is Dex, though not entirely. "I'll be back soon," I say, deciding I need to find Kenton. "I have a friend to catch up with."

I walk down the hall and take the elevator up to his Ave. My knuckles still when I hear a murmur of voices. Royce is inside, and they are in a heated discussion. I open the door, and as soon as they see me, they stop. Kenton looks away and doesn't make eye contact with me, while Royce stands up straighter and turns to me.

"Anson," she says in her usual motherly tone.

"Royce," I reply in a short tone.

I know very little about Kenton's mom, except she was one of those modern feminists who refused to change her last name when she got married. His dad hated it. He used to say that it was a blow to his ego, but I don't think it really ever was. Royce always seemed to be her own person and make her own decisions. The second she was told that it was expected for her to do something she wouldn't do it. You need to stay at home, no. You should cook the family dinner, no. You should take your husbands name, no. She was never cruel or malicious about her stance, just firm. She wouldn't be anything other than herself. I admired her for that. Kenton's dad died when we were young, and his mom wasn't around as much as Kenton would have liked. She was always busy with work and left Kenton to figure things out on his own. When she would work he would stay at my place, my mom made sure he was never really alone.

From what I knew Royce was a doctor and only took rare cases, the ones that were interesting and dangerous. Kenton didn't talk about her career much, but from what I gathered from the stories my mom told me, she specialized in innovation—creation. She and my mother were complete polar opposite, yet they were close friends. I figure that's why Kenton and I were such good friends—though, I guess now, he goes by Vaughn.

"What do you want to know?" she asks. Her shoulders finally give in to a slouch.

My jaw tightens. *I want to know everything. I want to know nothing.* All I can mange is, "Will she remember?"

"I'm confident she will," Royce replies.

Kenton's eyes narrow in confusion. "What happened?"

"She attacked Ana, but it is normal for her to feel that way," Royce explains.

Kenton stands, and in moments, he is at the

door. I know where he is rushing off to, and Royce knows too.

"She's in quarantine. Unless you're a part of the Board, you will not be allowed in," I state the rules almost like I'm rubbing the fact that he can't go see her, but I can, in his face. "At least for the first twenty-four hours," I finish, hoping that it makes me sound a little less jealous than I am.

With his back to me, he slams the door shut and faces us.

"Why are you with them? Why are you with Andrew?" I don't mean to lose my composure, but I can't help it.

Kenton looks at me. "A few months before it hit, I was with my mom. We were taken to a facility in the east. A few weeks later, your dad showed up. He came for my mom."

"It couldn't have been my dad," I argue.

"Why?" Royce asks curiously.

"He died in a plane crash a few weeks after we got here," I say.

"Crash?" Kenton replies, his gaze shifts to Royce.

"What about your mother?" Royce asks.

I shake my head no. "She's gone."

She flashes a quick look to Kenton. "I'm not sure about the time, but after we met with him, we were taken to Andrew Sawyer's facility in Alaska. After the initial meeting, we never saw him again."

I see the corner of Kenton's mouth tug, which is his tell for when he is lying. *What are they hiding?* "I don't understand. If my father organized for you to go there…that would mean he was involved?"

Royce squares her shoulders toward me. "Anson, there's a lot to fill you in on, and I'm more than willing to tell you, but right now, we need to focus on the bigger picture."

"Which is?" Kenton asks, mocking his mom.

"I have to go check on this boy Tucker and then check back on Henly, but you need to gather the Board as soon as you can."

"No," I respond. "You've kept me in the dark before to get what you want, and I won't allow you to do it again." I stand firm by my words. "If you want my help, you'll tell me your plan."

She shakes her head no. "I can't until I know that Henly is okay. She's the key to all of this. If she can't testify in front of the Board, then all of this will be for nothing. If her memories have returned, no one can know. Not yet at least," she adds right before she leaves.

"Why? Part of your secret plan?" I scoff.

"Yes," she says as she closes the door behind her.

I turn to Kenton. "What did they do to her?"

His head drops. "I don't know how bad she is or how far he went with her memory. One day in surgery, my mom triggered something in her brain that returned some of her memories, but it backfired. She went crazy. She fought every one who got in her way—killed two nurses. They had to confine her for weeks. A few days later, Ana contacted us. We met her a few miles from the hospital gates, and she told us the truth about Henly, Andrew, the deviations, and deniferia. She told us we had to stay and watch over Henly. It was the only way we could end whatever they had created. She told my mom how to restore Henly's memories and what parts of the brain to avoid."

My hands clench into fists. She will never change. I used to feel bad for Ana when Henly would go on one of her rants and portray her mother as an ice-cold villain capable of all kinds of evil, but now, experiencing it all for myself, I see that Henly was right.

Davis's words come back to me: "She is a slave to her ambition." There is a bigger reason she has stayed, beyond her fear of Henly being harmed. *She is a slave to her ambition. There's something in Henly Ana needs. There is a different reason Ana wants her back, but what is it?*

"How did she contact you?"

"A message through a nurse who was a friends of hers. I don't really know, my mom tells me very little," he huffs.

"Why bring her back? Why now?" I ask.

"She wasn't going to survive much longer."

"And you two are…"

"I don't know," Kenton replies. "You and her were…"

"Yes, we are…or were." I don't continue. Instead, I tell him, "You should go see Zoe. She'll be happy to see you."

"Where are you headed?"

"To gather the Board," I respond and leave the room.

CHAPTER 11

HENLY

The chains dig into my wrists every time I move. For some reason, they thought it would be a good idea to chain me to my bed in my cell. I woke hours ago to the slight drip of water slowly drumming from my sink in the corner of my cell. It still drips, and with each *tap, tap, tap* the water makes against the metal sink, I lose a little more of my sanity. After my eyes adjust, I realize where they put me, and the moans from the other cells only confirm it. The moans are from people who cry out as the virus courses through their veins and from those who whimper, asking when they will be allowed to leave. I hear one of the medics get thrown from the room. An alarm is sounded, and then there is a sharp snap followed by silence.

Before working for my father, I would have been terrified simply being near those noises—the way they'll do anything to get out of their cells. Now, being down here seems fitting. With every groan, they take me back to my father—to Alaska. It was a place that made sense, and only in the confines of this small room, I can admit I miss it. When I was there, I had purpose, a reason, but here, I am a monster. I'm nothing more than a prisoner chained to a past and a present that is muddled into one big pile of chaos. No matter where I run, I can't escape that.

My hands reach for the tears that stream down my cheeks, but the chains restrict me from even that basic comfort. Apparently, trying to kill your mother after all she has done to you is not justified. Tracing the links of my chains, I feel where they are weak and weigh the idea of breaking them and running. *Where would I go?* At this point, it doesn't matter. I just need freedom. I crave it. Pulling my wrists, I feel the handcuffs dig into my skin. The small drips of blood trail down my wrists until the pain subsides and the cuffs are gone. Lying still, I hear the heavy thumps of footsteps. They are slow at first and then gain haste. I pull a piece of metal from the foot of the bed and take a few steps to the edge of my cell as footsteps approach. It was stupid for them to think they could keep me locked away here. I will get out, and when I do, I will run.

But as the anticipation builds, my limbs grow tired; it is as if I have been treading water for hours. The door opens, and Royce appears. For a moment, she seems relieved.

"You're awake. Good." She smiles as she closes the cell door behind her.

"Royce?" I cough.

"How are you feeling? I see you're already redecorating," she says, motioning to the metal pole in my hand.

When I let the metal clink to the ground, the deviations in the cells around me react, thrashing against their walls. "I'm tired," I admit.

"Come, sit. We have a lot to discuss."

I lean my back against the wall across from her. I keep as much distance from her as I can. "I don't want to talk. I want to go to my room."

She looks up from her notes and exhales. "With what happened this morning, I'm not sure that will happen."

"Okay…" I exhale and continue on with what has been eating at me. "How long have I been gone?"

"Two and a half years," she replies.

I've been gone two and a half years? The memories whirl in and out of focus. They found me months ago, but made me stay with my father. A different kind of anger begins to build in my hands, and I feel it flow through me. A quiver in my arms reminds

133

me of the wounds on my wrists, but as I glance at them, I notice they are already healing. Soon, my memories will be no more than a small scar to match the others.

"Is it over?" A part of me already knows the answer. *It is never over.*

"Almost," Royce says empathetically.

"Where's Davis?"

"Soon. Let's debrief you."

I feel the tears hit full force as my new memories burst against my old ones. I remember the person I was and see the person I have become, and it frightens me. Two and a half years I have been missing. No, not missing—misplaced. They knew where I was, but I didn't. My hands clutch my head in hopes the pain of trying to remember will stop.

"It will get easier to decipher which memories are real from those that aren't," she explains.

I shake my head. I'm suddenly aware of the emptiness inside me. "They're all real. That's the problem."

I stare at the woman I once trusted with my life. The horrors of what we have done can never be undone. In a matter of seconds, I have to fight the rage that fills me, and I lose focus until Royce places an arm on my shoulder.

"Don't," I say, responding to her gesture that no longer comforts me.

"Henly, we need the notes and documents you concealed. Did you bring them with you?"

"Yes, you told me to write down everything. You planted that memory. I remember." I exhale. The small memory springs awake in my mind. Two years ago, I agreed to this, and Renner, he knew the whole time. It all suffocates me. "Reina," I whisper. I turn to Royce, my glare ice cold. "You let me kill her!"

"Who?"

"You know who!" Of course, she might not. Our list of experiments is endless, but I don't dare say her name aloud again—I'm not brave enough. "All of them…" The words flitter out. The weight of my replaced conscience consumes me.

"They had to die," Royce says.

"No, they didn't," I say through gritted teeth. "They were innocent!"

"They were your father's orders. You adored him. You obeyed every single one without hesitation. I couldn't intervene. I couldn't change them. If I had, he would have known."

I study her face. Her expression surprises me. She is sad. *Could it be she didn't want them to die?* The room seems to shrink as I walk toward her and take a seat on the bed next to her. I look at her and wonder at what point did I lose my innocence. *At what point did they steal it from me?* Exhaling, I realize, with parents like mine, I never stood a chance.

"We need those documents before the Board convenes," she says softly.

I nod. "Where are my things?"

She stands and motions for the guard to open the door. Quickly, she is handed a bag full of my belongings, and then the door is slammed shut. I hear the heavy heartbeat of the Militaris soldier as he reassumes his position on the other side of the cell.

They should be afraid of me.

Royce looks at me with a smirk. "Can you blame them? They don't know what you are."

They don't know what I am? Do I know what I am? "Do they honestly think they can contain me?" I threaten.

Royce places my pack on my bed and then turns to look around my cell. "Your mom helped design this. I would say they're confident." She pauses and then looks me in the eyes. "Can they contain you?"

"The hinges on the door aren't reinforced with steel; they'll break easily. Based on the pitter-patter of footsteps, there are what, three—no, four guards waiting outside my cell. There are four more by the door to the elevator, which comes down every thirty to forty-five minutes. Each one is heavily armed, but knowing my mother, they're ordered to keep me alive. The buzz from their shockers are awake, waiting just in case I try to escape, but if they knew anything from what happened today, they would know I would feel nothing more than a prick. There's a nurse whose heart beats too loudly; she holds the syringe to sedate me." I look up to Royce and ask, "Isn't that right?"

"So, why not escape?" she asks curiously.

I shrug my shoulders and stare hard at Royce. "Same reason you chose to come down here to see me personally—curiosity."

She smiles and hands me my bag. "Good."

I search through it and find the notebooks. "Here." I hand them to her. "What do you need them for?"

"Proof."

"Of what my dad...Drew...has done?"

She shakes her head. "No, proof of your loyalty." She flips through the pages and then looks back at me. "You're going to help me take down Andrew."

"How?"

"In time," she replies as she heads to the door. "Henly, one more thing."

"What?"

"For what it's worth, I am sorry." Her words ring through the air. I know she is, but that doesn't make a difference. *Does it?* "Prove it," I challenge.

"I'll make sure you get out soon."

In true Royce fashion, she walks away without looking back. At times, I wonder if this is just a wall she puts up so she doesn't have to feel bad for what she has done. In her eyes, it doesn't matter what harms she has caused as long as the outcome is good. My fingertips trace the grooves of the gray walls that surround me, feeling every soft dip of the mortar as it intersects with the next brick. Through the walls, I can hear everything. At first, it was hard to control what I could hear, but I learned to manage it, and it soon became something I liked. I can hear a woman in a cell through at least five walls who chants the rosary over and over again. I can hear her heartbeat, and it is strong, unlike the rapid beating of the deviations down the hall. She will live.

"Henly Marie Sawyer?"

His voice carries through the crowded hallway, but I would know that voice anywhere.

"Dex?" I whisper.

I hear his footsteps until he is just outside my door.

"Militaris four-nine-seven, here to see holding patient eight-two-four."

"Denied. Cleared personnel only," a voice declares.

"I'm cleared through Board member one-seven-three, Anson Renner."

There is a short silence and then a loud buzz. Only a few seconds pass before we are in each other's arms.

"Are you okay?" he asks as he grabs my face in his hands.

"I'm okay," I whisper between breaths. "Are you okay?"

He laughs. "I'm okay. I'm sorry it took so long to find you."

I shake my head in an attempt to regain my

composure. "What are you doing here? Don't you know I'm a threat?"

He smiles. "She deserved it."

The door closes behind him, and he follows me to my bed. Before we sit, we just stare at one another, taking in all the lost time. His appearance hasn't changed much: same brown eyes, same smile, same demeanor. In the last two and a half years, he has grown, and more hair and stubble decorates his face. His eyes, they show the same kindness they did years ago when I first met him.

"I see you got new clothes while I was gone?" I inquire.

He looks down and shrugs a bit before he says, "I switched titles."

"What? That isn't allowed."

He grins. "When you have a Board member on your side, anything is possible."

Matching his grin, I reply, "Well, there you go."

His voice turns serious. "So, this morning…"

I shrug my shoulders. "Yeah…I don't know what that was."

"Are you going crazy?" he asks as his finger

rises and begins to make loops near my head.

I swat his finger away from my head before it can make any more crazy loops. "No," I say. "At least I hope not." I force out a laugh.

Suddenly, I hear a buzz and look around the room. The buzz is quiet at first, and then it grows into a loud hum. We are being watched. I can sense it. My index finger hovers over my lips as I motion for Dex to stay quiet. Closing my eyes, I try to focus. I try to separate the heartbeats from the feet that shuffle in other cells. I separate the noise of Dex's breathing from the buzzing and feel the energy that beats off the floor beneath my bed. I sense the small camera's movement above my head and act.

Some things started off as a hindrance when I got my enhancements. At first, everything was too loud. The sound of my own breathing would cause a migraine, but now, my enhancements are an added strength. I take the piece of metal I ripped from my bedframe and smash it above my head where the first device is. Then, I find the second speaker beneath the bed. I wait a few more seconds to feel the vibrations in the room, but the buzz wears off. I look at Dex, who wears a strange look on his face.

"They were watching us," I confess.

"And now?" He looks around the room.

"We're in the clear," I reply.

"I'm sorry…"

I shake my head and realize he is about to give me the apology he has been waiting to give me since the day he left me behind in Havre. It wasn't his fault, and I wish he knew that. But nothing I say will make him realize that, so I let the silence linger, and to be honest, he and I know silence well. We have always been connected by our unspoken bond, and we have never really needed words to be comfortable with one another. I remember all the times before we would just sit and share one another's company, knowing we were never really alone. In this moment, here with him, I realize again I'm not alone. I have my friend back.

"I haven't told Davis anything," he whispers after some time has passed.

"Don't. There's no point." The cell seems to close in a little. "I don't want her down here, and I don't even know how long they'll keep me here."

"You won't be here long."

"Have they said something to you?" I ask.

"Renner is working on it," he says, but there is

an uncertainty in his voice, or maybe it is frustration.

Renner. He was at the bottom of the list of things I wanted to face here, but with each one that gets knocked off, he moves up on the list. For a moment, I try to find things to put at the top of the list: find Dex—check; get out of this cell; see Davis; say sorry to Quinn; find Vaughn; figure out Royce's plan; kill my dad; and then face Renner. But, at this point, I feel like I might want to add "apologize to Ana" for, oh, I don't know, strangling her. Honestly, I will do anything to keep him at the bottom of my list.

"How's Quinn?"

He lets out a small breath. "She's good. Keeps busy, but good."

"I let Ellie die…er…she died while she was with me, and if you could pass on the message that I'm sorry…" I pause, knowing the apology should come from me. "No, wait. I'll tell her when I see her."

Dex nods.

"I saw Adam when they dragged me down here. He seems to fit in. And the others?"

"Hill is here working in the medic unit, DJ is training to be in the Militaris, and Tucker is being monitored in the medic unit. Luke, he travels a lot. He and Quinn fizzled out a few months ago."

"Who knew you'd be so up to date on all of the gossip." I laugh.

"Well, she didn't have Ellie, and you were—" He stops when he sees my face. "That's not what I meant...I just meant that she felt alone."

I place a hand on his shoulder and force my regret to the back of my throat. "I know."

"I just, it was hard. It was hard without you. That's all."

I'm not one who is fond of being touched, but when he embraces me, everything is right in the world. It is different; he has always been my friend. We left Aurora together, and he was there when I had to face my dad, and he is here now when I have to face all of this.

"I know what you mean," I say.

"You didn't even know who we were!" he scoffs.

I push away from him a little harder than I mean to and watch his face turn serious. "Sorry, I don't know my own strength sometimes." I clear my throat. "I knew something was missing. It's just, I'm different now, but I knew."

"Nah, you're the same, just a little stronger."
He stands. "I wish I could stay longer, but I have drills
to run. I just wanted to come and see you while I
could." He embraces me again.

It is strange. With all the memories I have, this
is one that burns alive in my head: Dex's embrace. His
embrace is tight, but not suffocating, and long enough to
let me know he really cares. He feels like family. I smile
knowing some things will always be the same.

"You'll be back soon, right?" I ask.

"Of course." His hug makes me feel otherwise.

The room echoes as the door slams shut behind
him. Even with all of the memories that suddenly seem
to fit into place, I know I'm not the same person I used
to be. I can't be that person. It is not that I don't want to
be, but time won't allow me. Being here in Aurora is an
even louder reminder of that. With all of my
modifications, I can't go back. I can't pretend.

I stare at the mirror in front of me that reflects
my cold green eyes. They resemble much of my
mother's coldness. My runner's frame even has her
familiar curves now. I squeeze my eyes shut a few times
in hopes that when I reopen them, I won't see Ana
staring back at me. But she is. I see her in my beige skin

and in the small freckles of emerald in my eyes. I think my father saw her in me too. Sometimes when we would be up after surgery researching, I would catch him staring at me with a mixture of awe and sadness. It was almost like he missed her and he wanted to be a normal family again. Sometimes I thought his gazes seemed regretful, as if he felt he had words left unsaid from a fight they never fixed, but now I understand it wasn't that type of regret. He regretted that she didn't join him. She didn't believe in what he was doing. Even now, she is more redeemable than I am. She got out, literally ran away from him as fast as she could. My fists clench, and for a moment, the memory consumes me.

My father's affection for me was never real. I was, and will always be, just an experiment to him. The moment whirls through me, and I don't know whether to cower or fight. I have to get out. I have to breath. I take a step to the door, and my fingers freeze on the handle. *Where would I go? Home? I don't have one anymore.* I walk back to the small sink in my room and wash my face. The chilling numbness of the cold water trickles down my neck, and it is barely enough to shake me from the fear that, in more ways than one, I am becoming someone I never wanted to be—my mother.

I lie back down in bed and kick at my pack until I hear it *thud* to the ground. I know I can't keep hiding from the truth. Royce's plan is crazy, but I have no choice other than to follow along. I let out a heavy sigh. I stand and find the picture of my dad and me sitting next to each other in one of my many recuperation rooms. His arm is draped around my shoulder as I lean into him. My eyes are closed, and his lips are on my forehead—a very Kodak moment. But staring at the photo brings me to a false memory. *At some point, he had to have loved me more than an experiment. I mean, I am his daughter!* There is a knock at the door, and quickly, I push the picture back in to my pack and shove my pack underneath my bed.

CHAPTER 12

RENNER

I can't focus. I replay the conversation I had with Royce. She has a plan and I'm not privy to knowing all of the details. *How can I work with that?* I can't focus. I have yet to see Henly since she had her memories returned. I made it as far as the quarantine floor before I turned away. I couldn't force myself to go in. I'm not sure what is holding me back. So for now, I force myself to move and focus on something else.

I reach the boardroom and start making calls. My requests for every member to attend tomorrow's meeting are met fairly easily. All but one agrees to make an appearance. Word has gotten out that we have Henly, and I'm sure the Board members are in a rush to get here, to analyze her and see if she is as special as the rumors say she is. My role in all of this doesn't sit well with me, and I can't help but think calling this meeting is a bad idea. I can't explain why, but there's a gut feeling that leaving the entirety of tomorrow's meeting to what ever Royce has planned makes me uneasy. I keep thinking back to when she talked about my father, speaking in present tense as if he were still alive, or at least very recently deceased. There is something more to Royce's plan. I can feel it. There are too many gaps in her story for all of it to be true, and I'm going to figure out what she is hiding.

I leave the boardroom, but instead of going back to my room, I walk down several hallways, down the elevator to G-4, and past the quarantines. A small hallway takes me to a restricted area where I type in my access code: one-two-nine-three-six-four. The light flashes blue and then green before the door slowly opens to the archives. I gently close the door behind me as the lights flash on one unit at a time, exposing history.

Before civilization had ended, a unanimous vote assured certain relics would be saved. These relics were supposed help us rebuild our new civilization. Though, looking around, I'm not sure how all of these artifacts will serve as blueprint. It is not that easy. For us to grow and reestablish ourselves, we also have to adapt, to learn, to evolve. At times, when I feel as though things will never change, I come down here and look at the archives and remember we are capable of creating a society that is united, a society of liberty and of justice.

I follow the rows of history, and on any other day, I would sit and read through military strategies from WWI, WWII, and WWIII. The way a powerful man can influence the masses to perpetuate his own agenda baffles me. This is real Machiavellian type stuff—make them love you or make them fear you, and if you're really good, make them do both. But today, as I walk through the archives, I can only think of Henly and her father. Her father's own agenda is what got us all here.

I want to be there for her, to save her, but if she thinks I left her in Alaska, then she will never forgive me. Before, I would have ignored her wishes and pushed my way through the walls she built around herself, but not now. She doesn't need me. I can't chase her now, especially after what she has been through— especially after what I did with Zoe. *Zoe.* I haven't spoken to her since the other night, and to be frank, I'm not sure what I would say. This whole situation is a real mess. I look around. Henly would have liked this place. She liked stories, at least the stories her father used to bring her after one of his many trips. *Liked—I keep thinking about Henly as if she is in the past and not locked up in a cell a few floors below me.*

Before I allow myself to fall any harder for a girl who is no longer mine, I leave. I take the same hallway I came through, but stop halfway and look down to find my hands shaking. I'm nervous. *Go in. Just go.*

"Renner?" Adam says as he looks down at his sheet. "There are no transfers scheduled for tonight."

I shake my head. "No, I'm not here for a transfer. Just…can…can I get…Sawyer's room code?"

He hands me a sheet of paper, and I look at the numbers on it. The codes change every twenty minutes.

"Down the hall, last room on the left," he replies and then chuckles. "You won't be able to miss it."

I nod and take the walk down the long hallway. Each step takes me farther into the quarantine where the soft whimpers from those who are waiting to be moved to the upper levels change into groans, but not the pained kind—no, these groans are vicious, enraged. I open a latch and peer into the room through the viewing pane to see a deviation thrashing against the cell walls. It has just turned. Her eyes are almost clear, her flesh fresh and clean, but her mind is gone. She is lost to us. Right then, I stop and think about what I'm doing. *What am I thinking? I'm going to break her out of here and then what?*

"Hey! Don't just stand there. Keep walking. I have a headache, and you're making them get louder!" I hear Henly yell through her cell door.

I slide the latch closed and fumble the key card in my hand, still undecided of what I'm going to do next when I hear her whisper.

"They're too loud." She sounds exhausted. "It's all too loud."

All in one motion, I grab the paper in my hand and walk to her cell. I input the codes to her door. When the light flashes green, I turn the handle and take a step inside. She is sitting on the edge her of her bed, her pack barely visible behind her legs. She's surprised to see me. Did she not expect that I'd come see her? If I'm being honest, I didn't think I would show up here either.

"Need a break?" I ask her.

For a moment, her face scrunches together like she is unsure of why I came, but she quickly recovers behind a calm, blank stare. She looks around the room and exhales before she speaks.

"Breaking me out jail? That's not the Renner I remember."

"You're not in jail," I respond.

She mocks my answer. "Then why don't I have a key to my own room, I mean *cell*?"

Her tone is sharp like glass. She sounds just like her mom: clear, cutthroat. I take a step back.

She motions to her surroundings. "You can see why I'd be confused?"

"Do you want out or not?" I reply, losing my patience.

She studies me. It takes a few seconds for me to realize that she must think I'm armed. I raise my hands in the air and do a quick circle to show her I'm not here to hurt her.

"What are you doing?"

"Showing you I'm not armed," I answer.

She snickers underneath her breath. "As if that would make a difference," she says as she walks past me.

I follow her a few paces down the hall until we come face-to-face with Adam. He looks at Henly like she isn't a person. He looks at her like I would a deviation—up and down, assessing to see if she needs to be sedated or shot. I don't blame him. When I first saw her, really saw her, in Bowden, I looked for any threats that she could possibly present. The soldier in me forces me to weigh potential risks, and I had to look at her that way. In the end, we don't know what Henly is, which makes us all tread cautiously.

"Taking her out for a walk?" Adam asks nervously. "Make sure she stays on the lower levels. Royce and Hill don't want her interacting with others yet."

"Excuse me?" Henly scoffs, taking a step toward him.

Adam ignores her and hands me a vial. "If her vitals go crazy and her rage appears, inject her with this. It will keep her out long enough to get her back to her cell."

"Cell," she says triumphantly, as if her point earlier has been proven.

Smartass.

"What's this?" she snaps.

Adam takes Henly's hand into his hand and places a metallic bracelet around her wrist. He grabs the light from his inner pocket and flashes it in her eyes, watching her reactions. "It's to track your whereabouts. It also checks your vitals around the clock, and it makes sure you won't go all big green on us."

"Big green?" She asks.

Adam turns to me grinning. "Like the Hulk. *Smash!*" He begins to smash the air around him with his fists.

I crack a grin. Adam is strange, but at least he knows how to diffuse the tension. Henly, on the other hand, doesn't find this funny, not in the least. She looks like she could kill him right here.

"Let's go before you start smashing him." I laugh as I lead Henly out into the hallway.

"Stop laughing! It isn't funny." She huffs as I head down into the archives.

I turn to her. "It's a little funny."

She clenches her jaw and shakes her head no.

I stifle my disappointment and keep walking. That is another thing to add to the checklist of things she has lost: her sense of humor. We get to the door of the archives, and I type my code into the panel. The short walk from the quarantine to the archives has seemed like a marathon. The light turns green, and I let her in before me. She takes a step inside, and I hear a sharp intake of breath. *I knew she would like it here.* She turns to me, and for the first time in months, she actually looks me in the eyes and speaks to me.

"What is this place?" There is an awe in her voice that makes me smile.

"The archives. It's where we keep history." I point across the room. "You're going to want to look over there first. That's where we keep all of the literature."

She turns to me and studies my face, but doesn't say anything. Instead, she follows my guidance to the shelves that hold stories upon stories. Her fingers trace the shelves, reading each title as she passes them.

"Spend a lot of time down here?" she asks.

I shrug my shoulders. "Lately, yeah."

Her lips curl into a mischievous grin. "Nerd," she says, but then turns suddenly serious. "Why are you doing this? Why did you bring me here?"

"I don't know," I answer honestly.

I watch her as she pulls a book from the shelf and flips through the pages. Her hair falls around her face, leaving only the book visible. I close my eyes, and just like that, I feel like things are normal again, like I am back on that hill outside of the compound memorizing her dark hair, her green eyes that bore happiness into mine. This Henly is engrained into my memory. I will never be able to forget her.

"Guilt," she whispers.

I open my eyes. "What?"

"Your guilt. It won't allow you to let go," she adds.

"No," I almost yell at her. "That bullet wasn't meant for you." I flinch as I remember the way her father put her in front of the bullet that was meant for him. He used his daughter as a shield. It makes me sick.

"Funny, seeing how I'm wearing the scar." She places the book back on the shelf, and I watch as she tucks her hair behind her ears. "I hate you for making me stay. I hate you for making me go through that for your greater good. I hate it. I hate you." Her eyes are glossy as she starts to yell at me. "You could have freed me, or at least let me know what the hell I was agreeing to! You could have let me be aware of the choices I was making! You could have saved me!"

"What are you talking about? Henly—"

"No! You don't get to stand here and act like you get it. You don't get to bring me here and act like everything that happened was okay! You couldn't even be the one to give me the orders to stay."

I look at her with confusion. *What is she talking about? I didn't make her stay. I spent the last*

two and a half years looking for her, disregarding my
assignments and orders so I could search for her.

"You may think you have brought me back, but you didn't. I died there," she finishes. "The girl you think you brought back doesn't exist anymore. She died in Alaska, so don't visit me again hoping to see her." Her final words are pleading.

I look up and see tears running down her cheeks. I want so badly to reach out to her, to fix this mess, but as I stare at her, the truth becomes more prevalent—she is gone. What hurts the most is staring at the shell of someone you used to love and watching them change and being unable to change with them. This is Henly now. This is who she is—a stranger.

"Henly, I-I-I'm—" I stammer before she cuts me off. I'm unable to get my bearings; she has caught me off guard. I don't know how to respond, how to make her understand.

"You're what? Sorry? You don't get to be sorry for what I had to go through. You get to stand there, tall and strong, knowing you did the right thing. That's what you're all about, isn't it?" She walks past me, and her final words sting. "I can find my way back, but will you?"

Her words sit with me long after she is gone. *Will I find my way back? Will I make it back to a place where she isn't my focal point?* I turn around and stare at the door she walked through hours ago. I can't get my legs to follow her. I can't make myself go after her to demand an explanation—to explain myself. Eventually, I make my way to the door, turn off the lights behind me, and head for the surface.

CHAPTER 13

HENLY

"Where are you coming from?" Hill asks as he sees me.

"The archives."

"They trust you enough to let you go walking around?" he questions as Adam walks up behind him.

"Renner took her," Adam answers.

Hill looks at me, and for a second, I think he can see right through me, like he knows what happened between Renner and me and wants to comfort me, but he can't.

"How are you feeling?" he asks.

He looks different. The worry lines on his forehead mask his handsome features, and his eyes seem darker than I remember. *Spending time with Ana will do that.* My tongue searches the top of my mouth for an answer, but no matter how hard I try to force myself to respond, I can't, so I shrug my shoulders. "Been better."

He checks a box on his paper in front of him and motions for me to go ahead of him.

"I have to grab my pack," I say.

"No need, I got it," a Militaris soldier responds a few meters back.

"One Sawyer, Henly for transfer," a transporter announces.

I take the bag from the soldier and follow Hill into the hallway. The guards have doubled and each carry sedation guns, just in case I lose it again. *Good idea.* At least this is an improvement from the last time they transported me. I'm impressed. I strap on my pack and stand taller. I follow them out.

As we turn down the hall, I catch a glimpse of Renner getting into an elevator. He doesn't see me, but the mere sight of him flurries my doubt. *Should I have yelled at him the way I did?* It doesn't matter. Everything I had to say was said, and I meant it. Everything I went through could have been different.

"What's in the bag?" Hill asks, breaking me from my thoughts.

"Nothing, just random clothes, nothing deadly." Instantly, I regret my word choice. "I mean, I'm not going to kill you." That doesn't ease the growing tension.

He looks up, his brow arched. "I figured as much. Are you ready?" Hill's voice carries loudly across the sullen medic room.

"For what?" I reply.

"No one told you?"

I shake my head no.

"We reset her memories only yesterday morning," Royce says as she enters the room behind Hill. "Grab your things. Let's go."

"Your vitals looked good as of two hours ago." He smiles at his chart and then to me. "A lot less crazy going on up there," he says as he points to my head.

"You haven't even evaluated me, " I respond. The last time Royce came to see me, she had all kinds of contraptions to determine my condition.

"We didn't have to. The room was doing it for us, that is until you decided to kill our sensors." Royce's voice lingers on the edge of agitation.

"Oh, you mean my jail cell that you bugged?" I ask with a grin.

"Stop being so dramatic," Royce replies. "Please go with Hill so he can check your vitals."

When I turn the corner, there she is—my mother. It is the second time I have seen her, but the first time I have seen her since I attacked her. The marks around her throat are covered by white gauze; however, she looks like she is back to her usual self, completely submerged in charts.

"I'm surprised they let you in here. After all of the chaos you caused, I figured you would be dead already." I taste my words, and they are bitter. They don't mask the rage I feel inside.

"Nearly strangling me to death wasn't enough? You still feel the need to insult me?" Her words reach me, but her gaze doesn't. Her voice is hoarse and cracks with every other word.

I look down at my hands and remember how they felt wrapped around her neck, unapologetically strong. Her eyes are immersed in the charts in front of her.

"You tell me," I say as I lift the hem of my shirt and expose the scars left behind by my father.

She finally looks up, her lips pressed together. Her face softens, and right when I think she is going to respond, she doesn't. She shrugs me off and turns back to her work. She is still the same woman who traded one daughter for the next. She left me in Alaska to be tortured and dissected like an animal. My hands begin to tremble, and I'm afraid I will lash out again. The room shakes, and it is as if I am losing control of my emotions. This is something my mutation isn't supposed to allow—emotions. A while ago, my father had injected a serum into my nervous system. He said it would help me remove emotion from any situation, which is supposed to help me think more logically. I have been learning how to adapt to this change, and for the most part, I have been able to keep it under control, but this is not one of those times.

"What's happening to me? Why am I losing control?"

Royce speaks up, "We don't know."

"That's why you're here," Hill responds. "We need to do some blood work to see if we can figure it out."

"This happened to you a few times when you were in Alaska. Drew couldn't pinpoint the problem, but during one of our last surgeries, he finally found something."

"What did he find?" my voice cracks as I speak. *I'm afraid to know.*

"He never told me. The only thing he let on was that you were to go through the final stages."

"What are the final stages?" Hill asks.

I don't need to ask what the final stages are. I put people through their final stages, but the only thing that catches me off guard is that the final stages were left for those who were to be made an example of or who had information that would benefit us. The final stages were always reserved for those who reacted to the virus and were becoming deviations, but that couldn't apply to me. My eyes narrow as I try to remember if I had felt that way, if I had felt as though he was going to kill me. But as soon as I catch onto a memory, it blurs into another. *Was he going to turn me into a deviation?* I look up and find Hill with a syringe in hand, motioning me to sit.

"How are you going to get results from my blood. I'm the only one like this."

Hill shakes his head. "No, you're not. Not anymore. That night in the compound when we were attacked by the deviations, Tucker was shot. Do you remember?" Hill asks. "You matched his blood type."

The memory is vague, but as he tells it, I begin to see it more clearly. I remember running back to the compound with Renner. I cringe at the memory of the wind that lashed and pulled at us. We barely made it over the fences in time. Tucker had wandered out in the middle of the night, and the soldiers shot him.

"The blood transfusion," I whisper as I trace the small needlepoint scar on the inside of my elbow.

"Your blood was infected with deniferia, and you passed it to Tucker," my mother adds. There is a slight sound of disgust in her voice.

"Take as much as you need," I say, feeling exhausted.

I sit down and feel his fingers roll up my sleeve. I hear everyone in the room gasp, except for Royce; she was there for most of the creations of these scars. Even Ana can't look at the way the scars crisscross against each other. Quickly, they turn away, and in that brief second, I can only imagine what I look like through their eyes. I'm a monster of sorts, like Frankenstein. Hill ties an elastic band on my arm, flicks at my vein, and then inserts the needle.

"I'm sorry," I say.

He looks at me, his eyes full with sadness. "Me too."

It doesn't take long for Hill to have what he needs.

Turning to Royce, I ask, "So, what's next?"

"The next phase," she responds.

"Of testing?" I ask. It seems like I'm the only one in this room concerned about what my father's plans were. The others just want results, but I can't blame them. I want to know too.

"No more testing. If my suspicions are correct, we don't have much time."

I'm about to question her suspicions further, but my attention is caught by the file my mother is carrying. I look at Hill, who gives me a nod and walks into an office I assume is his with my vial of blood. I follow my mother. I stand at the entrance of her office, arms crossed, watching her work. She pulls blood into vials and exchanges them with others. Nothing has kept or will ever keep her from her work.

"Do you know what she is?" I ask, keeping my tone low.

Startled, my mother drops the stack of papers and turns to face me. "Know what?" Her voice cracks when she speaks.

"After everything I've seen, you're going to act like I don't know anything?" My voice is no higher than a whisper, but it is sharp.

She looks to the file on the table and hands it to me. "It is dormant," she says.

I take the file and look through it. "How have you kept it dormant?" I ask as I scan through several test results.

"I've created a temporary serum for Davis, but her cells keep evolving, adapting to whatever I give her. So therein lies my struggle. I have to keep creating something that will outsmart deniferia, but I have found a positive strand that has become a foundation for testing a long-term vaccine for all those infected." She turns back to the vials on the table.

"A cure?"

"Essentially...if I have enough time."

The charts reveal what I already knew about Davis, what my father told me about her. Davis is infected, another test subject for my father's ruthless experiments—only he doesn't know where she is. I scan the sheets that barely make any sense, but keep reading them over and over again in hopes they will become clearer. *My mom found a temporary fix. Is it possible she can find a cure? If only we had some people to test the possible vaccine on, we could do trials and make an effective cure. Infect them and then vaccinate them. The lives we could save.* I look up to find my mom analyzing me.

"What?" I ask defensively.

"You like it."

"What? No," I respond quickly.

"You do."

"No."

"I know how your father is, the types of things he likes to learn, and the extent he'll go to to learn them. He skips animal trials and goes straight to the real thing—human testing. If you want real results, then you have to test the real thing. You have the same gleam in your eyes that he gets," she says as she leans against the shelf, looking pleasantly surprised. "Of course you're curious. It's in your blood to be curious."

For a moment, I don't understand what she means. *Am I curious because I want to know what is happening to me or because I'm their protégé?* She stares at me, waiting for a response. My back burns up my spine and settles into small tingles around the nape of my neck. "I'm not like you," I spit out.

"*That's* what you're worried about? Being like *me*?" she asks, amused by my sudden defensiveness.

"I'm not like you," I force myself to say again. But to be honest, I'm not sure I believe it.

"No? Perhaps you're like your father." She

takes the file from my hand, turns back to the vials in front of her, and then begins to work through them.

Her words sting and leave me unable to respond. She is right though; if I am not like her, I'm like him. Both of them, like the virus, are in my blood, and I fear I will never be able to escape either of them.

CHAPTER 14

RENNER

The chopper lands a few miles outside of a city west of the Aurora. The streets are nearly vacant as the sun makes its way down the abandoned buildings. It is a ghost town. Oddly, it is as if the buildings and cars are waiting for someone to inhabit them again, to make them useful. Things have gotten worse—less rescue calls and more control calls. Somehow, the virus is still fiercely spreading. Earlier today, we got a transmission call from survivors in the area. It has always amazed me that after all this time there are people who refuse to seek help.

"All right, let's get a perimeter set up. I want men securing their area for the next two blocks. After it's secured, we'll send out a transmission and make contact with the survivors. Let's be sure we get them out quickly and quietly. Ferruli, I want you and Johnson in the chopper with Edelstein and Rivera. Any movements, you let me know." They nod and head to the chopper. "Riddle, you and I will head up ground zone."

Formulating the strategy is always the easy

part, but complications always arise when getting to the survivors. This area is easily one of the most heavily populated with deviation interactions, which makes this rescue that much more intense. I tug on my equipment, making sure everything is secure. Nothing can go unnoticed. I look around for any details that seem out of place. Something feels strange. I tighten the strap on my pack, and with my rifle raised, I decide to head over to Ferruli. I feel uneasy about the quietness, but in unison, we move forward.

I came out here to forget about this morning's revelations and all of the chaos that awaits me back at Aurora, but I can't. I grit my teeth, *let her go*.

"All clear in the sky. Over."

I grab my radio. "Anything seem out of place? Over." I ask.

"No, not a thing. We're ready when you are. Over," Johnson says.

Why does his voice sound muffled? Is he getting out of range? "Stay in the zone. If you go out of it, we'll lose you. Over," I reply.

"Will do. Over," Johnson says, his voice distorted by fuzz.

"We got the clear. Let's go," I say as my finger

circles the air above me.

We make our way down the streets easily. Actually, there is no sign of anything really. *This is too calm,* too *quiet.* I look over my shoulder, but see nothing behind me or in front that should cause concern.

"So, she's back," Riddle says as he comes up behind me.

I nod yes, but keep my attention ahead.

"How messed up is she?" he asks, and for a moment, the question makes me defensive, but I know he doesn't mean it as a personal jab. It is just another question Riddle would ask anyone else who had been captured.

"Pretty bad," I respond.

"Is that why you're out here?"

I shrug my shoulders and stop short when my radio fills the quiet. "Renner, you got a pack coming on your flank—no, your rear—wait, they're surrounding you!"

I don't wait for the next report. I search my surroundings for the best possible outcome, and set my sights on a fire escape that leads straight to the roof. I get Riddle's attention and point to the fire escape. He directs the rest of the Militaris to the ladder. As we are ascending the ladder, a voice booms over my radio.

"Renner, get out of there now!"

It is too late. They are flooding all around us. I grab Riddle by the shoulder and bolt into the street. I look back to see some Militaris soldiers are following us, but the others who made it up the ladder now fend for their lives. I want to help them, but there is no way we can fend off an attack this massive. *The right thing…think! What's the right thing?* I push them from my thoughts and focus on the men I have left.

"You are my eyes, Johnson! Get us the hell out of here!"

"Left, down the back alley, and then right!"

Johnson continues to guide me in and out of alleys until we reach a building. "Where now?"

"They're coming from all sides."

"There's no entrance! Just a brick wall and a parking garage!"

"They stopped," he shouts back.

"What?"

"The ones ahead of you aren't moving, and the ones behind you have stopped."

I switch gazes between Riddle and the handful of Militaris soldiers who linger behind me. "All right, we're going into the garage. We need to make this quick—in and out." I look behind them. The deviations are banded together to form a long wall and are slowly making their way toward us. "We leave no one behind," I finish.

I stare into the dark garage and flip on my light that sits right above the scope of my gun. *This is not what I had in mind when I left the quarantine this morning.* I grab my radio and order Johnson to find me the nearest exit, but as luck has it, there isn't one. We have to go through the garage and make our way up. Up and out.

"Johnson, I need you to send a transmission to the survivors and let them know we've been delayed. Over."

"We've been trying to send a communication since we got in the air, but there's no response. Over."

"Something isn't right," I say to the dark garage

"I agree. Let's get the hell out of here," Riddle answers.

Looking behind us, I motion the rest of the men to follow me in. The farther in we go, the more every noise echoes off of the walls and the more tension builds in my muscles. It is pitch black, and the flashlights barely give us enough light to see a few steps in front of us. We search the walls until we find stairs that lead us into the building. I'm getting impatient I need to get my soldiers to safety.

"Over here!" Someone shouts.

I flash my light on the door and motion for Riddle to open it. Quickly, we file into the building. A bitter smell overwhelms us. The floor is slick tile looks like its been recently cleaned, shiny to the point where I can see our reflections. I give orders to scope out the area. The building looks like it was used for some fancy office job. Some of the old furniture has collected dust and cobwebs. It seems this building was once filled with regular, uninfected people who sat at their desks thinking about what would constitute an appropriate time to clock out. How strange to think of the world as it was before to what is has become now, and not even be able to connect the two.

We set out down the hallway to find stairs or anything that will lead us to the roof. When we finally do, something hits me. I turn back to the way we just entered. *The floors are clean. Next to nothing is broken or damaged.* The only thing that is remotely dirty is the dust that has gathered on a few tables. This building no longer seems so abandoned. I look over my shoulder to Riddle who seems as confused as I am. I watch as he grabs his radio.

"What's it looking like out there? Over," Riddle asks.

"They're waiting for something. Just stand—"

"Johnson? Hello, are you there? Ferruli? Over," Riddle repeats, but there's only static.

Whether they have gone down or our communications have been lost, we are now on our own. I walk back to the door we entered through and peer back into the parking garage. The deviations are right outside the door. As I turn away, I hear a pounding across the hall.

"Stairs!" someone shouts.

The rest of us rush to the stairwell and take the stairs two at a time until we finally reach a door on the fourth floor. I can hear my heart pounding in my ears, or maybe it is the deviations rushing up the stairs behind us. Either way, I don't have time to figure it out because the stairs end.

"What the hell?" Riddle pants.

"We have to go in and across! This style of building has multiple stairwells. If we're hitting a dead end, that means we have to go in and across this floor to get to the stairs on the other side!" a recruit shouts.

I look up and read "Peters" on his nametag. I have got to make sure I get to know the new recruits. I nod, and we break through the door to find a small makeshift hospital, or at least that is what it appears to be. Rows upon rows of beds line the room, and the people lying in them are each strung up to some kind of IV. I gesture for the others to be quiet and point to the door across the room. As we make our way, I look over each person who lies motionless. In the far corner, one of them begins to stir. I hold a fist in the air to signal the others to stop. I quietly push past a bed and head toward the woman who is stirring. It is then that I truly notice the others, their bodies. Some are decaying, but most of the bodies are healthy. They are not dead, just sedated. I stop halfway to the woman and slowly start to back up. *Someone is turning them. Someone is creating more deviations.*

As I turn back, my gun clinks against metal and sends a ringing sound into the air. That one small *ding* is enough to make the woman's eyes shoot open and focus on me. As she is about to pounce, I raise my gun and ready my aim. *Who would do this?* I fire a round straight into her heart. Suddenly, the others start to move, but before we can lose that fight, we run out of the room and up the stairs.

"What was that?" Riddle asks.

"They're changing them," I say.

His face pales to the revelation. "What?" he responds in disbelief.

"They're making more deviations," I spit out as we push up the stairs.

Before we make it to the last staircase, we have to cross another lobby. Riddle turns to me.

"Do you think there are more?"

"Probably, but hopefully they're sedated." I look down the stairs behind us. "We have no other option."

"We're delayed. Help is on its way. Over," I hear Johnson's voice boom on the other side of the door.

I exchange a quick glance with Riddle before we push open the door. The room is dark, and with the exception of Johnson's voice, it is quiet. Then, Peters walks in and the lights flash on, awakening a screen. Johnson's voice comes to a screeching halt, and the screen begins to flip through images. It starts playing as if it were on a timer, looping over and over. Slowly, we file in and barricade the door behind us with random furniture we find in the room. We are making our way across when her voice echoes throughout the small room.

"Davis, it'll be all right."

My feet have lost any motivation to continue on. I look up to the screen and see Ana cooing into her daughter's ear. The others continue on, but I'm frozen—fixated on the screen.

"Here—" Andrew hands Ana a needle "—inject this."

"Drew, I'm not sure she can withstand this."

"She can, and she will. Henly has already been infected, and the virus is dormant. Davis needs to be our fallback, our second plan." Drew speaks as if Davis were just another experiment.

Ana stands, but can't inject Davis. Drew grabs the needle and jams it into the little girl's arm. I watch as Davis lies limp, as if she were dead, and then suddenly, her body begins to fight whatever Drew has injected into her. Ana turns away, but Drew doesn't. He watches until she has stopped moving and then walks over to Ana.

"You'll have to make sure she stays medicated. If you miss a dose, she'll become active."

Active? I look to Riddle who is fixated on the same screen, but he turns away when there is a thrashing at the door. *Time to go.* I rip my eyes from the screen as it goes black. We don't wait a second longer to make it up the stairs. When we get to the rooftop, the chopper is waiting.

"What the hell happened to you?" Ferruli asks.

"Communications were lost," Riddle said, a little out of it.

"Let's get out of here!" Johnson yells over the blades.

I nod and wait for everyone to load before I get on myself. I look at Riddle, and he's wearing the same deep expression I am. *What the hell just happened?*

"We've been trying to connect with the survivors, but there's no response."

"There were no survivors," I say. "Someone wanted us there, but not to save lives," I finish.

"An ambush?" Riddle questions.

"What? How do you know that, Renner?" Ferruli asks.

"This is where we were supposed to find the survivors, but we found this hospital instead. The deviations only stopped chasing us once we got to this room full of people. They were hooked up to wires and IVs, a whole army of them."

"What for?" Ferruli asks.

I shake my head. "My guess, they're test runs. Fake rescue calls to test how well the deviations will do. Anyone who gets captured is changed."

Everything has led us to this. The silence on board is an indication that things are far from over. It all makes sense: this is what Henly's father is planning. He is creating an army. *An army for what?*

* * *

The chopper lands in the early hours of the morning. Dawn is peaking over the mountains, and I can feel it all catch up to me: the lack of sleep, searching for Henly, Zoe, and tonight's discovery. These are all things I'm going to have to face. Shadowing my eyes from the early morning sun, I make my way back into Aurora.

"Where are you headed?" Ferruli asks me.

"Grub and then sleep. I have a Board meeting in a few hours I have to prepare for. You know how those go," I say as we step inside Aurora.

Ferruli grabs my shoulder. "You have to tell the Board what we saw tonight. I know it might put your girl at risk, but they have to know what's going on outside these walls."

"Yeah, I know. If he's building an army, he is coming for something."

"Or *someone*," he replies.

I know who that someone is.

"Do you think he knows she's here?" Ferruli asks.

"If she's not with them out there, then where else would she be?" My voice is flat when I respond. By now he has to know.

Ferruli exhales deeply. "Maybe we should start training the new recruits twice as hard to get them ready."

"Yeah, I think that's a good idea. Get DJ to gather his unit and start training twice a day, starting today," I say. "Write up a report. Have Johnson and Riddle fill theirs out too. Get all paperwork together and meet me outside the boardroom so we can debrief the rest of the Board members."

Ferruli nods in agreement and leaves to meet up with Riddle and Johnson to get things in order. He is a good second in command. I take the stairs down by two until I'm standing outside of the elevator. When the doors open, to my surprise, I find my good friend Kenton on the other end.

"I've been looking for you," he says, his body blocking my entrance.

"Yeah? What for?" I reply, nudging past him to get into the elevator.

"I chose my title." He grins at me smugly.

"I'll set you up with Ferruli later toady."

"No, I want to train with my long-lost friend. I mean, you don't seem all that thrilled to see me," he says with a hint of laughter in his voice.

I press the stop on the elevator. "What is this about? Is this about Henly? I don't have time to deal with that. She's yours. All yours!" I yell without meaning to.

Kenton's back straightens, and he suddenly stands taller. "What the hell are you talking about?"

Gritting my teeth, I anxiously press for the doors to close, as if pressing the button again and again will make this thing go any faster. "I saw her last night. She thinks I made her stay."

He looks at me with sincerity in his eyes. "They play tricks on you. Get you to do what they want without caring what the repercussions are."

"What's that supposed to mean?"

"Think about it. People around here, or in Alaska for that matter, only serve one purpose."

Through narrowed eyes, I look at him with confusion.

"They either support the cause or they don't. Everything in the middle is fair game. Think about what she has been through."

I rub my forehead with my hand and instantly know what he is talking about. The elevator shudders. I look up at him when the light *dings* for the main floor.

"Come with me," I say to Kenton as I motion for him to follow me.

I tell him everything that happened last night while we were downtown. By the time we make it back to my room, he is caught up on everything we saw, including the people who were strung up and ready to turn. Kenton said he had heard rumors about this happening, but he could never be sure. Henly's dad never let him get too close to military strategy. I listen as he explains his own theory about what Henly's father is up to. At one point, he even lets my father's name slip. He said that when my dad was alive, he had been very much a part of this whole thing, but the way he speaks about my father makes it seem like he is still around.

"So what now?" he asks. "How do we prepare for this?"

I shrug my shoulders. "We first have to figure out what or who he wants."

Kenton sits back in his chair. "I assume that Henly is his main person of interest, but does Andrew know about that Tucker boy in your infirmary?"

I shake my head no. "No, not even citizens here know who he is." I lean my head against the arm of

187

my chair and stare at the ceiling. I have no idea how to connect the dots or even where to begin.

"Go back to the beginning." Kenton's words ring loud.

"Davis," I whisper.

Kenton looks at me with confusion. "Henly's sister? What about her?"

"She was in the video, the one in the hospital. Ana didn't want to inject Davis, but Andrew—he didn't care. He took the needle from Ana and jabbed it into Davis's arm. He said that if Davis was medicated she'd become active."

Kenton looks at me, and I can see his mind working. "If Henly is the perfect person, then Davis has to be the antithesis of that."

We look at each other, and at the same time, we say, "He wants them both."

CHAPTER 15

HENLY

A light tap jolts me awake. Quickly, I search my surroundings and discover I'm back in my room. The walls are the same cement gray as I remembered. Honestly, not much has changed. Lying back down, I stare at the ceiling and let my memories come over me. Memories from my childhood mixed with the lies my father has told me. Different images of Davis blur together. *I haven't seen her yet. What will I say to her?* I turn when I hear more taps at the door. As I walk to the door, I grab the sweater from my chair and pull it on over my head. I barely get the door cracked open when Davis's frail body bursts through the door and clings to me.

"Mom only told me this morning!" she shouts.

I wince as she refers to Ana as "Mom," but instead of acknowledging it, I reply, "I'm sorry. I was in quarantine. How are you?"

We walk together to my bed and take a seat next to each other, my arm hanging around her shoulders. I look at her. Her hair has grown back—still blond and still gorgeous. Her eyes don't shine the way they used to, but how can they after everything she has been through? As I hold her, I can feel her bones where more flesh should be. I take her face in both my hands and kiss her forehead. When I pull away, Davis wipes the tears away from under my eyes. I smile down at her, but she doesn't smile back.

"Are you okay?" she asks.

"Yes, I'm fine," I lie. I can hear the doubt in my own voice.

"Mom said you're different, but she wouldn't tell me how."

There she goes again calling her that. "I am different. Better. Why are you still skin and bones?" I joke as I poke her hip.

She finally smiles. "It's the medication Mom has me on. She doesn't know what Dad—Andrew has done to me, so this helps keep things at bay."

She doesn't know what she is?

After a few moments of silence, she asks, "Are you dangerous? Is that why they had you in quarantine?"

I look at her and am amazed that my mom—our mom—is still protecting Davis. She didn't tell her about me trying to strangle her or the truth about what our dad is doing. Ana is a parent to one of us, and even though my heart aches to know what that would feel like, I find comfort in the fact that at least Davis will have that with Ana.

I try to sound positive, but feel like I fail on my delivery. "I'm okay. They had me in quarantine as a precaution. But no, I'm not dangerous. I've got a handle on things."

She smiles and takes me in her arms. Her hug is warm and familiar. She is my family, and I have missed being around her. I have missed feeling like I am more than just a lab rat. I pull away and see she is now the one crying.

"What's wrong?"

"He didn't like me the way he liked you. The things he made me do…endure. The surgeries, experimentations—I only hope he didn't make you…" she doesn't finish.

Oh, no. She wants to talk about what has happened. I look between her and the floor. *How do I tell my sister I don't want to talk about it? I know she wasn't his favorite. I was—I am.* Suddenly, being so close to Davis doesn't feel that comforting anymore. I don't want to relive what I have done or been through out loud, especially with Davis. I can't sit here and pretend to share this with her. This will not bond me to her. This will push me further from her, and that will drive me straight into insanity.

I pull away from Davis. "I can't"—I gesture between us—"do this. I can't talk about it yet."

Her head drops. I know I used to be the person she would talk to; the one who would hear her complaints, pains, hopes, and wishes with ease; and the one who would help guide her. But I can't do that now. I can't hear what he has done to her. I can't relive what he has done to me. I can't place that on her shoulders. *I'm a murderous coward.*

"What title have you chosen?"

For a second, she is perplexed, and then she looks down at the floor. She stares at the floor for so long that I follow her gaze. When she speaks, it catches me off guard.

"They won't let me pick one." Her voice is as soft as a whisper. "I'm too much of a liability, so I just help wherever I can."

I want to disagree, but I hear my father's voice ring loud: "She's infected." *But what does that mean? What can she do?* When I look up, her eyes are fixed on me.

"You *are* different," Davis says quietly.

The statement affects me more than I think she means it to. I suck in a small breath of air and nod in acknowledgment. The worst part is that I can't even deny it. I am different, but not in the way she thinks I am.

A knock sounds from my door. I hesitate to answer it. I want to reassure her, tell her that everything is going to be okay, but those words don't come out when I finally compose myself.

"I just need time," I say. "Time." I exhale, trying to believe my own words, but I don't. Time won't change anything.

Another knock, this one more urgent than the last, startles us both. I open the door to find Dex on the other side followed by several Militaris soldiers. It is time to meet with the Board. I turn back to Davis and swallow the lies I have successfully fed her. There is no longer a familiarity between us. We are just two strangers staring at one another, hoping that one of us will make the effort to seem like nothing happened— like we are normal. I have missed her so much that it nearly drove me crazy to think she was gone. She was my confidant, the person I would turn to when our parents were driving me mad. She understood the struggle I was going through. But now, looking into her eyes, I see in her what I felt over the past months. She is mourning. The Henly she knew—the sister who used to make fun of her about boys, Ana, everything—is gone. She is now stuck with the robot our dad created.

"I have to go," I whisper, feeling ashamed.

Her expression softens when she stands and reaches out to Dex. "Okay. I'll catch up with you later?" She looks back to me. "Love you, sis."

"Love you."

The smile I give is forced, but I hope that it comforts her. We both know we will never be the same. I look past her to Dex who informs me to bring the journals and all of the photographs. As I grab the contents out of my pack, I catch a glimpse of Davis and Dex. The way he rubs her back, the way he is there for her, and the way they have grown into each other makes me nostalgic. In this moment, my memories with Renner come fully into focus.

Renner sat with me in the storm while we were trapped in the compound. I close my eyes, but Renner's face morphs into Vaughn's. He was also there for me, reminding me to live and to breathe when everything was so suffocating. They both helped me through different phases of my life, but here I am, icing them out.

"Henly?" Davis whispers my name.

I look up and wait for her to speak again.

"Henly, I'm glad you're back."

"I'm glad I'm back too…" This time, I'm not sure if it is a lie or the truth.

* * *

The elevator screeches to a halt as we stop outside the main level. In my hand, I hold the key to Royce's plan—a plan I'm not too sure of quiet yet. If she can pull it off though, maybe it can work. We can make it work. I flip through the pages of the journals as my nerves set in. Every five minutes Dex asks me if I'm okay. When it is time, we walk down the corridor, and the Militaris gathers around me, hovering over me like they could keep me contained. I wish they would realize I'm here on my own terms. If I wanted to escape, I would. I exhale and try to let it roll off of me.

"Nice to see you're being compliant," Royce announces as she greets us in the hallway outside of the boardroom. "Planning on fighting anyone today?"

"No. Here." I hand her the book. "This is what I wrote down. This is all of it."

She folds her arms across her chest. "Dex, give us a minute."

He doesn't move until I give him the go ahead.

When he is finally out of hearing distance, Royce speaks, "You know that charm you've got? You're going to have to dial it up."

"Charm? What are you talking about?" I ask. "What the hell does charm have to do with anything?"

"If this is going to work, you're going to have to ask to be a part of the Board. They have to accept you," she demands.

"No! There's no way. They won't. I-I-I can't," I stammer.

"Look, Henly, this must happen. You need to push out Anson. You need to make sure he's off of the Board. Do you hear me?" She looks over her shoulders as the Board members begin to arrive, filling the room one seat at a time.

"He is a founder's son. They won't let me push him out!" I shout.

She quickly grabs my shoulders. "Anson doesn't know his father didn't die in that plane crash. If he finds out, if he knows, he'll go to the ends of the earth to make sure he finds proof—finds him." She pauses to look at me. "Look at what he did to find you. Before we found you, he was relentless. He will be the same with his father. And when he finds him, his father will convince him that he had nothing to do with any of this, that it was all Andrew's plan, and Anson will believe him. Anson is our weak link here. His father makes him vulnerable. He's always had this odd desire to please him, and because of this, he'll think that it's right to give the senator a second chance. I cannot allow it knowing that the senator has been working with your father. Anson will bring the senator back here where he will find exactly what he needs to finish out the plan. And you better believe that if Anson leads the senator back here, your father will follow, and everyone here will be in danger."

I hate the words that leave her mouth, but she isn't wrong.

"How do I do it? How do I get them to push him out?"

"Five minutes," Slade announces as he walks past us and into the boardroom.

Royce smiles graciously at him before she

turns back to me. "Listen, we'll have to use you and his father against him."

"What?" I grab the folder. "What's in this?"

She exhales, and for a moment, I can tell she already hates herself for what she is about to do. "It's proof his father was a part of it all. If they think Anson could, in any way, be involved, they will suspend him until a further investigation can prove his innocence or guilt."

"Guilt? He's not guilty."

"Are you sure of that?" Royce's tone is accusatory.

"Absolutely. He doesn't even know his dad is alive. He wasn't a part of this. This isn't right," I whisper. "How does this help you? How does this hinder my father?"

With an exhale, she looks me straight in the eyes and says, "Look, his father is a part of this just as much as your father is. You both are linked in that way—sins of your fathers. To bring this operation down, we have to sever the arm of the giant. This plan will help us do that. If we can take down Anson's father, then we're another step closer to success. But I can't trust Anson to react in the way that would benefit us once he finds out his father is still alive. Not yet anyway. Don't throw away everything you went through in Alaska for *him*. Do you hear me? Make it count. Anson left you there to do a job, so do it. Do the right thing, and take down your father."

Her words light my fire. She is smart enough to know what to say to make me hate all of them. "You will tell me the entirety of your plan when this meeting is over. Not one second after."

"Fine."

"It's time," Dex announces.

I turn away from Royce before she can say anything else.

As I close the door behind me, Slade is already announcing me like I'm the plague. "Ladies and gentlemen of the Board, welcome. Thank you for coming and convening on such short notice. As you can see, Henly Sawyer will be joining us for this meeting. If any of you are worried about contamination, we have provided masks, but I assure you she is not contagious."

Do you hear that? I'm not contagious. Good to know. I turn to find nine of the ten seats full. In front of each person, there are small, rectangular metal plaques with their quarantines and names engraved on them:

Rosco, Ronald Slade—the same man I remember with beady eyes and a long bird nose, his skin still snow-white and taut; Holstein, Henry Glenn—a somewhat pleasant Asian man who is too tall for his chair with black hair and square black frames over his eyes; Jarrell, Susan Porters—a small pudgy woman who looks like she is on her last breath, and when she coughs, I smell her cancer, so her chair will be open soon; Duram, Christina Munn—a smiley young woman who is ready and astute with a pen in her hand; Bowden, Charlie Lancaster—a familiar face with concerned eyes; Edson, Geoffrey Scott—a paranoid man who quickly puts on his mask and who does not find it funny when I pretend to cough in his direction; Ecatepec, Juan Guillermo—an older man who reminds me of my abuelo as he leans back in his chair, stroking his black and white beard; Sinaloa, Danica Torres—a middle-aged woman who looks like she could be related to Ana; La Paz, Ulisses Petro—a man who doesn't seem to fit his name with his bright orange hair and beard a shade lighter; and Aurora, Anson Renner—the man I once thought loved me, and the man I'm about to hurt. His chair is empty. I look over my shoulder to Dex, and he sees it on my face.

"Take your seats," Slade booms over the quiet room.

"We're still waiting for Renner," says the woman from Duram.

I follow Slade's hand to a pair of seats toward the back of the room. "We'll begin without him."

We take our seats, and the meeting begins.

CHAPTER 16

RENNER

He wants both of them. I've been so wrapped up in Henly and the discovery of the army her father is creating, that I haven't been able to see the bigger picture. My only fear about presenting this new information to the Board is that I have no way to measure the ramifications of what could happen to Davis. She has always been quiet and kind, kept to herself, and follows the rules in the quarantine. Once, when she found me frustrated, she told me about a time when she and Henly were kids. They had gone on a trip somewhere. Their parents were out late when Davis had woken up from a nightmare. She said she had dreamt that her parents were mad scientists performing experiments on her. Henly had searched the apartment where they had been staying and didn't find their parents anywhere. So, Henly had stayed with Davis the entire night, even after she had fallen asleep. Davis didn't know for sure, but she figured Henly was staying awake to yell at their parents, and sure enough, in the morning, Davis had heard her ten-year-old sister yelling at her parents. Their father apologized, but Ana had gone to bed. Ana had refused to be lectured by her daughter. In hindsight, I realize Davis's dreams were real, something her subconscious was trying to tell her. She doesn't deserve this anymore than Henly does, but if she's a threat, she needs to be hidden.

"You're late."

I look up in time to see Riddle outside the door. "Have they started?"

He nods. "Yeah, and if I were you, I would hurry up and get in there."

I walk into the boardroom with Kenton on my heels. The tension grows as they all turn to face me. I scan the room and find myself halted when I see Henly in between Royce and Dex. My eyes narrow as I spot a folder in her hands. My gut tells me something is wrong.

"Mom?" Kenton whispers in confusion. He turns to me and gives me a look that only years of friendship could solidify. He has no idea what she is up to.

"Welcome," Slade announces. "It is nice of you to finally join us. Dr. Royce was about to debrief us about our current situation in Alaska and the miraculous discovery of Ms. Sawyer," his voice is less sincere.

I take a seat and motion for Kenton to pull up a chair next to me. As he sits, Henly stands, and her eyes narrow on us for a second too long. I have to clear my throat to get her back on track. The dark circles underneath her eyes are deep; she is exhausted. Her body isn't frail like I remember, but rather strong and full of purpose. She is not the same girl I saw the other night, and the notion of not knowing what has changed with her stings. Looking at her now, it seems like I'm staring at a stranger.

"Royce doesn't need to speak for me," Henly says finally. She takes a second to look at every single person and then at me. "Over the past few months, my stay in Alaska has been informative. While being held captive, I was able to gather enough information to help bring down Andrew Sawyer." She looks at Dex, and I watch as he hands her a notebook. "In this book is all of the information needed to infiltrate Alaska. The only thing missing is the information on his other facilities."

She divulges things that have kept me up at night, like where she was held, what procedures have been done to her. But what shocks me is the fact that he never treated her with malice. She was his project, and he had to protect his asset.

Time seems to stand still, but when I look at the clock above her head, I notice an hour has passed. I turn to Kenton, and his eyes meet mine and then quickly divert to the ground. Nothing is new to him. Then, I search the Board members' faces and read something different on each. One reads sadness, another pain. The others read with anger, disbelief, or disdain. I finally look back to Henly who has stopped talking. Each depiction of surgery and the many who have died through her father's experiments are exactly what I would have expected. Her descriptions of her father's projects are thorough and alarming, but not once does she mention the army he is creating, the hundreds locked in a building on the outskirts of California and who knows where else.

"And what are we to do with this information?" Slade asks, cutting through the ear-piercing silence. "We have no way of knowing if what you say is true." He sits up in his chair and looks at the other members of the Board. "This—" his fingers motion to the table and then to those around him "—could be a ploy to infiltrate our facility," he says with a sneer on his face.

"If that were the case, he would already be

here, and you would already be dead or worse—changed." The way Henly speaks mirrors Ana. Her raised brows exude annoyance as if their questions are absolutely absurd. She has always been to the point—realistic—but not this cold, not this calculated.

"Leave us the notes and findings, and we'll discuss what our next step is."

"No, after what *this* Board has put me through, absolutely not."

"Then what?" the Board member from La Paz questions, "You come here and expect us to trust you?"

Henly's eyes close, and her hands ball into fists. I motion to Kenton to ready himself just in case she loses control again. After a few moments, she opens her eyes and takes a shallow breath.

"If trust is what you are concerned with, then let me prove myself. Though, after everything I have done for *this* Board, I don't think that is necessary." She opens the documents in her hands and begins to pass photographs around the table. "When I returned and was given my memories again, it came to my attention that one of the men who helped my father orchestrate the attack and who helped him carry out his entire plan was a man by then name of James Renner."

My lungs pinch, like I have just taken a blow to the ribs. *My dad. She knew about my dad? Did she see him? Did she speak to him? She knew.* The entire room turns to look at me, but I don't protest. Kenton and Royce implied he was involved, and even though I'm not sure if it is true, I can't say for certain it is not, so I don't react.

"Renner!" Slade's voice booms across the room. "What is the meaning of this?"

"As you can see on the death certificate, he was identified by yours truly, Anson Renner," Henly says. "Isn't a little odd that *he* was the one to identify him as dead, yet he's alive?"

"No, this has to be a mistake," my friend from Duram says. Her fingers flip through pages of photographs.

I look up through blurry eyes, anger erupting, to glare at the girl I once knew. She is using what my father did against me as if I had known this whole time.

"There's no mistake," Henly announces firmly.

Kenton stands. He looks past Henly and speaks to his mother. "Is this your plan?" Kenton turns to me and then to the Board. "He never spoke about Anson, not once. Anson never knew his father was alive." He turns to Royce. "We both thought he was dead. He didn't know."

"And who are you?" Slade demands.

"Kenton Vaughn. I brought Henly home."

"You have no standing here. Either sit down and keep your mouth shut, or I'll have you removed," the woman from Jarrell yells.

"Thick as thieves," Henly says as she glares at Kenton.

"I can't believe this! I can't believe you!" Kenton shouts at Henly.

"That's enough!" Royce yells at her son. "Remove him! Now!"

Kenton is grabbed by Dex. "Let go of me!" Kenton shouts. I watch as Dex escorts him to the door. "Tell them! Tell them what they are! Tell them what Davis is!" Kenton insists.

I keep a steady eye on Henly, and her face pales.

The images of my father have traveled down the table to me. I pick up an image of my father standing next to Andrew Sawyer arm in arm, like friends. Slade slides the rest of the photos in front of me, and I can feel his eyes judging every expression.

My father's face has aged significantly, but his weathered features still looks the same. His shoulders seem taller somehow, like he has grown into his arrogance. His face is clean-shaven as it always was. There are a few marks on his right cheek that must have been from the accident—well, *faked* accident. He still wears the same tailored suits with a square knotted tie neatly pinned behind his suit jacket. I look up when I hear the room in an uproar. Henly stands on the other side of the long table, arms crossed over her chest, with an unreadable expression on her face. I wish for my anger to subside so I can deal with this logically, but it doesn't. I pull the piece of paper out in front of me and let Slade take the rest in his hand.

"Enough!" Slade shouts, his fists pounding into the table.

Royce stands. "We don't know if we can trust Anson Renner, and I motion for an investigation."

Slade replies curtly, "And what, leave Aurora in the hands of the Council?"

"No, I suggest we use our asset. We use Henly."

The room erupts in dispute. Someone shouts at Royce, asking if she has lost her mind, and I'm tempted to agree. Another shouts that Henly is a monster and can't be trusted. My eyes linger on Henly; she doesn't flinch at any of the accusations thrown at her.

"Did she or did she not just attack her mother?" Slade asks on behalf of the Board.

If I weren't so pissed, I would be in awe of how confident Henly stands and answers his question. "The attack was controlled, and I was under the influence of a vaccine your facility gave me."

Royce turns to look at Henly and then back to Slade. "Yes, she reacted negatively to the serum we injected her with. That, in combination with the return of her memories, led essentially to a neurological overload, which made her lash out."

"But how are we supposed to trust you, Ms. Sawyer? You have been in hiding with your father," a woman argues. I'm not sure who it was because I can't look away from Henly.

"I have information you need, and I know how to get to him without killing more people."

"And you won't share it with us unless we vote you in?" one of the Board members asks.

"I'm not sure if *you* can be trusted. With Renner on the Board and no positive determination of whether or not he's aligned with his father, I can't trust that whatever I tell you won't be fed back to the senator or my father." Henly's gaze stops on me, and she unclenches her fists. "Make no mistake, I'm aware that it was *this* Board that asked me to stay with my father. You all voted to make me his capture to gather as much information as possible—for *you*!"

"No, we didn't!" Renner shouts.

Slade pulls a piece of paper from the stack he has in his hands and gives it to me. "This is your signature, is it not?"

My signature. I find my name scribbled at the bottom. I read it further. The document is an order to keep Henly in Alaska, and my signature is at the bottom of it. *My* signature.

"I didn't sign this. This was forged," I say, and with a glare, I watch Henly as her face changes from anger to confusion. She looks at Royce, but she doesn't return my gaze. I slide back the sheet of paper to Slade. *I spent months searching for her, but this is what she thinks of me.* Kenton's words ring to mind: "They play tricks on you. Get you to do what they want without caring what the repercussions are."

"By the looks of it, there does need to be an

investigation as to what is going on," Royce says. "But in the meantime, Anson Renner should not be a part of this Board. He should not be making decisions if his judgment is clouded."

"How is my judgment clouded?" I protest.

"Henly," Royce states matter-of-factly. "You'll do anything to keep her safe."

I set my sights on Henly. "Which is Royce? Did I make her stay in Alaska, or do I want to keep her safe? Pick one."

Henly keeps her attention on the men and women gathered in the room. "Andrew Sawyer kept me as his prisoner. He created me to extinguish all qualities he considers weak, especially emotions. If anything, you could benefit more from me than I from you."

"Make no mistake, Sawyer, I have allowed your return, but I will not agree to you becoming a part of this Board," Slade responds to Henly. He then turns to me and says, "Though you have never given us any reason to doubt you, Renner, we have to investigate further to determine if you were ever involved with your father after his accident and supposed death. With this, I believe the best course of action is to—"

"Wait!" I say before I can stop myself. "What

about the army he is preparing? Why haven't you spoken to that?"

The room fills with whispers. Henly looks around and settles on Royce before saying, "There is no army."

I nod to Riddle who walks to the door and exchanges a few words with Johnson and then walks back with a folder in his hands.

Taking the folder from Riddle, I flip through it until I find the images from earlier. "Then what is this?" I slide the papers in Henly's direction. "What are these? He has hundreds of people strapped down, ready to wake for an attack. And this is just one facility here in California. Who knows how many he has or where they are." I look at the Board members surrounding me. "If you think I have any involvement in what my father has been a part of, you're wrong. Just last night, I was out with my men, and we found this, something *Ms. Sawyer* has so kindly forgotten to mention—among several others." I say her name with malice.

She opens the folder and looks through the pages. Slade stands and practically rips the folder out of Henly's hands.

"When was this discovered?" demands

Lancaster, the Board member from Bowden.

"Just last night," I say. "We were on a search and rescue when we encountered this makeshift facility. We were corralled into the building. There—" I point to the map in the folder. "Someone wanted us to know what was in there. It is was a warning."

"Your father," Henly whispers.

I narrow my gaze on her and say, "How could he? Isn't he dead?"

She flinches and her muscles around her arms spasm. She shakes her head lightly as if trying to gather her thoughts and make sense of what is in front of her. She seems unable to pinpoint which thought goes where. For a brief, fleeting moment, I feel for her. She is caught between different people who keep using her for their own benefit. She had a choice though.

"Exactly," I say. "She can't even discern what memory belongs where, yet she stands in front of us with false documents, forged signatures, and an order to release me for her own benefit." I look at her and see pain and anger cross her face.

"I have information you need," she says, but not to me. She speaks to Slade.

"Information fed to you by your father—" I

interject "—which is muddled by memories you can't even decipher. You're no good to us."

"No, not just my father, *yours* too," she snarls. "Remember that."

"How could I forget? Isn't that the whole point of you accusing me of treason?" I faintly mock.

"Enough! What exactly do you want in exchange? I will not release Renner without a full investigation," Slade states.

"To end this war—"

"It's not war! It's genocide!" a voice interrupts.

Henly clenches the table as Royce speaks, "When Henly first accepted to stay with her father per our request—"

"No, per *your* request," I say, speaking this time to Henly. Her eyes catch mine, and for a brief moment, she softens, but it is not enough for her to believe me.

"We confused some existing memories so her father wouldn't be able to understand the truth. However, when she was rescued, we were able to return the memories we had tampered with," Royce finishes.

"You've already said that, but why is she

really back? Is she finished there? Has she gathered all the information she could?" I ask.

Royce's jaw lifts just a little as if she were trying to remind me of her authority. "She discovered enough to know what his next move is."

A mocking breath leaves my lips before I reply, "Is that why she knew about the army he's building?" I say sarcastically. "Why is she really here? Did she realize she was going to be terminated, so she fled to save herself?" My glare focuses on Royce.

"That doesn't mean—"

"Of course it does. Suddenly she's here willing to tell us everything to save her own skin, and you want us to take your word for it without presenting any evidence, right?" I question and wait for a response. My jaw hardens when I see the pained look on Henly's face from my words. At this point, she has made it clear who she is loyal to. *There's no turning back now.*

"I'll leave nothing unanswered. You will know everything I know," Henly declares.

The room is quiet until Porters speaks up, her voice slightly tainted by the machines, but not enough for us to hear the worst possible idea. "That isn't enough. Renner is right. I don't trust her. I trust Renner.

He's never led us astray. I'll only vote if the two of you work together."

Across the table, Henly turns to face Royce, who seems to be pulling Henly's puppet strings. Royce's gaze meets Slade's, who eventually looks to me. It is one giant game of pass the buck. I sit back in my chair and shake my head, still unsure of what I want.

"She *would* be an improvement to the Board. She knows things. Henly, you would be willing to divulge them?" Slade questions.

"Yes," she says as she stands taller, but she still doesn't look at me. "But I will not work alongside the senator's son. I have endured too much," she finishes.

I want to fight back, but what can I say to that? She has endured too much already, and I now know my father was there aiding Andrew in his endeavors. He was there, and I couldn't do anything about it. I spent months searching for her, and all the while, she thought I had left her there. Now I know—some things can never be undone.

"Let's take a vote," Slade announces.

"No," I say standing. "Right now, Henly knows far more than I can help with. I'll take my leave and stay head of the Militaris until further notice. I caution you all to keep an eye on the decisions being made in my absence." Turning to Slade, I finish, "You begin your investigation on me, and when it's finished, I'll take my place again."

Henly's eyes are wide.

"Renner, that is absurd. We cannot allow a Sawyer to be a part of the Board!" Munn from Holstein yells.

"I will reclaim my seat as a governor with the Council. Slade and the rest of you will oversee her decisions and make sure she doesn't step out of line. While I am away, Slade will take charge of the Board. She will not have final say," I finish.

Henly drops the pencil in her hand and looks stunned. I take a sharp breath and shift my focus from Munn to Slade. He sits up, amused by what is unfolding. He is satisfied. Slade has now attained the position he has coveted for years. He is now the leader and the head of the Board. But I don't mind giving up my seat; this will make it easier for me to remain under the radar, to come and go as I please—to search for answers.

"Are you sure that this is what you want?"

Slade asks me.

"No, but this is what is best for the Board. And I too agree that I cannot work alongside someone I do not trust and has been programmed to follow orders," I say with malice and keep my gaze on Royce.

"I follow no one's orders," Henly spits at me.

"Yeah, whatever you say," I scoff arrogantly. *Two can play this game, Sawyer.*

Slade stands. "All those in favor, raise your hand." I watch as all hands but mine rise.

I'm neither for nor against Henly joining the Board, but I'm shocked as to how many hands went up in her favor. She may have pushed me out, but the only thing I can see is a girl who has been broken and is still being used by those around her.

"Opposed?"

No one raises their hand.

"Welcome to the Board," Slade says to Henly.

Henly pulls out a medium-sized notebook from her back pocket and smacks it on the table. "I wrote as much down as I could in here. Everything you will need to know about Drew's facility is in there."

Slade takes the book and hands it to me. "Take copies of these, would you? Make sure every Militaris soldier knows this book inside and out. Every detail needs to be recorded."

I take the notebook in my hand and head for the door, but before I can get out of the room, Slade adds, "Renner, make sure you verify Henly's story as soon as this meeting concludes. She will need to be vetted further."

I can't catch a break.

"That's an order," Slade says with a smile. He likes the sound of that.

I open the door and give Henly the courtesy of heading out first with Royce following suit. When Henly is a few paces ahead, Royce turns to me.

"There is a point to this. I promise."

I grab the back of my neck and feel the day already weighing on me. "I knew this was all you—the forged signature and pushing me out. My mom was right by telling me to watch out for you," I sneer.

"Your mother—God rest her soul—and I were friends. I tried to help her get away from your father, so this is personal for me too."

I look at her in confused anger. "You failed then, and you're failing now. You think Henly is up to the task?" I take a step away from her. "I have a verification process to begin."

She doesn't stop me. I walk up to find Dex and Henly talking and catch the end of Dex's words.

"You did what? How could you do that to him? Push him out like that?"

"That's what I'd like to know," I say to both of them.

For the first time today, she keeps eye contact with me, and I feel a piece of myself return.

"I don't know. I barely found out that this was a part of the plan," Henly says.

I motion to a room down the hallway. "You don't know." My brows rise in feigned surprise. Lifting my fingers, I say, "Puppet strings."

"Screw you." Her jaw is tight when she finishes.

"Hey, whoa," Dex interjects before the tension can escalate.

I give in and say, "I'll set you up with Riddle and have you verified."

"They were *your* orders, weren't they?" Henly asks, and I sense a hint of worry.

" I thought it'd be better this way since I'm not to be trusted," I say.

"What? What exactly happened in there?" Dex asks the both of us.

I smile, trying to bury my frustrations. "Not sure, but can you set Kenton up with the Militaris? I need him ready and prepped quickly. We have orders." I motion to the notebook in my hand.

Dex takes a step back and looks at Henly sympathetically. His look makes me almost feel bad for her—almost. For the first time since she has been back, I see a flash of humanity cross her face, like she is terrified to be alone up here.

"You have to do it," she whispers.

Through narrowed eyes, I look down at her and whisper back, "Why? Because I know about Davis?"

"No, because if I lose it, at least it will be you I go after," she says with a glare.

"Perfect, an angry ex-girlfriend to be locked up with," I say sarcastically. The words taste bitter when I see her flinch at them.

I take her to the verification room a few levels down. We walk side by side with an uncomfortable tension between us.

"Is this where you take me into that room and

show me the video of my parents because I don't think I need to see it again." She laughs a little. "I believe you. They did it."

I shake my head no.

"It's not a practicum, is it?" she asks with worry.

"No, I'll inject you with the verification serum to make sure you're telling the truth. I'll ask you a few questions about what's happened. Then, I'll take you to see Quinn. She'll analyze your mental and physical health."

"The serum will be pointless. With all of the enhancements, it'll burn through my system too fast to actually work."

I press my lips together tightly and nod.

She looks at me and exhales. "Right. Let's go then."

We walk into the room, and I ask her to sit down. I walk over to the camera and shut if off.

"You have a habit of turning cameras off when you interrogate me," she says over her shoulder.

"*That* you remember? The first time I interrogated you? Of all the things…" I reply harshly.

This is the part of the verification I don't want

them seeing. I'm pissed at her, but I want her to know that I didn't have any part of keeping her in Alaska.

Taking my place in front of her, I begin. I pull out the pendant that has been weighing on me ever since Davis gave it to me and set it on the table for her. She takes it between her index finger and thumb and rubs it back and forth.

"Thank you," she whispers.

"I didn't know," I say again, my eyes glued to the pendant in her fingers. I can't look at her, not yet.

"Didn't know what?" she asks, empty of any emotion.

"Any of it—what was asked of you."

"Your name was on it. Signed in your hand—"

"*Forged*. It wasn't my signature. I didn't know." I look at her finally. Her green eyes, filled with understanding, quickly brim with tears.

She looks away from me to her hands. "Figures." She rubs her hands together and laughs. "Why am I not surprised? They would have done anything to get what they wanted." She plays with the pendant, pulling the chain over her neck. When she is done, she looks up at me and asks, "Why didn't you tell me yesterday?"

At that moment, I feel the old, familiar ache to comfort her weasel its way back in, but sitting here across from her, I don't know how to. She may look like Henly, but after everything I have seen, I know she is not.

"Whatever I would have said wouldn't have measured up to everything you've gone through. You would have only heard empty apologies. It was too late..." I exhale deeply. "It *is* too late.

With both palms, she rubs her face. "It is." Her hands fall away from her face, and she struggles to hold back the tears.

"I just want you to know," I say to her, "I would never have made you stay."

She looks up at me through her lashes. "Can we get this over with?"

I smirk, pointing at my shoulder. "As soon as you apologize for shooting me."

The corner of her mouth twitches. "I guess we're even." She points to her shoulder, and I wince from the memory of the bullet that hit her.

"I meant to shoot him," I say seriously.

She laughs. "Hopefully, your shot has gotten better. Mine has," she says as she eyes my shoulder. "If

I'd wanted you dead, I would have killed you. So, you're welcome, I guess."

My eyes narrow.

"Lighten up, Renner. We're both alive...for now at least," she says.

I don't know why she thinks this is funny. I walk over to the camera to turn it on to start the verification process, but I stall when Henly starts talking again.

"We can't go back. I think that has been made pretty damn clear. Maybe we could work on being friends. Instead of this fighting..."

Her smile is soft, and before I have time to stop myself, I've forgotten all of the anger and hatred from before and smile in return. "We could try that."

Her soft smile breaks into a wide grin. "So optimistic."

"Ready to get this over with?" I ask.

"No." Her eyes meet mine.

I can't look away. Once again, whoever this version of Henly is, she has taken hold of me, and even if I wanted to deny her, I couldn't.

"Wait, what do you know about Davis?"

I place my finger over my lips and motion to

the door, hinting to her that, though the cameras are off, we might still be heard.

Suddenly serious, she sits up straighter and says, "Let's do it."

CHAPTER 17

HENLY

The verification process is over quickly. It is not like I remembered it; there were not any serums or needles. At this point though, I'm sure they have realized those won't work on me anymore. Renner and I linger in the room. Now that I have been properly vetted, we finally have a chance to talk about what is really going on without cameras on us.

"Royce, with the help of Slade, has been stacking the quarantines in her favor." I whisper.

Renner's forehead creases with confusion. "Why? Why does she need them?"

"When the time comes, she wants to make sure everyone on the Board will rule in favor of her plan. As of today, it's working."

"Today…" Renner's voice sounds defeated.

"At least she's doing something."

Renner shakes his head. "By manipulating the Board? The Board was created to represent the people. All she's doing is representing her own self-interest. It isn't right."

"She may have manipulated them today, but

what were we supposed to do? Wait for politics to play out? This is how it has always been. People sit in rooms talking, waiting, and then people die. We can't just wait around for a group of people to decide what is best anymore! I may not know her entire plan, but I can live with that. Renner, we have to take action before he does! That is, unless you are working with him." I can't look at him. I accused him of being in cahoots with his father even though I know he isn't.

"You know for a fact that I have nothing to do with him."

My eyes narrow to match his glare. "How would I know?" I lie, pushing him closer to anger.

"Really? You're going to play dumb? You know *something*. After all, he created you—"

"He did, and I do know something. But here's the thing, Anson, I don't answer to you anymore," I say as I stand.

"Is this how you want to play it?" he demands.

A smug smile spreads across my lips. "In fact, you answer to me now," I say with a condescending tone.

"You're just a pawn. You may not answer to me, but you answer to someone. You think you're free from him—you're not, and you never will be."

His words are hard and cold. I hate him. I hate him for addressing something I was trying to avoid.

"You knew about my father, accused me of being aligned with him. You hook up with my best friend, get me suspended from the Board, and to top it all off, here you stand with a smug smile? If you're going to act like you're above it all, make sure you actually know what the damn plan is." His voice isn't angry when he speaks, just defeated—we both are.

He slumps down in the chair across from me. He is staring intently at his hands, and as the silence rings, it is the first time I notice how dark the bags are under his eyes. The length of his hair is longer and curls right beneath each ear. Tired or not, he still looks handsome, and something about him still makes me feel hopeful. He is the reason why I'm fighting so hard. If only he knew that the one thing keeping me glued to my seat is the weight of his words. *I don't hate him—not even a little.*

"I didn't know," I say, breaking the silence.

He turns his eyes to me, but he doesn't seem convinced. "Which part? The Board, Kenton, my father?" The anger in his voice is something entirely new, and a part of me is taken aback.

I take a sharp breath before I speak. "You know what? I knew it all. I knew who Vaughn was, and I knew about your father." I glare back at him, but I don't know why I'm doing this. It is petty, but I would rather him think I don't care than for him to see me hurt because he already sees me for what I am.

Without another word, he stands and opens the door for me, but that only angers me more. I want a response. I want him to feel as pained as I do. *React! Do something*, I want to shout.

"What? Nothing to add?" I scoff, but he looks right past me. *What have I done?* I escape into the hallway and shiver as he slams the door behind me. I lean against the wall, and my chest moves up and down rapidly. The air tastes sharp, and it feels like I'm breathing glass. Up and down, my lungs pump, and I feel like my heart is going to run away from me. I cling to my chest and feel an all-too-real pain. It is crushing me. My head feels heavy.

"Renner!" I shout, but the pain pinches my lungs even tighter.

The door behind me swings open almost as quickly as it shut. Bits and pieces of Renner come in and out of focus as he kneels before me.

"Henly, what—hey, stay with me." He tries to calm me.

I shake my head. "I can't breathe…"

"Someone find Royce!" he shouts.

"No! Get Ana! Get my mom!" I scream through the pain, worsening the pinch behind my lungs. Black dots dance in my vision.

"I've got you. I promise." He scoops me up, and suddenly, I'm weightless.

* * *

I lie in a bed in the medic unit draped in a blue cotton gown. For a second, I panic. I fear I'm back in my father's grasp. My breathing quickens, and the monitor spikes as I rip the tubes from my arms.

"No…I won't go through this again. No," I whisper firmly.

"Henly, hey, it's okay. It's *okay*. You're still here. I've got you." I look over and find Renner pulling the tubes from my hand and giving them to a nurse to reattach.

I grab onto his hand and squeeze it tightly to

make sure he won't leave me—ever again. When he flinches, I loosen my grip a little, but I don't let go.

He looks at me, tucking a strand of hair behind my ear. "You've got to stop doing that," he whispers.

"I'm a damsel," I say with a laugh.

"Yeah, I wouldn't go that far," he teases. "Just take it easy."

"I'll try," I reply.

The corner of his lips curve into a smile, and oh, is it a good one. "You're welcome."

I raise a mocking brow. "Thank you…" He stands to leave, but I tighten my grip. "Don't," I whisper.

He nods and sits down next to me. "Do you remember what happened?"

I shake my head. "A little?"

"Ana said you were over stimulated. Apparently, it's a side effect from your memories returning, something in the serum."

"Makes sense," I say.

He shrugs his shoulders, but he isn't looking at me anymore. His gaze is fixated on the monitors behind me. *Something isn't right.* There's a look in his eyes that seems distrusting.

"What?" I ask.

"Nothing."

"Something is wrong. I can sense it," I say as I point to my head.

"You can?" he asks.

"No, I'm not a psychic, but tell me."

His face loses its hard exterior and softens. "I don't buy it—their explanation. I don't think it's something in the serum. There's something else going on. I just…something is in those tests that they don't want you to know about."

I laugh, and by the look on Renner's face, he must think I'm going crazy—maybe I am.

"It's Ana. She's always lying about something."

"Yeah." He exhales deeply.

I turn over his hand and trace the calluses on his palm; they tell a story of strength and bravery. His hands hold years of a life I have never heard about.

"Thank you," I say sincerely.

His thumb caresses my wrist as my finger trace his hands. "You're welcome." He smiles and looks up at me through his lashes. "Didn't think I'd ever hear that…"

I wrinkle my nose. "In case I forget to say it later."

"Later?"

"I have a history, I think, of forgetting to say it, so thanks...for the future stuff."

"That you do." His finger softly taps the side of my head jokingly.

His hand moves down and cups the side of my face. His eyes focus on mine, and in this moment, I want to tell him so many things, but the silence between us remains.

A knock on my door forces him to pull away. I turn to see who it is, feeling the heat of his hand still on my cheek. Vaughn lingers, leaning against the doorframe, eyes fixated on Renner.

"Sorry to interrupt," he says, and under the burn of his glare, I feel my hand in Renner's.

Instantly, I let go and clear my throat, avoiding eye contact with either of them. I don't really know where they stand, and to be honest, I don't know where I stand either, but it doesn't look good for me.

"I should go," Renner says as he stands, but I cling to him again.

"No, don't," I whisper.

He pulls his hand from mine. "You're in good hands." His pained eyes meet mine, and his jaw tightens at his own words.

He'll never change.

"I'll keep an eye on her," Vaughn states.

"I'm all right," I say to Vaughn.

Vaughn looks at me and seems wounded.

"I'm just tired," I say, but not to anyone directly.

"All right, Sawyer. I'll swing back in a few." Vaughn smiles. Out of habit, he takes a few steps toward me and places a kiss on my cheek. My body tenses, and I see Renner look away.

Without another word, they both leave. Resting my head back on the pillow, I close my eyes and pray that sleep will come. Rest is what I need to not feel like I'm dying again, but it doesn't come. I'm too focused on the footsteps I hear coming into my room.

"I'm all right, really, Vaughn..." My words are left in the air when it's neither Renner nor Vaughn.

"They left," Quinn answers.

"Oh...good...right," I babble.

"How are you feeling?" She fiddles with wires above my head.

"Okay...good...better." *Why do I keep bumbling?*

Her smile is kind as she scribbles something else on the notepad in front of her. When she is finished, she takes a seat in the chair next to my bed. I catch her eyes as they trace the lines of scars up and down my body.

"My dad and my mom, but mostly my dad..." The words feel like sandpaper as they leave my lips. "They would wait for the storms to test the virus on me so the cracks of lightening or whistling would mask my screams." My eyes widen when I realize what I have just confessed. I look at her, and her face is calm. "I'm sorry," I whisper.

"For what?" she asks.

"For telling you that, for everything—for Ellie."

Her jaw tightens at the mention of her mother. After a few moments, she answers, "It's okay."

I nod, but still feel the guilt. *Could it be that the list of people I have killed is getting longer than the list of those I'm trying to keep alive?* I am racking my brain, trying to find the next topic, something to say, so the silence isn't as suffocating, when she finally speaks.

"Want to go see Dex?"

Dex. The only person who reminds me how good silence can be. I nod as she brings in a wheelchair.

"Dex is in with Tucker. He makes sure to visit him when DJ is away."

Quinn helps me into the chair, and for a moment, it feels like Ellie never left. But as I look over my shoulder at her, I know things will never be the same. No amount of wishing will ever bring back the past.

I sit quietly as Quinn wheels me down the hallway to Tucker's room.

"Dex, look who's awake," Quinn announces as we enter the room.

"Hey." I smile.

"There she is. How are you?" he asks.

"I'm good."

"So good that she has two men vying for her attention," jokes Quinn.

"Oh, yeah, I'm such a hot commodity!" I say playfully.

"It must be a Sawyer thing." He laughs.

"Gross! I saw the way you were looking at Davis. Are you dating my sister?"

His eyes widen as he stares at Quinn. "No?"

"They're hanging out." Her fingers draw air quotes.

"Well, take her on a proper date!"

"What?" He laughs. "I know. I will. Things have just been crazy, but she is amazing."

"I *know* she is. Take better care of her than you did with me." I laugh, but my joke lingers in the air, and I feel like I've pushed it too far. "I'm sorry. It was a joke...I meant it as a joke."

"I know," he responds, but his smile is gone.

Quinn stands. "I should get back to work."

"I'm sorry..." I say to the both of them. "I didn't mean to..."

Quinn looks at me and says, "You have nothing to be sorry about. I'm sorry we couldn't get to you sooner."

I nod and look at Tucker who is asleep on his bed. "Is he always sleeping?"

Dex shrugs his shoulders. "For the most part. They want to keep him sedated until they know what he can do."

"Is DJ usually this busy?"

"He's in training. Some days are longer than

others."

"Quinn said Militaris?"

"Yeah, he's really good at it, moving up quickly. He comes by when he can, but he's pretty focused on his training."

"He's so young," I whisper.

We don't share another word. We sit in the silence, and I enjoy every bit of it.

CHAPTER 18

RENNER

The thought that Ana and Royce are hiding something eats at me, so I head back to the medic unit. I need to find out what is really going on. As I approach the unit, I see Kenton leave the medics in a rant of anger. I can't help but chuckle; Henly is difficult. Before I go in, I make sure no one sees me. I stop and wait for one of the last medics to leave the office before I sneak in.

The shelves stacked against the wall are filled with varying types of paperwork. I find a stack of files near the bottom of the first shelf, followed by a locked compartment box.

"What are you doing?"

I look over my shoulder to find Quinn leaning against the counter. "Looking for Henly's file."

"This one." She hands it to me.

I take it and set it on the table in front of me, but as I scan the chart, I realize I can't read anything. Handing it back to her, I say, "Is there anything that doesn't seem right?"

She shakes her head no. "No, she was so

overloaded with memories that she crashed."

I rub my hand against my face. "Quinn, something isn't right. I can feel it!" I yell as I sweep the file off the table. "Why is that locked?"

She looks at me and raises her brow, half in surprise half in annoyance. "Case sensitive files are in there, like Tucker's."

I look at the safe. I feel it in my gut—whatever is wrong with Henly is in there.

"Quinn…"

She walks past me and enters in a code, but the compartment buzzes red. "That's weird," she says.

"What?"

"My code should open it. I should be able to look at those files."

As she is about to type it in again, I look over my shoulder and see Royce walking in through the main entrance of the medic unit, giving us only a few minutes to get out before she catches us.

"Hey, Royce is coming."

She stands and gathers the papers from Henly's file that I spilled across the floor and quickly places them back into the folder.

"I'll figure out what's going on," she says as

she tucks the folder under her arm. "In the meantime, lay low. They've already let it trickle down the chain that you're suspended and waiting for a proper re-evaluation, so don't get caught doing anything dumb. I'll swing by your room later if I find anything."

"Okay," I let out.

In my quiet attempt to sneak out of the office, I hear Henly's voice. I slightly push aside the curtain and see her in a wheelchair at the end of Tucker's bed. Dex is in the chair next to hers.

"I liked it," Henly whispers.

Dex uncrosses his arms and sits tentatively.

Henly tries to hold his gaze, but it falls to the floor. "The way they would change—become something new, something for me to study, to create. I had all the power." Her eyes fixate on the palms of her hands.

For a second, I'm taken aback. The Henly I knew would never relish in power. She detested it, hated what it did to people and what it did to her parents. This conversation I have stumbled upon hits hard. I mean, I know she isn't herself anymore, but the small ounce of hope I had kept hidden has now been crushed. She is simply something her father created.

"Everyone has darkness," Dex finally responds.

He's right.

She lifts her gaze from the floor. "You don't."

He shakes his head, and his back straightens as if he is suddenly uncomfortable. "No, everyone does."

"But *you* don't," she says again. "I've seen others' darkness's—my mom's, my dad's, Royce's, and Vaughn's. They're all mine to share."

"What do you mean they're yours to share? Henly, you're not responsible for their actions."

"Aren't I though?" She exhales deeply. "We're here because of something they found in me, something he made me. I mean, in the end, had I been destroyed, this would never be—"

"Henly, you can't think like that," Dex replies. He pulls her chair toward him. "You can't. You're here, and it's not your fault."

After a few moments, I hear my name slip through her lips. "I'm *his* darkness…Renner's."

"What? You're not his darkness."

"I am. I knew about his dad this whole time, and I haven't…I convinced him that we should be friends, but I'm killing the one thing I've always admired about him." Dex turns to her and waits for her to continue. "I've always admired his ability to do what is right. He'd do anything for me. He even gave up the Board."

Her words trail off, leaving me at a loss. She sits back in her chair with her shoulders sagged in defeat. She drops her head so it rests on the blue fabric of the wheelchair and stares at the ceiling. Her expression reads with disgust. She is angry with who she has become. *She is my darkness.* I mull over the words.

My life has always been a struggle, long before she came into it. Losing my parents was a burden she made lighter. When they took her, the burden grew at an overwhelming rate. All the darkness I struggled to keep away swam back to me and tormented me in new ways, ways that reminded me Henly was gone and in the hands of a masochist who would do whatever he had to do to secure his most valuable possession. *No, Henly isn't my darkness. She is the reason I am still fighting.*

"But you," Henly whispers, "I've looked for yours, and all I have found is that you've lost people and seen horrible things, but you're still you."

He shakes his head. "I'm not what has

happened to me, neither are you."

"You all look at me and expect me to be someone, someone I'm not…maybe I never was. He wants someone I can't be, and now, things with the Board and Royce…" she starts, but doesn't finish.

"Henly, Renner was a wreck. All he did was look for you. That's it. The Board tricked the both of you."

"What am I supposed to do with that?" she asks him.

"Anything you want," he replies. "You are what you choose to be—nothing more, nothing less."

"When did you become so wise?" she responds with a small laugh.

"When Renner didn't blame me for losing you." He doesn't meet her gaze.

"Dex?" she whispers, but her words fail her as she begins to cry. "I don't blame you either."

He stands and grabs her out of her chair. "You're no one's darkness."

Her grip tightens on his shirt. "Dex."

"You were thinking it, and you're not."

She nods as her sobs soak the shoulder of his shirt.

"He's a lot stronger than you give him credit for."

She laughs, and the noise is nice to hear, but I have seen and heard enough to feel like I have, in some way, betrayed her. Slowly, I back up and walk out of the medic unit. I head straight to the surface, toward the helicopters, and find myself enlisting in a search and rescue mission. I need to get away from all of this and gather my thoughts. It is a strange feeling to wish to be someone else, someone whom she trusted enough to tell all those things to, but she has always kept me at a distance. She has always preferred Dex. He has always been able to make her feel safe, whereas I have only pulled her into dangerous situations, made her feel vulnerable. To say that I am jealous of Dex would not be too far of a stretch. As I strap my weapons to my back, her words ring through my mind. Her words are not true. She is not my darkness. I will always do what is right. Always. And she is what is right.

CHAPTER 19

HENLY

A small tapping behind me jerks me back to reality. Vaughn stands a few steps from me, hands behind his back. My nerves burn down my spine, causing me to sit upright and attentive. *How long has he been standing there? Did he hear what I confessed to Dex? How did I not notice?* Dex holds my gaze for a moment before he looks away to Vaughn.

"I should go. I told Davis I would meet up with her for lunch."

"Okay," I say. "I should go too. I have to start training."

Vaughn scoffs, "Train? After you went all crazy this morning?"

"I'm fine," I say as I glare at Vaughn.

"Do you want me to take you to your room?" Dex asks, completely ignoring Vaughn.

"It's fine. I can take her," Vaughn says. "You have somewhere to be."

Dex blocks Vaughn from my line of view. "Do you need me to take you, Henly?"

Vaughn laughs. "Really? What am I going to

do? Run off with her?"

"You did that once already," Dex says.

"I brought her back to you people," Vaughn replies. "And by the looks of it, she's no better here than she was there."

Dex is about to say something when I speak, "Dex, it's all right. You should go."

Vaughn grins and slides out of the way for Dex to leave.

"You need anything, you know where you can find me," he says, and I nod.

"Didn't he say that to you last time when he left you?" Vaughn mocks.

"Vaughn stop." I glare at him before turning to Dex. "It's okay, I'll be okay."

He's not happy about it, but he turns and goes. I stand and feel the room spin. I try to refocus, but it is useless, so I sit back in the wheelchair. Vaughn is immediately by my side, helping me and asking me questions. When I open my eyes, he is kneeling down at my eye level. He does this; it is his way of showing he cares, of showing me I have his full attention.

"Are you okay?" His face registers concern.

"Yeah, just tired," I say.

"You? Never." He smiles.

For a moment, I smile at him the way I used to, when things between us were normal. Back in Alaska, he was the first one waiting at my bedside after surgeries. He would be there to distract me from post surgery pain. He was there—always. Through all of the times I felt like I was going to die, he made me feel alive. It is strange though. Now, sitting with him, I don't feel alive. I feel like my illusion of security has worn away, and now all he brings are memories of being cut open or hooked up to wires. He brings back all of the tortures I keep trying to escape.

"You have gotta stop being a dick," I say to him.

He smiles. "It's a joke. Besides, he did actually leave you."

"No, my dad kept me there, and *you* helped. Don't think you have fooled me."

His smile disappears. "Fooled you?" he questions.

"Should I call you Kenton or stick with Vaughn?"

"What?" He rolls his eyes. "What are you talking about?"

"You have this whole different life that I'm just learning about, and I'm supposed to trust you blindly? Vaughn—Kenton—I don't even know what to call you."

He laughs loudly as if my doubts were irrational. "Are you serious?" He waits for me to smile, but I don't. "Okay…" He exhales. "Anson and I were friends before this happened, ever since I moved in next door to him when I was seven. It was right around the time my dad died. Our families were close. Since he and I were the only kids in our families, we'd do everything together. His mom was like my second mom, mostly because Royce was gone so much. When everything went to shit, he says they tried to come for us, but we were already gone. His dad had already taken us to Alaska. At least, that's what my mom said. We're still friends, or I think we still are, but he calls me by my first name. You and my mom are the only ones who call me Vaughn."

I nod. "The truth?"

"Yes."

"Why did you bring me back?"

He shrugs his shoulders. "It was time."

"Was it? Did Royce order it, or was it your

conscience that told you to?"

"Dammit, Henly. I kept you safe. If you knew the truth, you would have made everything so much worse." His voice begins to rise. He inhales sharply before he speaks, "I'm not Anson, and he's not me. Stop comparing us like we are one in the same."

"I'm not comparing you! I just want to know the truth!" I shout at him. I lean my head back against the chair and breathe. "I wish I could trust you again...I just want to trust you again," I whisper.

Vaughn swallows hard. "I'm sorry...I just couldn't risk you knowing. I didn't know how you'd react."

"So you lied," I reply harshly.

"I didn't lie." His voice is low. "I just did what I had to."

I think about it, and I probably would have done exactly what he had expected. I know I would have fought my father, but I still deserved the truth. I deserved to know my father wasn't some doting dad who wanted to heal me. But no one told me, no one thought I should know. His silence is the only answer I need.

"Can you take me to my room. I'm tired," I

say finally.

He wheels me to my room in silence. Nothing is the same, not even the enhancements my father has given me. They are changing, becoming weaker, and I find myself missing them. I miss the way they made me feel powerful and strong. It has been so long since I have felt vulnerable to anything that I now understand what my father was trying to achieve. I shudder at the idea of understanding him the way I'm beginning to. He wanted a better future at any cost. When we reach my room, Vaughn helps me into my bed, but his eyes are unable to meet mine.

"How are you feeling?" he asks again.

My brows furrow. He doesn't usually have to ask how I feel. He has always known the answer: not good and then great.

"Tired," I say, playing along.

"How are your abilities? Are they wavering?"

I swallow hard. "Yes. Why are you asking me these questions?"

He smirks, but I see his worried demeanor hiding behind his facade. "Such distrust…"

I smile. "The part you forget is that I know you. Not once in Alaska did you ever ask me how I was or about my abilities. You were always determined to distract me."

"That's when I got to see you. Now, I barely even get to look your way without being scolded."

"What aren't you telling me?"

He stares at me and clenches his jaw.

I'm right. He is keeping something from me.

"If you ever really did care—if any part of this was real"—I gesture between us—"then you will tell me. You have to give me a reason to trust you," I say finally. Although I hate my manner of manipulation, I have to know. No, I *deserve* to know.

"Your dad, before we left, told me to keep an eye on you. He said things were decreasing, that the virus was mutating…"

"What? How?"

"I don't know. You were changing, and he could tell that this part of the experiment would be coming to a close."

"Coming to a close?" *He was going to terminate me.*

"Yes. I don't know if he was going to send you through the process, but I couldn't let that happen. I didn't trust him."

"*That* is why you got me out?" I ask, a little disgusted with him, and to be honest, I'm not sure why. If anything, he saved me, but I still can't help but feel anger toward him.

"What?" His brows furrow.

"You brought me back because you thought I was dying, not because it was the right thing to do!"

"What? Does it matter? I brought you back!" he replies harshly.

"Get out!" I stand from my bed. For the first time in the last twenty-four hours, I feel strong again. It's as if I'm feeding off of my anger, like being angry brings back my strength.

"Henly," he pleads.

"Out!" I yell as the tears fall.

Defeated, he exhales and walks out. I brace my head in my hands and scream until my throat hurts.

It shocks me that my dad would ever actually think to terminate me. He reminded me every single time he prepped me before surgery that I was special—his design. My fear was that if I ever stopped being useful, he would get rid of me—dispose of me like the others. I just never thought he would really do it. With every surgery, he learned all the ways deniferia did and didn't work. I would apply his findings in my own experimentations. He molded me, made me think I was doing the right thing. What eats at me most, though, is the truth behind his surgeries on me. He was using me. I wasn't special. He just needed me to learn more about deniferia before it was too late. As soon as I stopped showing results, I was useless to him—another failed experiment. Deep down, I knew this would happen. I just...I didn't want to believe it.

He will kill everyone who is deficit by his standards, which now includes me. There is no changing him. He will erase anyone's memory and turn him or her into a mutt for his cause. So many others will become projects, vials, and experiments if he is not stopped. I wonder if my father found it amusing that I would join those who I had experimented on. The irony of it definitely wouldn't have evaded him to know that soon my fate would align with all of those experiments. But what he doesn't know is how quickly the virus is mutating. He doesn't know what exactly is happening to me. If I can find out, then I will have the upper hand. The room slightly spins, and I feel dizzy. *If Davis is the virus and the virus is changing, then what does that mean for me?* As soon as I steady myself, I head toward the only people who will be able to answer my question clearly.

I move as quickly as I can through the halls until I get to the elevators. I press the button continuously, waiting for the *ding* to announce the elevator's arrival. The elevator takes too long though, so I bail and take the stairs. Moving quickly, I push past random people talking or walking too slowly. They grumble and snarl at me to slow down, but I can't. I have to know. I finally find myself outside the medic unit and feel my feet freeze. Just beyond this point, I will find out what is happening to me, and for a moment, I wish I didn't care. I wish I didn't want to take down my dad. I could just die and finally be free. But I can't. I owe it to all those lives I took for him. I owe it to myself to finally know the truth, even if it may be too late.

I muster up the courage and push through the doors. "Is the virus inside of me mutating?" I ask Hill, forcing myself to keep my voice even.

Hill's eyes dart to Royce. She awkwardly uncrosses her legs and then crosses her left leg over her right again. She is nervous, but remains silent.

My eyes dart between them. "Say something!"

Out of the corner of my eye, I catch a nod from Royce, but she is staring at Hill.

"Yes," Hill responds.

I turn my full attention to Hill. "And...what does that mean?" I ask.

He stands from his chair and crosses the room. He shuffles through papers on a shelf for a few minutes and then places a stack of documents in front of me. My fingers hesitate, hovering over the stack. Here, in front of me, are the answers to all of my questions. I quickly riffle through them.

"Do you remember the time in the compound when you fought Reina?"

Reina. Her name brings a million slow motion images, her pleading for me to stop while her body lay bruised and broke. Her name exposes how hollow I feel, and I know that no amount of atonement will be able to make up for that.

"When I first took a sample of your blood, your white blood count had several abnormalities. Then, you healed too quickly for the injuries you had sustained," Hill explained.

"That is what you meant to tell me before I left?" *That feels like a lifetime ago.*

"Yes. You were the one infected, not your sister."

I nod my head, and I feel some of the memories come in and out of focus. I place the documents back on the table.

"When we tested you again, your white cell count was different—lower."

"Okay…What does that mean?" I inhale, waiting for him to continue.

He rubs his eyes. "I don't know. Normally, it would mean you don't have enough white blood cells to fight off future infections, so you'd be more susceptible to infection and illness, but in your case, I have no idea."

I feel it again: they're keeping something from me. "What does that mean?" I ask again, this time directing my question to Royce, but before she can answer, someone else does.

"It means that Mother Nature always finds a way of curing the world of its abnormalities."

I turn to find Ana in the hallway, her lips pressed tightly together. I notice the marks around her throat are nearly gone, but parts of her flesh are still raised from when my fingers were around her throat.

Her words echo loudly through the small room.

"We don't know if that's the case," Royce says.

But I can't look away from Ana because she is right. I think back to the solutions from previous generations: vaccines. Polio, bird flu, the bubonic plague, you name it—if there hadn't been a vaccine, they would have died out on their own. *Is that what's happening to me? Am I dying?*

I swallow down her hypothesis. "Am I turning into one of them?" My voice quakes before I can control it.

"No," Royce answers immediately, but doubt lingers.

"I'm feeding off of my anger. When I'm angry, my enhancements come back, and I feel strong."

"That could be a side effect—" Royce begins.

"You said yourself my father found something. Vaughn said it earlier too. Did he know? Do you know when it's all going to happen? Do you know how long I have?" My questions tumble out one after another. I'm afraid.

Royce shakes her head. "Yes, he found something, but it's not that."

"Do you know what he found?" I ask, but she shakes her head no. "Of course you don't. He would never tell anyone if I were changing." I pause to look at my hands and study them, searching for any sign of my change. "How do we find out for sure?" I ask finally, but it takes minutes for anyone to answer.

"Your father," Ana says without an ounce of emotion.

I try to keep the lump in my throat hidden. "How do we find out what he knows?" My voice cracks, and this time, Ana notices.

For the first time in my life, she is unable to meet my gaze. "You go back."

The rest of the room is dead silent, and I know their lack of protests only verify my mother's words. *I have to go back to my father. I have to go back to the surgeries and scars. I have to go back to the lies and the tortures.* All at once, I force myself to go numb.

"She can't—" Royce tries to protest, but I cut her off.

"I'll go back," I say as steadily as I can.

"Henly, you don't have to do this. We can find another way," Hill objects.

"There is no other way, right?" I say, looking

at Ana.

She continues to avoid my gaze. "No, not if we want quick results."

I take a minute to compose myself and then ask, "How do we do it? How do I go back without making him suspicious?"

"We'll find another—"

"Stop!" My voice rises. "I go back. That is the only way"

"Henly," Hill protests, but it is too late. I have made up my mind.

"How are we going to pull this off?" I ask a little louder.

Hill looks to the doorway where Royce lingers. "We'll have to fill in the others and get a team prepared."

I know who he is talking about, and I won't agree to it. "No, we do this on our own." My voice is hoarse when I think about betraying Dex, Quinn, and Vaughn. I refuse to think about Renner. He will protest this more than the rest, even if it is the right thing to do. *I really am his darkness.* Either way, he has no say anymore, but I do. I can make this easy for me, disguise this any way I want to, because if he finds out, he will go to any length to keep me here.

Royce pushes herself off of the door. "So, how do we get you back to Drew without telling anyone?"

I feel my shoulders sag. I know what she is about to propose. "You really want to send him back with me?"

Royce lowers her eyes. "Drew won't hurt him."

"He *will* if he finds out he's in on all of this," I say to Royce.

Hill starts tapping his foot against the tile. He does this every time he tries to refocus. "We can sedate her. We can make it look like Vaughn found you."

"What about you?" I ask Royce. "What will your excuse be for being gone so long?"

She shakes her head. "I'll think of something." She takes a step toward Hill and me. "But you'll have to be convincing."

"I fooled him before."

"Barely," she responds. "We muddled your memories because you, yourself, weren't sure you could keep the truth from him. He didn't have a reason to suspect before, but now…"

"We could temporarily alter her memories

again," Hill announces—the tapping of his foot quickens.

"What?" I say to Hill, but find his focus on Royce.

"Would that work again?" she responds.

"It could," he persuades.

"How?"

Hill tilts his head sideways. "It's risky, but we did it once. We can do it again."

"No," I try to interject.

"It was risky in the first place, but now…" Royce says, completely disregarding my objection.

"No!" I say again.

"You would have to show me your notes," Hill responds to Royce, ignoring me as well.

"Enough!" Ana shouts.

They both blink their eyes, waking from their tunnel vision.

"She will go back and be convincing. Won't you, Henly?"

My throat is dry, and it hurts to swallow, so I nod.

"What do you suggest?" Royce asks curiously.

"He won't know. He'll be too excited his

experiment is back," I say sarcastically.

"Henly, he was going to terminate you because he didn't know what you were becoming. You won't have much time once you're back," Hill says softly.

I swallow away the lump and force my voice to stay neutral. "Then we better hurry, or Mother Nature won't need to fix his mistake. Wouldn't you say, *Mom*?" I lock eyes with Ana.

Her eyes narrow briefly before a small smile creeps across her lips.

"Always *so* dramatic," she whispers.

CHAPTER 20

RENNER

The chopper lands early in the afternoon. Patrol was a bust and did absolutely nothing to ease my frustrations. Since Henly had me suspended from the Board, I can't go around asking questions. Instead, I go to the one place where I know I will find answers. Quinn has agreed to help me figure out what is going on with Davis. I feel a strange freedom now that I'm just another founder's son. There is nothing I have to tend to—not a breach in quarantine, not a capacity issue, not even a law that needs to be enforced. I just have to make sure my men are ready when they are needed.

I have Ferruli overlooking most of the corps. Johnson is training the new lieutenants and has high hopes for DJ, the kid we brought with us from Havre. He and Dex have taken it upon themselves to train Dex's dog, Gray, to help in the search and rescue convoys, but at this point, Gray can only smell the difference between a treat and a human. DJ has yet to go out on a search and rescue, but when he does, I have a good feeling about him.

I turn the corner and see the medic wing in sight.

I take a quick glance and check to see if Quinn is around, and one of the medical assistants points to her office. I walk into what used to be Ellie's office. All of the photographs on the wall almost bring Ellie back to life. Years ago, Ellie started putting up photos of people she had helped or grown close to. Quinn has never changed them. She has always wanted to keep this part of her mother alive, at least the memory of her. I scan the frames, walking by each one and looking at the people in them. Most of the pictures are of strangers, but then I see one that brings back old memories. It is one of Ellie and me. We were sitting outside on the outer decks on the east wall, right off the ridge. I think it was midday, and we had just come back from our very first search and rescue. It was a rather grim one; we didn't find a single person alive. I remember I looked at her and felt heavy from the day's disappointments. She turned to me then, and with her always-wise words, she said, "You know you can't save them all."

"I'm not trying to save all of them. Just, what is the point? They're gone." My voice was short and full of anger.

"You can't save her," she had said.

My head snapped in her direction when she

said the words that had been on my mind. "I know that," I had whispered, less convincing than before.

"Do you?" She turned to me, her gray hair tied up tightly in a bun. Her voice was kind, and for a moment, I envisioned my mom sitting in front of me. It threw me. My eyes closed, and I wished that for once my mom would be here when my eyes opened, that she could speak to me. My reply had gotten wedged in my throat, and I couldn't force my words past the dryness. I did the only thing my body would allow and nodded.

"I think, now this is just me, but I think the point is to try. We have to make sure we keep the good of humanity alive until we can fix it. We have to make sure we keep helping the ones who need it."

When I opened my eyes, she was looking at me. Her lips turned up into a soft, almost insignificant smile. She nudged my shoulder with her own, and I smiled back at her.

"We will win. We will fix this."

At the time, her voice was so confident that it was easy to believe her, but looking at the picture now, I'm not sure if I can anymore.

Ellie had pulled out a small Polaroid camera that she had found on the trip and whispered for me to smile.

"Really? A picture?" I had whined.

"Yes, for the days I'm discouraged. I can look and remember that we're out fighting the good fight."

I wrapped an arm around her shoulder and forced a corner of my mouth to smile again. I didn't want to admit it then, but she was right. A part of me has always known we have to fight to keep what is left of what is good. *I miss her.* Since then, whenever I had had a hard day, I would come and sit in her office and look at all the photos. Today is no different. My eyes trace more faces and become fixated on one across the room from me.

"Hey, sorry if you've been waiting long," Quinn apologizes as she enters her office.

"When was this taken?" I ask her.

She sets the papers in her hand on her desk and walks over to me to look at the same picture. "Not sure. A few weeks after she was here." Quinn glances at me briefly. "She was in here a lot at first." She laughs.

Back then, Henly spent her first few weeks constantly in and out of the medic unit. If she wasn't getting strangled, she was either getting put under by Zoe or running away from deviations. She has had an eventful life to say in the least.

"She loved her like a daughter," Quinn says softly behind me.

I turn to her when she lets out a small breath. Quinn has a way of hiding how she feels and putting on a brave face. She, unlike Ellie, is very hard to read.

"Do you want to talk about it?" I ask.

She shakes her head. "It's surreal sometimes that she is gone." She chuckles. "I still catch myself talking to her. It's strange."

"I did that. After my mom died, I used to walk around talking to her like I would anyone else," I confess. "The strangest parts were those moments when I'd forget she was gone, and I'd pause to wait for her reply."

Quinn looks up at me, tears in her eyes. "Yeah, then there's the silence when they don't respond. It sends you through it all over again." She wipes her eyes as she speaks, "Like with these stupid files. I was in here last night trying to work through them, you know, trying to figure out what the link is, what Mama Crazy is hiding, but I couldn't. Last night, I was thinking through it all out loud, and then I asked her what she thought, but of course, she didn't respond."

The files on Henly can wait. Quinn is usually

reserved and keeps to herself. She used to have her mother to confide in, but now it dawns on me that she has been keeping this in for months. I sit down in the chair next to her and let her lean her head on my shoulder. She squeezes my arm, and it is nice to feel that some part of me still has a bit of family left. We just sit, looking around the room at the pictures of Ellie. It is true: she would know how to fix this. She always knew how to fix everything.

"I try not to hate her for it though," Quinn whispers. "I try... I blame Ana, sometimes Davis, but I try not to hate Henly."

"I blame my dad."

Quinn sits up straight and blinks at me.

"Did you know my dear ole dad was a part of all of this?"

Her eyes narrow in confusion. "Your dad? The *senator*?"

I nod yes. "How is that for a game changer?"

"He's still alive?" she asks, looking puzzled.

"No, he was shot in the raid in Bowden, the one where we found Henly," I tell her.

"Wow. How's that sitting?"

I shrug my shoulders. "I mourned him a long

time ago. Now, I'm just empty about it."

"Rough," she says with a laugh.

I laugh too. "Right." After a few seconds, I ask, "Can I ask you something?"

She nods.

"Why do you blame Davis?"

Her arm reaches and tugs at a strand of hair that has fallen in front of her face. She tucks her hair behind her ear and loosely plays with the end of the red curl, twirling it between her index finger and thumb. She is nervous to answer.

"Honestly, I don't know. She doesn't stand up to her mom for what she's done. She's always scurrying along behind her like she's some brittle being, like if she is overexposed, she will blow up. I just don't get…" Quinn stops playing with her hair and looks up at me. Her eyes widen and her hands grab ahold of the chair. "Thank you, Mom!" she shouts.

"What?" I ask.

"That's it! *She*'s it. Okay, so we already know she had something, was something. I mean, why would they keep Davis all the way in Havre if they didn't want her? I mean, they would have killed her, right? Andrew Sawyer only cares about innovation, about creating, and she is something! She *is* the virus!" She looks at me and is confused by my lack of shock. "You knew that already?" she asks rhetorically. "Okay, so if I'm Andrew Sawyer, I like to experiment on people, right? I would want living forms of deniferia to extract, test, or use to infect. I would need two samples: one that is positive and one that is negative. I mean, it is true they both carry it, but only Henly's blood has helped Tucker get better. Do we even know what Davis's blood would do?" she asks, but mostly just to herself. "To make more deviations, he needs Davis. The virus has remained dormant in her somehow." Quinn is up and at her desk in a matter of seconds, searching through piles of paperwork. "Look at this." She shows me, but quickly realizes I just see numbers and colors, nothing coherent enough to gather a conclusion. "Right, well, Ana is making a vaccine, a shot of some sort that is keeping Davis alive. Therefore, she is closer to curing deviations." Quinn narrows her eyes at me. "She is trying to *fix* this mess. That is why she is down in quarantine so much. We already know if Andrew gets his hands on Davis, he could use her like an atomic bomb to wipe out the weak and see who survives. That is, if he knows *how* to use her."

"He can't know or he would have already used her."

She shakes her head. "I'm not sure. He didn't have a range, and I read your report about the deviations on your last search and rescue. It may be that he didn't have a place large enough to test."

"Range?"

"Yes—" she shakes her head "—think about it this way, say you have a new missile you want to test, but you don't have an area large enough to test it on. You would want to check for radiation levels to see how far it would affect people and what the damage would be, right? He needs to see how far her range of infection will go. That's what he's unable to do. He doesn't have a location large enough that is filled with uninfected people to test her on."

"Davis is a liability to everyone here," I whisper. "If he finds her, he could use her to test deniferia on the quarantines."

"Maybe, but if Ana is treating her, maybe not. We don't know until Ana divulges what she knows. I suggest you call an immediate meeting with the Board and make Ana tell us what the hell is going on."

I shake my head. "I can't do that. I'm

suspended, pending an investigation."

She stops and looks up at me. "What?"

"Yesterday. When the news came out about my dad's involvement, the Board reacted in a rather unsavory way. The Board wants to make sure I didn't know about it. That, and Royce and Henly are up to something."

Her brows rise in amusement. "And I thought I had a busy day."

"I know…" I reply. "So, do you think Ana is testing deviations?" I ask.

Quinn sits back in her chair and looks at me in dismay. "I think so."

We both let out a shaky breath.

She stands up and puts a few pieces of paper into a folder. "Can you have Henly look at these? I mean, she should know what's going on, but be careful since she got you kicked off of the Board. Make sure you can trust her."

"I'll figure it out," I say, taking the papers. "What are you going to do?"

"Head down to meet with Ana in quarantine. I want to talk to her in a place where she can't kill me. I'll keep you posted on what I find out."

As she walks out, she turns back to me and says, "Thanks for the chat."

I nod and speak up before she walks out, "You still have Ellie's Polaroid?"

"Top drawer, to your left," she responds.

I walk around her desk and pull open the drawer. Right before me is Ellie's clunky, chipped black and green camera. I walk over to Quinn and snap a quick Polaroid of us before she has a chance to object. "Now you can start your own series of people you've helped."

"Got to fight the good fight," she says before she leaves.

CHAPTER 21

HENLY

My lungs pinch to the point of making me feel like I'm going to suffocate. All I want is to wish away my selfish desires, but I can't. I have to know what my father has done to me. If I do nothing—if I don't go back—I will never find out what is wrong with me. It is in moments like this I wish I could confide in someone. I wish I could tell Renner everything, but what good would it be? If there is something wrong with me, I don't want to give him false hope that everything will work out. I could very well die in the near future. Still, I'm torn. I know I should leave and not look back, but after wandering these halls for hours, I look up to find myself outside of Renner's door. I raise my hand to knock, but second guess myself and lower my fist. *What am I doing here? I must be desperate if I'm here. There's no argument about that.* I can't tell him, yet here I am, unable to walk away. I don't want to leave again without saying goodbye. A part of me wonders if this will be the last time I see him, and if it is, I at least want a solid goodbye. I stifle my pride and knock. I hear a small shuffle before the door opens.

"You?" I question. I look down both ends of the hall to make sure I haven't wandered into another Ave.

"He's not here," Zoe states coldly.

I can't stand her haughty demeanor. I've never been inside his room—rather, I have never been invited inside his room. At this point, my jealousy can't be disguised.

"Sorry," I sneer.

She stands in front of me. If I could guess, she likes where we stand—her on the inside and me out in the cold.

"Did you need something?" she demands.

I shake my head. "No."

I turn away from the door and walk down the way I came. *I guess he has Zoe now, and I have Vaughn, though I don't really have Vaughn. Vaughn was playing his part in a life I was trying to fit into.* Here I was, thinking that it could be that easy. I should have known better because, lately, everything has shown me that if it is too easy, it isn't real.

When I turn the corner to my Ave, I see Renner pressed against my door, asleep.

"Renner?" My voice stirs him.

His eyes flutter, blinking the sleep away and trying to wake up. It takes him a few seconds before he registers where he is.

"What are you doing here?" I spit out. The image of Zoe in his room comes back to me.

He rubs his eyes. "What?"

"Zoe's in your room. She's…uh…pleasant as always," I reply bitterly.

"Who? You went to my room?" he asks with surprise, but he can't meet my gaze.

"How long have you been here?" I press, hoping that he missed my small fit of jealousy.

"Not long, just since I got back," he replies, still rubbing the sleep out of his eyes. "You were looking for me? Why?"

My eyes search the wall above him for an answer, but I come up empty. I can't really tell him why I went looking for him. "You fell asleep?" His tired eyes and disheveled hair make me smile. "Where were you?" I coax, unlocking my door.

"Search and rescue detail and then random Militaris work."

"Oh," I say, and I find myself worriedly looking at his body for bruises or scrapes.

"I'm fine," he replies. "My new job." He tips his head to me.

I know what he means. It is my fault he got demoted, so I don't push it further.

"You don't look fine."

"I am," he says, lingering in my doorway.

"What are you doing here?"

"Yeah…"—he stands taller—"can I come in?"

I open the door wider. "Sure."

He walks past me and sits on the bed. In the brief silence, I take a few seconds to study him. He has had a hard day. Perspiration has built up around his temples. The veins on his neck seem to thump quickly, and the way his chest falls makes me see how exhausted he really is. *Why is he here?* A part of me wants to reach out to comfort him, but I won't allow myself to be clouded by what I have to do. I stay where I am and choose to lean against the wall across from him.

"What are you doing here, Renner?" I repeat.

"Davis."

My brows narrow as I wait for more.

"She's the virus. Your dad is essentially making an army, but the new deviations—their deterioration is decreasing, and they look almost human.

When we found them in a building, a video flashed on a screen with a little girl crying for help. The little girl was Davis. The way Davis is reacting to deniferia is different than what's happening with your father's trials. He's trying to create an army, but he needs Davis. He needs to recreate the serum Ana initially created so that he can figure out the best formula for it. I found this, and—" he hands me a stack of papers "—I think it talks about the treatments your mother is administering to Davis, her trial runs, and her conclusions."

"What?" I ask, somewhat in disbelief, but also in amazement. He has done it. My dad has found a way to control them. When I was with him, he was working on finding ways to control deviations from a short distance. He tried implanting a microchip that would help control the deviations' rage and deliver commands, but only some took to the chip implant; a majority didn't respond at all. Even worse, the chip only worked in a short range and only for a varied amount of time. From what I can remember though, he had been working on this long before I had arrived. This project was his and the senator's biggest hurdle, and I guess he has finally overcome it. *He may have figured out how to control them, but there's no way my dad knows what my mother is doing to Davis. Does he? Could he have figured out that she's just as useful as I am, if not more?*

I let out a sharp gasp when I look up and find a near replica of the senator standing in front of me. *I never realized how much they look alike.* I open my mouth to tell him what I know, that maybe his father didn't die, that he could very well have escaped and be in Alaska right now, but what good would that do? To tell him his father could still be alive would be torturous. He would do anything to see the senator, to question him. I know because that is what I would do. *No, don't tell him. Don't be his darkness again,* I convince myself.

"What is it?" he asks.

I force my legs to stay planted where they are. The silence is so entrancing that I jump when there is a knock.

"Expecting someone?" There is an edge to his voice that reminds me of how I spoke to Zoe. He is jealous.

I shake my head. I push off the wall, and I feel Renner's eyes watch me as I reach the door. Opening the door just enough, I see Vaughn. I step out into the hallway and quickly shut the door behind me.

"We leave at zero four hundred," Vaughn says.

"All right?"

"They have a meeting sometime tomorrow for votes that we will unfortunately miss."

"Royce?" I ask.

"She and Ana are going to get the approval for a small search party. That's how they're going to disguise this," Vaughn explains.

"Vaughn, does he know about Davis? What she is?" I ask him, but I'm not sure I want to know.

"Yes, he wants her just as badly as he wanted you."

Wanted. The way he says it hits a chord that makes me almost sad I'm not my father's most prized possession anymore. "How do you—" I don't finish. I know how he knows. For a while, the only other person my father trusted me to was Vaughn. "Never mind," I finish.

He turns away from me and snickers. "Don't forget to offer my friend a nightcap."

My hand pauses on the doorknob. I watch the back of Vaughn's head as he turns down the hallway. It is so like him to have the last the word. I walk into my room and find Renner standing, his eyes full of questions.

"Who was that?" His voice is low, defensive.

I don't hesitate to tell the truth. "Vaughn—Kenton."

For an instant, his face softens into hurt, but then it bounds back to its cold exterior. "Yeah...Sorry to ruin your plans. I just needed to know about Davis."

He steps past me to the door.

"Renner, is that really why you came?" I turn to face him, his back toward me. "To fight? Or did you feel bad about Zoe?"

His shoulders sag, and his fingers release the door handle. "What about Zoe?" he asks. His eyes are cold.

I bite my lower lip in anger. "Are you two a thing now?"

He mocks me when he replies, "More like a phase."

The harshness in his voice makes me want to hurt him as bad as I ache. "That didn't take long."

He lets go of the door handle and throws his hands in the air. "Twenty-four months! Twenty-four months—two years—of thinking you were dead, and now you're—"

"I'm what?"

He takes a step away from me, presses his hand against the wall, and takes a deep breath. When he looks at me, he pleads, "I thought you were dead."

I grit my teeth. *Not this conversation. This is not how I want to say goodbye. I don't want to rehash the past.* I've been trying to ignore this conversation for as long as I could, but here it starts. Being angry with him had made it easier to do what I have to do in the morning.

"A few weeks after the raid in Havre, we'd gotten word that your father might have transported you elsewhere." He turns his back to me, both hands braced against the wall.

I take a few steps back and inch myself across the room to stay away from him. He walks to a chair across from me and takes a seat, gripping the arms of the chair. His grip is so tight his knuckles shake.

"When we got to the small facility in Seattle, the gatherers found a video of you."

"I was never in Seattle." My voice is soft, almost nonexistent.

He exhales, and I can feel the exhaustion in his voice as he continues to speak, "So it seems."

"And?" My voice shakes.

"You pleaded with me to stop looking for you, that others would pay the price if I kept searching." He drops his gaze from mine. "Three weeks later, a crew of gatherers found a body—your body—though, I realize now it wasn't really you. 'Your' body had been dumped out in the middle of nowhere." He looks up at me. "That was a little more than a year and a half ago."

My mouth feels dry, and my back burns from the weight of his story. His eyes are glossy as if he is in some distant place, telling the story for someone else.

"Holding on to you. Loving you—*losing* you like that—" he looks up at me "—almost killed me. But now, you're here, except everything is different. *You're* different. Zoe was here, and I thought I could forget you. I thought she could make it go away."

My throat is suddenly dry and itchy, making it hard to breathe. I stand and walk to the other side of the room. I lightly cough, hoping to suppress the drowning I feel inside. My eyes burn as the water spills over, leaving salt streaks on my cold face. I hurry to wipe them away before I speak, "It is what it is." I say the words without meaning them.

He stands and, in a few strides, closes the gap

between us. "It isn't." He shakes his head as he continues, "Even when I think I can, I can't get you out of my head. Not then, not now."

"Oh," I respond, frozen by his words.

His pleading eyes search mine. "What am I supposed to do with that?" he whispers.

He is so close that I can feel the vibrations of his words on my lips. Instead of answering, I pull him toward me and kiss him. Kissing him is different than I had remembered. His lips are frantic and hard against mine. Our hands pull at one another, trying to empty the space between us. My heart flutters awake as his lips trace my jaw, down my neck, and then back to my lips. I have lost control of my hands as one slides down his cheek, while the other gets tangled in his chocolate hair. I press my lips down into his neck and reconnect with a part of myself that I thought I had lost. I'm trying so hard to make up for lost time that I don't feel when his hands freeze.

"Oh, Henly…" His fingers trace the scars on my stomach.

"Please, just help me forget." I react carnally, and I kiss him again.

"Henly," he whispers in between breaths. His

hands stay firm at my hips.

"Please?" I plead.

His hands cup my face. "Not like this," he whispers. "Not like this."

I open my eyes and whisper in his ear, "Why do you always have to do what's right?"

We both laugh, but it fades when he asks, "These are from your father, right?"

I look away, but his eyes follow me until I'm forced to see the specks of hazel that implore an answer. "Yeah, surgical scars."

His face softens. "Why would he cut you open?" he asks delicately.

"He wanted to see what the virus had mutated inside of me. He wanted to know what had been enhanced and what hadn't. He wanted to know if things like an organ full of cancer cells would kill me or if the virus could heal me. He wanted to know if he took out a part of my kidney whether it would grow back or not." I look up at him. "It did."

Renner's hands cup my face as he presses his forehead to mine. Really, there isn't anything he can say that would make what has happened okay, so we stand in awkward silence as he traces the scars my father created. Then, he locks eyes with me, and his breath becomes uneven. I find his eyes staring at my lips, and without warning, I press my lips to his again, and the room fills with heat. His hands run through my hair, and I move into him. Our chests pound in sync. I haven't felt this alive in years. My hands run down his back to the hem of his shirt, and in one smooth motion, we find our way to my bed, his body hovering over mine as I pull him closer to me.

"I'm sorry." He grins.

My eyes narrow in confusion. "What?"

He shakes his head and smiles. "I should go."

"Of course. Your roommate is waiting for you," I reply sharply.

His laugh is intoxicating and booms through the room. "What are you talking about?"

"Zoe was in your room…"

"Right. Why *did* you come to my room?" He smiles as his hands brush my hair from my face.

"No reason," I deny, but it is futile because he is at my lips again, distracting me from my anger.

"Then I'll stay here with you. If you'll have me," he whispers between kisses.

Even if I could force him to leave, it is not

what I want. What I want is to spend the last night I have here with him. I take his hand, and we lie side by side, staring at the ceiling. For the first time, it feels as if no time has passed.

"Zoe was just…" he whispers, interrupting the silence.

I clear my throat before I say, "I know…I was dead, but you can't be here if you're supposed to be there."

He turns his body to face me. His hazel eyes keep focus on me until he speaks. "I'm where I'm supposed to be," he says. For a moment, he pulls away and looks at me. "And you? Are you where you want to be?"

I look at him and feel the fear of returning to my father pull at me. This sudden rush of guilt makes the truth dance on the edge of my tongue; I want to tell him that, in a few hours, I will be on my way back to my father, but for reasons I still don't understand, I can't. This is where I want to be, but this isn't where I get to stay. Either way, the truth isn't something I get to speak anymore, not with him at least. If I tell him, he will want to sacrifice it all and go back with me. I can't have that. I can't have him risk anymore for me.

"For now…" I whisper with a grin.

Rolling his eyes, he lies next to me and pulls me closer to him. "I won't let him hurt you," he says as his arms tighten around me.

I swallow hard, a mixture of fear and guilt beginning to consume me. My continued silence only furthers the fact that I'm lying. I need to protect him, but a part of me worries that not telling him could damage him more. I can't let my mind go there. Instead, I think about Dex, Quinn, and Davis. I have barely seen my sister since my arrival, in part, because I can't handle her resemblance to my father, even her mannerisms mirror his. Every little thing that used to make me feel like home has turned into my own personal house of horrors with her. The way she wants to share each other's pain isn't therapeutic for me. It just pulls me further into the darkness that reminds me I'm more like my parents than anyone here knows. This is why I have to go back. I have to face what my father has done, so I can stop running from the people who mean the most to me. I want to be free. Slowly, I convince myself that telling Renner won't matter. When he wakes tomorrow, I will be gone. If I tell him everything tonight, he will try to convince me to stay, and I can't. I need to go, even if he doesn't agree. Right now, I just want to enjoy him.

Renner's lips press to my lips, drawing me from my trance. I close my eyes, and for the first time in months, my nightmares stay dormant.

***

My eyes fly open, and panic ensues when I blink through the darkness. I sit up and see the clock tick toward four. Quietly, I untangle myself from Renner and watch as his dark lashes flutter in some dream that keeps him asleep. Finding my bag, I quickly pack my things and set them next to the desk. Before I leave the room, I spot a pen resting on top of a piece of paper. *The least I can do is leave them something.*

I start my first note, scribbling Davis's name at the top of the paper. I explain myself the best I can. I tell her I will be home soon, to be careful, and that I love her. I tell her to take care of Dex and Gray. I fold the paper closed and write her name on the outside. I move on to the next letter. This one is harder to write.

I try to think of all the words that might comfort Renner after I'm gone, but I know there are none, especially after tonight. Instead, I just scribble "sorry." I close the note, folding it in half, and write his name on the front. There have been so many goodbyes between us that I don't think I could live through another one. I set it down next to him on the bed and walk out of the room as quickly as possible. If I hadn't, I would have stopped and stayed in this place with him forever.

The ride up the elevator seems to take forever as if the hoists were covered in mud, slowly sticking after each floor. When I finally get to the top, I see a small group of Militaris soldiers gathered around. I move close enough to hear the rough, jagged voice that sends a shiver up my spine.

"Dex?"

He looks up and grins. "Hey."

I scan the group and see Vaughn purposely looking away. "Vaughn," I say louder. "What is Dex doing here?"

Vaughn doesn't look up when he speaks, "It was volunteer only."

"You *let* him volunteer?"

He finally looks at me, his blue eyes piercing through me. "It was volunteer only, and he volunteered."

I grab his collar and pull him to the side.

"What the hell are you doing? He can't come back with us."

"And why not?" he asks.

"My father knows who Dex is. As soon as he sees Dex, he'll know and get us killed."

"I'll tell him Dex is a recruit. Don't worry," he responds as if my worries aren't valid.

"That's not enough." I turn to Dex. "You can't come. He knows you, and he will kill you, or worse, he'll make me change you."

"I'm not letting you go to that sociopath alone," he responds defensively. "Not again."

"Dex, stop trying to be the hero. We both know I am capable of taking care of myself."

"Yeah, until he realizes you know everything and that you're a traitor. Then what will happen? You think he's just going to let you go? I know you don't need protecting, but I won't let him keep you again."

"Dex, I can't lose you…" I say, but my words trail off because I know the dangers of going back to my father. "This isn't a game, and your life isn't something I want him to play with."

"I'm a big boy, Henly. I know what I'm doing," he says.

I turn to Vaughn after Dex heads back to tend to his pack. "If anything happens to him, I swear I'll make you pay."

Vaughn laughs. "You need to relax."

"No, what I need to do is make sure my father believes this new lie. This half-witted plan we have concocted has to work. It has to fool him. If it doesn't, he'll go after everyone I care about." I strap my guns to my back and ready myself for this. I look back to Dex. "That includes you."

Vaughn looks at me through narrowed eyes like he is trying to see if I'm telling the truth. Once he has decided I am, his expression softens. "Then we better make sure that doesn't happen."

"What did you tell Davis?" I ask Dex.

"The truth," he replies.

My jaw drops a little. How is it that he can be so good and honest, and I'm just a liar who walks through the shadows so Renner won't discover what I have been hiding?

"She wasn't happy, but she understands," he says glumly.

Before I have a chance to reply, the alarms blare.

"Time to go!" Vaughn yells.

I roll my eyes at Vaughn, but he is right. "You don't have to do this," I say one last time to Dex. "Please, don't do this."

Dex hugs me and whispers, "I'll be fine."

He is my brother, and I don't want to lose him, but I understand his choice. I would make the same one if the roles were reversed.

We grab our things and climb into the chopper as the wings spin awake. When I look up at Vaughn, his eyes are narrowed and focused on something in the distance. I follow his eyes to see what they are fixated on. *Him.* His run is desperate. He makes it to the gate, but the chopper lifts off the ground. He is too late. His hand grips tighter around my note, and I watch the hurt on Renner's face turn into frustration as the distance between us grows.

PART III

CHAPTER 22

RENNER

I stand in the wake of the turning helicopter blades. My jaw clenches when I spot Kenton firmly seated near a window in the chopper. *How can she do this?* She sits a little taller and whispers the same five-letter word that was in the letter she left me. I can't keep chasing her if she keeps running after her own grave. After last night, this stings like betrayal.

I didn't want to believe it when I heard Davis's voice through the door, pounding and yelling Henly's name. She was so distraught and kept muttering something about Dex and Henly leaving. I should have known, but it wasn't until I found the note with my name scribbled in her handwriting that I fully realized what she had done. After everything we have been through, all she wrote me was "sorry." I can't bear to look at her anymore. I can't bear to watch her leave me again.

Without warning, I take off running. I burst into the medic unit and find a startled Quinn. She stands and rubs the sleep from her eyes.

"What's going on?"

"Where is she?" I ask.

"Who?" her voice is raspy from sleep. "I haven't seen Henly since yesterday afternoon—"

"No, she's gone. Where is Ana?"

"Gone? Wait, what? Gone where—when?" She follows me through the hospital until I stop outside of Tucker's room.

"Ana. Where is Ana?" I ask again.

There must be something in my voice or in the way I look because she turns and gestures for me to follow her. I have no idea where she is going until we reach the lower levels of the quarantine area. I watch as Quinn's hands turn into a fist, but she hesitates to knock.

"Dex went with her." The words seethe through my lips and are meant to ignite anger in Quinn. I can't be the only one who feels betrayed. I know how she feels about Henly. She was angry her mother died protecting Henly, so I can understand why she is hesitant. She has tried hard not to blame her, but if something happens to Dex, she will never forgive her. But I know the truth about Dex's alliance will anger her enough to find him, which will then lead me to Henly. It is a poor parlor trick to manipulate her this way, but I'm too desperate to care about morals.

"Ana!" she shouts as her fists bang against the door loudly.

Down the hall, I hear the stirs of the deviations as they come awake. Their poundings echo against the walls.

"What?" she spits out as she opens the door. "I'm busy. What do you—" Her voice stops when she sees me. "I see she made it out?" Ana's voice is surprised. "And I see she left the two of you behind."

My glare narrows, and I have to fight the impulse to take her down to one of the deviations' rooms and let them rip her to shreds. "Where is she?" I say through gritted teeth.

"Not my jurisdiction," she says as she is about to the close the door. "And it is not yours either. Last time I checked, you're not part of the Board."

I throw open the door. "Where is she?" I repeat myself, this time with more conviction.

"Does it sting? The fact that she didn't trust you?" Her voice is mocking. "If I know my daughter well enough, I know she left without even a goodbye, didn't she?"

I take a step back. She doesn't care what her

daughter is walking into. All this woman cares about is her labs and their results. Instead of playing into Ana's games, I realize who I need to find if I want any answers. I turn around and leave, slamming the door shut behind me. Quinn is quick to follow and closes gap between us in no time.

"Henly wouldn't take Dex back with her, would she? Right? She couldn't take him to her father. What if he recognizes him from before when they were in Havre?" Quinn demands as we turn past the medic unit and up to Royce's office.

I don't respond because I don't have to. We both already know Henly would. She and Dex have some strange relationship that, if I'm being honest, I hate. I hate how she confides in him, the way they know each other's secrets, and I hate that she trusts him more than she trusts me. But more importantly, I hate how she took him over me.

As I turn the corner, I catch Royce unlocking her office door, her expression tightened. She is not surprised to see me.

"Renner. Quinn," she greets us and then gestures for us to make our way into her office.

"This won't take long," I say, trying to contain

my anger.

After she closes the door, Royce gathers a few documents into her bag and nods. "I agree. I have a plane to catch." She looks at me. "Can you talk and walk? I need to be there before their helicopter lands."

"So they did go back?" Quinn asks as we head out of the office.

Royce looks from Quinn to me. "Yes."

"How could you let her go back?" Without meaning to, I have pushed Royce into a corner and have my forearm pressed up against her windpipe, but Royce's eyes give nothing away. She has always been a mastermind at keeping her emotions in check.

"Renner," Quinn whispers as a pair of Militaris pilots come into view.

Slowly, I let Royce go.

"Control yourself," Royce whispers. "I know your ego is bruised because she didn't take you with her, and I can't pretend to stand here and know why, but she didn't. Deal with it. Stop letting your emotions control you, dammit."

I take a step back. It has been so long since anyone has spoken to me like my mother used to—straightforward, no malice—just the truth. This was why Royce and my mother got along so well; they were essentially the same woman. My mother's words were never meant cruelly, like my father's were. No, she liked to call herself a romantic realist who saw the world for what it was, but she refused to let the dullness of the truth paint her world black and white. She always taught me to acknowledge reality, but never to fully accept it. She taught me instead to make it my own, to never bend to its will, but rather to make it bend to mine. I control my future, not the other way around. It always baffled me how a woman like her could end up with a man like my father, someone so cold and direct.

"I'm sorry," I finally say, but my words fail to convey how many times I had uttered this phrase to my own mother.

"Ma'am, we're ready when you are," the pilot announces through the door.

Royce nods to the pilot. "One minute." She turns her attention to me.

I don't press her for information. At this point, it would be useless. I stand back and stay quiet.

Royce smiles weakly, but then turns to Quinn. "Make sure Tucker gets his vitals checked around the clock." She then looks at me. "Make sure there are two

Militaris soldiers guarding him around the clock as well. No strangers in or out, just you and Quinn."

"Why?" Quinn asks.

Royce's eyes are fixated on me. "Trust me, Anson. Please, just trust me. If you don't hear from me in a week's time, you take Tucker and move him to a discreet location, another quarantine or somewhere far away from here. Make sure you, and only you, know where he is. Do you hear me?"

"Yes," I reply like a child eager to please a mother.

She reaches for me and takes me in an embrace. At first, I hesitate, but soon I rid myself of my insecurities and hug her back.

"Be careful who you trust, Anson," she repeats in a whisper before she walks out the door.

CHAPTER 23

HENLY

Out of the corner of my eye, I watch as Aurora fades into nothing but jagged rock and mountain terrain. The landscape begins to change from beautiful and green to dry and brittle. I suddenly ache for Aurora. It is the closest thing I have had to a home in years, and though my stays haven't been too long, I miss the cold comfort of the bland gray walls. I miss *him*.

The way he looked as the helicopter took off burns into my memory, like he knew I was capable of something like this, capable of hurting him, or like I did it on purpose. My eyes fall to Dex, and I see a necklace loosely hanging around his neck. The closer I look, the more the pendant seems familiar. He clears his throat and wakes me from my trance.

"She made it for me." He smiles as he takes the pearl in between his index finger and thumb.

I grab my matching pearl and rub it between my fingers. "Of course she did." I smile back and show him mine.

He tucks the small pearl back into his shirt and smiles at me. "I guess she wasn't okay with me leaving."

"Can you blame her?"

His gaze falls to the window. "No, guess not."

I'm not exactly sure what he is to Davis, but he is my best friend. I'm glad they have found comfort in one another. They will have time to figure out what that means. *Or will they? Dex being here with me, trying to save me, could get him killed. It would rob Davis of ever truly getting to know him.* Again, the images of Ellie dying come to mind, but her face is distorted with his. My head spins. Grabbing my forehead, I look out the window and try to focus on anything other than the images exploding in my mind. When I can't handle it anymore, I look up and see a city come into view over the faint light of the sunrise.

"Denver?" I whisper.

As the chopper begins its decent, Dex gives me a quizzical look. He is just as confused as I am.

"Why are we here?" Dex's voice is on edge, and I can only assume it is due to our last adventure here—the same adventure where we lost Ellie and where he eventually lost me.

It doesn't feel like any time has passed since then. I can see the crimson color painted against the white snow. I can hear the groans of the deviations as their black eyes hunted us. I can sense their desire to devour our bodies. It is like the last two years never happened, but they did.

"We can't show up in a Militaris chopper and expect him to be excited about it," Vaughn replies to our confusion.

"So, we land and then what?" I ask.

Vaughn's lips curl into a devilish grin. "Take me home, Sawyer?"

My eyes narrow. "What? No."

"Sawyer, whether you want to agree to it or not, that is where we're going. And I'm going to credit Dex for bringing you to me." He grabs Dex's shoulder. "My guy on the inside." His eyes study me as he speaks, "That's how *we* keep him alive." He points at Dex. "If I make it look like he and I were on the same team the entire time, he'll believe that we saved you. It'll show him our loyalty."

I follow his blue-eyed gaze and see my house a few miles away. I sit and brace myself for what is to come. *I chose this,* I repeat.

When we land, I expect memories to burst in my mind like before, but there is nothing. To be honest, there is not much left of my home anymore. My neighborhood now is only broken-down fences and homes that are burnt to ashes. The roof of my house is filled with holes and the windows have been left shattered. As I walk toward my house, I take in a world that used to seem familiar. Though now, it feels like a jagged memory, like this didn't happen to me. The earth seems untouched by the last few years. The vibrancies of the early morning sun reflect off of the snow. The snow finally brings back memories. One in particular, of my family and I playing in the snow, seems too real.

It was the first snowfall of the season in Denver, and I was six or seven. Davis and I were in the yard building something, at least I think Davis was there. She fades in and out of the memory, so I can't know for sure. I shake my head to gain some kind of clarity, but it is all a blur. I can't tell if it is a real memory Royce replaced or if it is one implanted by my father. The thought of him makes my jaw tighten, and I feel a warmth stream through my veins. *How strange is it that my affection for my father has changed so easily into something I can't even recognize?* Hatred isn't a strong enough word for all of the rage I feel toward him.

"Henly," Dex whispers as we walk up the front

steps to my house. "Hey, are you okay?"

I don't reply. My hand lingers on the door, but I can't force myself to open it.

"Henly," Dex whispers again with his fingers on top of mine. My breath catches as his fingers tighten. "We'll do it together."

Together, we turn the doorknob and slowly push it open. I step into the room that used to hold our belongings and find it completely empty. My whole house has been wiped clean. There is nothing, like no one ever lived here.

"Did the Militaris do this or my father?" I ask to no one in particular.

"Ana," Dex responds. "After you went missing, she told the Board that the best chance of finding you would be in this house somewhere, but she never found anything."

I purse my lips. "She found something. She always finds what she's looking for," I respond, and I can't help but laugh. In the end, my mother, the wily one, always gets what she wants.

"What now?" Dex asks.

"Knock me out," I say to both of them.

"What? No!" Vaughn rebuts.

"Then what? If you knock me out, it will make our story more believable." I pull off my hoodie and lay it down next to my pack. "You should probably radio in soon. Do it." I turn my attention to Dex while Vaughn tries to reach Alaska. "I don't want to be awake when they get here. I don't trust what I'll do."

"I...we can figure something else out," Dex says.

"No," I say sternly. "This is the way. Be careful." I turn to Vaughn after he finishes radioing in our coordinates. "Take care of—"

"Take care of Dex. I know. I will," he interrupts.

"Him, but you too. Please don't be stupid," I finish. *See you soon, Dad.*

CHAPTER 24

RENNER

I couldn't go back to my quarters, so I went to Henly's. My hand shakes as I reach for her door handle, like my brain is warning my body not to go in. *This is a bad idea.* I inhale sharply and force myself through. I don't know what I expected to find when I walked through the door, but every trace of her is gone. All that is left is an old stripped bed and a metal desk. I close the door behind me and take in the emptiness. I don't know how I should feel. I want to hold on to her—the way she tastes, the way she feels, the person she is—but I can't keep going after her. I know it is time to let go. She left me with nothing more than a single, five-letter word scribbled on a piece of paper. This time, it is all on her, and I have to accept the choices she has made, and she will have to accept mine. I close my eyes and let myself fall onto her bed. For a moment, the idea of letting her go simplifies my world. It would be easier to move forward without any emotion; it would be a nice change. Royce's words ring in my ears, *Stop letting your emotions control you.*

Exasperated, I sit up and stare at the blank walls.

Something by the far side of the room catches my eye. I walk over to it and find a photograph of Henly and Andrew taped to the front of a notebook. I stare at the picture in my hand and try to find a resemblance between Henly and her father, but I can't find any. In the picture, the two sit, smiling candidly as if this were a normal relationship. His arm is around her, and his grin is wide as he looks at his daughter. Henly smiles, but her eyes are focused on something in the distance. Flipping it over, I see it is recent, maybe a few months old. My fingers trace the lines of the journal, deciding whether or not I should read it. This journal looks different than the ones she handed me during the Board meeting a few days ago. The edges are creased, and as I flip through it, small keepsakes fall out—pine needles and a few pictures of Davis and Kenton. I take the notebook with me, sit on her bed, and then open it to a random page.

November 22

Her name was Reina. She knew me. She knew who I was, but how? She even knew Senator Renner. How did she know any of this? I'm so confused. I'll have to discuss this with Royce, but

she was there. If what she said were true, Royce
would have stopped me, right? She wouldn't have
let me kill her...

"Reina," I whisper. My finger traces her words again. *She killed Reina.* From what I've read, the process was quick, but she killed her without a slight ache of concern. I look deeper in the journal for the girl I just spent the night with, trying to find a piece of her that hasn't changed. I want a reason to keep holding on, to keep fighting for her—something that will redeem her—but I can't find one. She has no moral compass anymore. I knew she had killed people, Royce had warned me of that much, but to keep it from me...*that* I just don't understand. Or maybe I just don't care to understand.

I flip through the pages, reading line after line, trying to cement the truth into my mind. As I read on, it is like she had snapped. One minute, she had morals, and the next, they were gone, replaced by the desire to research, experiment, and invent.

The first pages are mild, like she was fighting something, but as they progress, she cares less about the person she was experimenting on. Toward the end, she had lost all sight of what was right or wrong. All the lives she took were to advance her father's research.

I spend hours comparing each and every page. When I finally look up at the clock, it is late in the afternoon. I tuck the book under my arm and head to my room. Before closing the door behind me, I look at her room one last time. I feel the break in my heart as I shut the door. I stand on the other side of her door not wanting to move. *I don't want it to end like this, but what choice do I have? I have to accept her choice.*

When I get up to my room, I throw open the door and toss the book on my desk. I pull off my shirt and throw it in a pile on the floor. The late evening air brings chills to my skin. I search my desk for the journal Henly gave me during the Board meeting and find it in my top drawer. I haven't had a chance to read it yet. As I pull it from the drawer, I notice a piece of paper folded on my desk. I set the notebooks on my bed and open the piece of paper. A part of me hopes it is from Henly, and I'm disappointed when it is not.

Hey,

I came by to see how you were doing. Hope everything is okay.

–Zoe

I crumple the sheet of paper. I'm not sure how to tell her, "No, everything is not fine. Sorry about the other night. It was a big mistake. Oh, and leave me alone. I've got some things on my mind that I have to figure out." *Yeah, I'm sure that will go over great.*

I flip open both journals and go over them together. I find a similar date, but they don't read the same. The one I found in Henly's room is mostly about her day-to-day experiences. The other has more detailed explanations about what procedures her father did, what tools he used, and the methods he implemented. The journal she gave the Board for me to dissect was full of entries about how she would infect those who were given to her. This is where I found the most similarities between the journals. While one discussed how each procedure was done, the other explained how she had personally felt about it and what she had hoped to accomplish. These seem to go hand in hand. I keep reading to the last page of the journal.

December 7

He found me—the one with the hazel eyes from my dreams. They brought me to this place they say I used to call home. It doesn't feel like home. I saw Royce this morning, and she told me to write down everything before they returned my memories, so here it goes.

My dad had me in Alaska. I left a few days ago to go to a rally in the north. I was sent there to gather more test subjects. We're close to perfecting deniferia. I know it. Looking at my research, it is clear that he, my father, and I have done everything to help the world evolve. It will be better because of the things we have done, but I digress. We landed in the northern territories at zero eight hundred. It was cold and muggy, but the messenger we had sent out weeks ago made sure to spread the word. There was a great turnout. The senator was getting ready to speak to begin the rally, but the Militaris showed up. They came to kill the people at the rally; they thought they were infected. They captured me, but I saw Rathe and the senator evacuate onto a plane. I think Senator Renner is still alive, but I can't be sure. I tried to follow him, but was accosted by a Militaris soldier and was taken down. I'm now here, and I'm ready to see my sister.

My hands start to shake as the last part drums again and again: "I think Senator Renner is still alive, but I can't be sure." *He was there. Yes, I knew that, but he got on a plane? He wasn't killed?* A hard knock on my door causes me to look up, but I can't move.

"Renner! It's Quinn! You in there?" She repeats the question a few more times.

Can it be? Is he alive?

"Renner!" Quinn shouts again. "Royce is on the line!"

I still can't move. I'm frozen. Everything is sinking in.

At some point, my door opens. I look around the room and find Quinn kneeling in front of me.

"Renner? Royce is on the line. She doesn't have long."

I lock eyes with her and whisper, "He's alive."

CHAPTER 25

HENLY

Slowly, my eyes open to the sound of machines beeping. Everything is blurry, but soon it all comes into focus. I shudder with fear. The room has the same tiled black floors and bright white walls, and the many beeping machines bring on déjà vu. My throat tightens, trying to suppress a scream forming in the pit of my stomach. My fingers walk up to the small bump at the base of my head where Vaughn knocked me unconscious. I pull the IV from my wrist and peel the oxygen from my face. I'm going to have to face him soon. I'm not sure what I will do when I see him, but I know I need to be ready. My heart skips frantically when the door swings open and *he* walks in. I realize no amount of preparation could have made me ready for this. Every part of my body freezes as if I were stuck in place by thumbtacks. Hesitantly, my eyes reach his. Tears fill his eyes as he pulls me in an embrace. For a moment, I think I might actually be sick.

"Shh, kiddo, you're back. I got you back," he whispers into my ear, but every touch hurts, not from literal pain, but because I know his embrace shows his relief in being able to continue his research.

My fists clench together, and the rage I feel is all consuming. My body trembles in fury under his cooing. This moment, right here, is a measure of self-control. I want nothing more than to kill him slowly, to make the pain last like he has done to so many others. I could do it. I know I could. My hands could easily wrap around his throat and squeeze until there is nothing left. The world would be a better place without Andrew Sawyer.

"Kiddo?" He pulls away from me and clasps his hands around my face, searching my eyes for something. He stares at me, trying to register what it is that I'm feeling. Only, if he knew, he would have me locked up.

"Dad..." I force myself to whimper, and once again, he cradles me in his arms. "How did you find me?"

"Vaughn and Royce found you. They had a man on the inside."

"Who?" I whisper, my voice on edge.

"One of ours. You'll meet him soon." He pulls away, staring at me with what I used to believe was love, but now I see it for what it really is: amazement of his creation.

His thumb caresses my cheek, and this one act sends me into a whole new level of anger. *It's just a lie—it was all a lie.* My mind races as I begin to think about all of the ways I could overpower and kill him. These thoughts are the only things that help force a smile to my face—the thoughts of *him* in pain. I can't bear another moment alone with him. I keep my hands busy by gripping my bed, and I'm thankful when the door pushes open.

"Look who it is," my father says as he faces the door.

I look up to see Dex standing behind Vaughn. *I have to pull myself together. I have to play this off just right. I have to. Dex's life if is on the line if I don't.*

"Vaughn," I whisper. "Thank you—" I look behind Vaughn to Dex "—and thank you...for bringing me home." Without looking at me, Dex clears his throat and nods like a good soldier would.

"Do you remember what happened to you?" my father questions me.

"No...I remember trying to protect the senator, but I got shot, and the rest is a blur." I wince.

"Vaughn reported that one of his men found

you on enemy territory. You're lucky they didn't know who you were. Thanks to Vaughn's friend, Private Buhl, we were able to get you out." He touches the bump on my neck and adds, "As safely as we could."

I avoid Dex's gaze and set my attention back to my father, but I can't look at him without feeling enraged—without wanting to squeeze every last bit of breath from him. *Focus, Henly. Calm down. Dex's life is—ah! Why does my side hurt*? I feel a sharp pang next to my ribs. It throbs and burns like waves across my torso. Instinctively, my hand reaches for the pain, and I find a small gauze patch beneath my medical gown. *I've only been back a few short hours, and he has already cut into me.*

"What happened?" I try to mask my hatred as fear.

My father's hands once again clasp around my face. "You were badly injured when they brought you home, and I had to fix you up."

He is lying, but I nod anyway. I know Vaughn hit me in the head. I asked him to. If I don't hurry and find out what he is up to, I will die. He will kill me, and there will be no remorse other than losing another test subject.

"When can I go back to my room?" I ask.

"Now actually. Vaughn came to escort you."

I force a smile, but it soon fades when he leans in and presses his lips to my forehead. "I don't know what I would've done if anything had happened to you," he whispers.

"Right…" I whisper. It takes everything I have not to flinch away from him.

"Henly, I mean it. Kiddo, you mean everything to me."

He looks into my eyes, and I almost forget about everything that has happened. He has that effect on me. His eyes remind me so much of Davis's that I want to believe him. "You will have a couple days to rest before we go back in to make sure everything is running okay, all right?"

This is how he has manipulated me my entire life. Beneath my hatred, all I ever wanted was to believe him, but he has told me time and time again who he is, yet I still hope for a better version of him. I want to believe he is better than this, but I should have been listening better to his actions. I pull him into an embrace and accept this moment is the last one for us as father and daughter. This is goodbye.

"Sounds good," I say.

As my father walks past Dex, I catch him take a second glance at Dex as if he thinks his face is familiar. It is, and it won't take long for my father to figure out why.

"Love you, Dad," I say in hopes to distract him from his fixation on Dex.

Caught off guard, my father turns to me and smiles. "I love you too, kiddo."

He walks off, and I feel the facade fade. "He *will* figure out who you are," I say to Dex. "And when he does, you'll be dead."

Vaughn hurries to my bedside like he used to and helps me up. Like old times, I take his shoulder and plead with him, "You know I'm right. Send him away. *Please.*"

"Royce vouched for him. He'll be fine," Vaughn replies. "As long as we stick to our plan, everything will work, and we'll be gone before he knows."

"Henly, I'll be fine," Dex repeats.

"Yeah? What about Davis? If something happens to you…" I almost yell, but I feel the incision on my torso sting.

Vaughn puts his finger in front of his lips, gesturing for me to be quiet. "I couldn't send him away even if I wanted to. Your dad has already debriefed us. There's nothing I can do, so stop."

We make our way down the hall. Vaughn carries most of my weight while Dex follows a few paces behind us. If I wasn't so worried about Dex, it would be like it used to be.

I squeeze Vaughn's arm. "Remember that time? It was late, and you came to my hospital room dressed in scrubs and broke me out."

"I thought you could use a little therapy," he confesses with a laugh.

His laugh feels good. "Yeah, we ended up getting stranded in the mountains. We had to call for an evac…" I continue.

He looks at me through a sideways glance, his eyes as clear and blue as a midday sky. "If you hadn't pushed the snowmobile that hard, we would've been fine," he teases.

"Sure…" I mock. "Then you disappeared for days."

The smile fades. "Your dad had me whipped…took a few days to heal."

"What?" I stop in disbelief.

"Yeah, you weren't exactly coherent after, and I didn't want to add to it."

"You should have told me!"

He shakes his head. "Why? There was nothing either of us could have done."

I ponder on it for a moment, and I realize he is right. The person I was before would have found a way to blame Vaughn and remove any blame from my father. Again, he has this effect on me—or should I say, had. My father will pay for the pain he has caused.

"I'm sorry," I whisper.

"You should be." He smiles again, but this one is forced and not from nostalgia. "He gave me an extra beating since the snowmobile broke."

I shake my head. "Vaughn, I'm—"

"Stop. It's okay."

For the first time in a long time, I *really* look at Vaughn. His face is scruffy, and the smile he wears is weathered and feels a little bit forced. His shoulders seem stronger, not anymore muscular, but more resilient. He refuses to lose himself in this process, and I admire that.

"So, how long have I been here?" I whisper.

Dex doesn't look at me when Vaughn speaks. "One week. Seven days."

"What?" My eyes feel like they are about to bulge out of my head. "How has it been a week? What was the surgery for?"

"We don't know. When we landed, you were rushed straight into surgery." He looks around before he continues. "I was in and out of interrogation with Dex for the first few days, making sure everything went smoothly."

"Hey, how about you two finish this conversation later?" Dex interjects.

I look over my shoulder to a fast approaching Rathe. If she is near, something has to be wrong. When my memories returned in Aurora, I realized what she is—a glorified babysitter. She watched me and reported back to my father, but Vaughn made sure to keep me safe. He always made sure I was okay. I glance at him and see he has never wanted to lie to me, and without reservation, I reach out for him. He doesn't hesitate to grab on to me, and I feel like I can conquer anything.

"Sawyer, you're alive?" Rathe says as she slaps me on the shoulder.

I wince, but the pain soon fades to anger and

mockery. "Not what you expected?"

Her eyebrow rises. "For being so perfect, I'm surprised they could contain you."

"It is hard to fight back when you're sedated." I stand taller against Vaughn, and I can see him step closer to Rathe.

"Step off, Rathe," Vaughn spits out.

She rolls her eyes and mocks Vaughn. "Good to have you back." She then turns to me. "We have a session this afternoon."

My eyes narrow in confusion at her wink. "A session? What? Why are you winking at me?" I question, completely oblivious as to what she means.

She looks from me to Vaughn and then to Dex. "Do I know you from somewhere?"

Suddenly, all of the air leaves my lungs, and I feel panic wash over me. *Does she remember who he is?*

"Yes, you interrogated me," Dex replies without missing a beat. He stands taller with a whole new sense of confidence.

"No, that's not it."

"Yes, it is," Vaughn says. "You and Kellan interrogated him last week. Where else would you have seen him?"

Finally, some air creeps back into my lungs. "What time is our session?"

Rathe's eyes narrow at Dex. "In two hours. I'll come by and grab you."

I nod as we reach the door to my room and open it. The three of us walk in, and Vaughn shuts the door on Rathe before she can think she is invited inside.

After I get settled in my bed, Dex asks, "What's a session?"

Vaughn and I lock eyes for way too long.

"Henly?" Dex persists.

As I look away from Vaughn, I'm shocked by his reaction.

"I'll give you two a minute."

Dex's expression doesn't soften when the door closes, and I realize Vaughn has kept another secret for me. I don't know if it is just being back here or if it is the distance between Renner and me, but I am reminded of how much Vaughn has done for me and how rude I have been to him for trying.

"What is it?" Dex pushes.

Taking a deep breath, I try explaining myself, "It's my job here. It's what I'm good at...*was* good at."

I pause as my throat suddenly feels dry. *How can I tell my best friend that I used to change people into deviations?* "I…I…"

"I know it's your job, but what is it? What did you do?"

His question has a double meaning. It refers to my past, but for me, it is all very much in the present. *What did I do? What do I do? I kill traitors, at least the ones I thought were traitors. I kill people—I killed Reina.* If I play this part, I'll have to do it again. I'll have to do it very soon.

"Henly?"

I try to focus on his words, but I don't know how to respond. There is no way to phrase it that will clear me from his judgment. Nothing I say will make it sound anything less than what it is—murder.

"That bad?" Dex whispers.

I swallow hard and force the words out. "I transitioned them, the captures, when they didn't cooperate."

"Transitioned to where?" He pauses and tries to put the pieces together, and I wait for his response. "If they didn't cooperate…" His eyes grow big as if the words finally click. "You *tortured* people!"

I wince at his realization, but don't deny it. It is as if in that split second, when he realizes what I am, the room heats up to an almost unbearable temperature. When I finally meet his gaze, my cheeks burn. I can't read his expression. First, he seems shocked, confused even, then he seems sympathetic, and then he is back to looking angry.

"I was different..." I try to defend myself. "My memories were lost...I was lost."

Dex takes a step back and squares his shoulders to mine. He just looks at me, examining me to see what has changed—or maybe to see what is the same. After his silence becomes unbearable, he takes a step toward me. His hands reach for my shoulders as he pulls me toward him, and he whispers in my ear, "I know...I know."

I sink into his embrace and instantly feel rejuvenated. I feel like my old, innate strength comes back to me. This is different from my enhancements; it is a strength fueled by love—by friendship—and I have been missing it since my memories have returned. I pull away from Dex, but before I have a chance to tell him, there is a knock on the door, and in comes Vaughn.

"You good?"

I'm about to respond to Vaughn when I realize he is not talking to me. He is talking to Dex. I turn in time to catch Dex's response as he nods yes. Looking between them, I feel anxiety building in the pit of my stomach. Soon, I will be back in the same room that fills most of my nightmares, doing what I do best—creating deviations.

"Henly, you have no choice. You have to be who you are." I lift my gaze to Vaughn, who seems to be bothered by his own words. "Who you *were*," he says, trying to correct himself.

Who was I? A monster. Who am I? A monster still.

He doesn't need to correct himself. Who I was then and who I am now is the same; they just won't accept it. There is no distinguishing my past from my present. Both sets of memories are mine. I created them. I am responsible. It wasn't some stranger doing these things on my behalf—it was me.

"Come with me?" I ask Vaughn.

Without any hesitation, he replies, "Absolutely."

Turning to Dex, I say, "You need to go. Lay low until Vaughn comes to get you later. Please, no matter what, get back to Davis if I can't."

"Okay." Dex looks past me to Vaughn. "She makes it back. No matter what."

They nod to each other, and as soon as Dex is out the door, I turn to Vaughn and punch him hard.

"What was that for?" He rubs his arm and gives me his signature grin. "Lighten up, would you?" He suddenly becomes serious. "You have so many people under your thumb."

"There's no one under my thumb." I glare.

Vaughn leans closer so I can feel his words on my skin. "Well, then maybe just me…"

Without thinking, the blue of his eyes captures my whole attention, and I lean forward, pressing my lips to his. I have done this so many times before, but this time, it is different. I try to convince myself that I didn't miss him, that our back and forth is a part of the show, but it is not. I care about him. I miss him. A part of me, though, still longs for Renner, and for a small moment, I let myself pretend I am with Renner again. I know it is wrong to kiss one boy and long for another, but right now, it's hard to separate them.

When I pull away from Vaughn, he seems relieved, like he has finally broken down the wall I had built up. I return his smile and try to rid myself of my guilt. I'm here with him and that is what I should be focusing on.

I look away to find Rathe leaning against the entrance to my room. Her eyes give it away. I follow her gaze back to Vaughn. It is the first time I have noticed the pain in them as she stares at Vaughn and me. Her cringe confirms it—she loves him. I don't hesitate to kiss him again. I take my time and enjoy the agony it must be causing Rathe. When I pull away, a smile hangs on the corner of Vaughn's lips.

Rathe clears her throat. "Time to go."

"I know," I say while still holding Vaughn's gaze.

He smirks, lifting his brow to study me. And then I see it come over his face. He gets it. The once flirty boy becomes hard and cold as he slightly shakes his head. Vaughn could always read me. Shame washes over me. I shouldn't have used him to get back at Rathe. I walk past him and turn at the door to wait for him to come.

"Are you coming?" I try to play off innocently.

He shakes his head as he walks over to me. "No, I don't like being used." He scoffs as his finger rubs against his lower lip. "Plus, Sawyer, it seems like you are back to your good ole self. You can handle this." He walks past me without another glance. "Good luck," he yells over his shoulder before he disappears around the corner.

I watch him as he goes, knowing I have bruised his ego. This fighting back and forth is new with him. I follow Rathe down the familiar path to work. I remember what I'm going to have to do again, and I grit my teeth as the anger boils beneath my skin, slowly coursing through me. For a second, it is invigorating to be reminded of just how strong I am.

We take the stairs down two levels and stop outside Level One as she types in her clearance code. We push through the door, and I'm sickened by how comfortable I used to feel in this place. The same five metal tables are still lined up against the far side of the room. The same machines are calculating the heartbeats, blood pressure levels, and pain levels of the test subjects. I walk by each patient, grabbing the charts that hang from the foot of each bed. This group is only in the first phase. They still have three more phases, each one taking them a step closer to becoming the perfect deviation. The second phase patients are kept on Level

Two, the third on Level Three, and the fourth on Level Four. During the second and third phases, they become more active. They wake up in a mist of confusion and rage, but that clears by the time they make it to the fourth phase, the final phase—that is, if they make it to the fourth phase, not many do. Those who really piss off Kellan in the first few phases, however, get roughed up a bit and then sent straight to me.

The day goes by quickly at first, but the closer we get to the final phase, the more I worry I won't be able to carry out this plan. I have been working myself up all day, wondering if I can do it—if I can kill someone again. I turn to Rathe. She has been eyeing me all day, making sure I do everything as usual. So, I do as I have done before: inspect, inject, and move on to the next. Today, I have already seen over thirty trials among the first three levels, and thus far, they have all been failures. None of them have been able to move past their rage and confusion. Across the room, Rathe checks the last patient's vitals on Level Three before she turns to me.

"We just have to go to Level Four and then we're done today," she says with a glint of excitement in her eyes.

"The joys of being back." My voice is monotone.

"Oh, come on! Remember the last girl we had up there? This one won't be nearly as much of a struggle." My shoulder tenses as she slings her arm around me. "I mean, he's an idiot for coming back and running his mouth."

I shrug her off of me and turn to look at her. "Who ran his mouth?"

"The messenger. The one we sent out to get more trials," she says as she points to the people being tested.

"What was he saying?" I ask as we take the steps up to Level Four.

"Something about the senator's son working with the Militaris. He said they were on this crazy mission to find you. Apparently, Vaughn took you to them."

I turn and study Rathe's face. She doubts me, but not enough to go against my dad. "This should be interesting…"

"How so?" she asks.

I look at her and shrug my shoulders. "I didn't even know the senator had a son."

Rathe smiles at me. "Yeah, he has a few photos of him in his office. He died when everything hit. Apparently, he took a bullet to the head by a deviation or something. He was pretty good looking though, a younger version of the senator. The things I would do to him."

I narrow my eyes at her in disgust. "Wow, really? That's how you talk about the dead?"

She laughs. "Oh, come on. If you saw what he looked like, you would too."

I shake my head no. "Let's see what he has to say, shall we?" I open the door to a preteen boy who is wide-awake.

"Hello, Liam," I say as I grab and read his chart.

I scan the chart and find that he is only twelve. He is young enough not to know that talking or getting noticed will get him killed. I look at Rathe as she narrows her eyes at me again. I know she definitely doubts me now because I have never talked to the people on my table before.

"I'm sorry," he says, his lips quivering. "I won't say anything again."

"I know. I know," I repeat as if it will make a

difference. There is no way I can change his fate, not now. One will have to die for the greater good.

"All right, let's take a look here. You have gone through all the phases, and now you've made it to phase four." I cross the room and check his vitals. "Not many make it here."

He looks up at me, his green eyes glistening with tears. "I'm going to die, aren't I?"

I don't answer. I can't. My voice has left me. I have no response for this kid who is afraid of what' is to come.

"Shouldn't have run your mouth!" Rathe yells. "Should've stayed loyal and not tried to stay with the Militaris."

"Enough!" I yell at Rathe. "Get out. I'll do this one alone."

She stands up, her hands in the air. "Whose side are you on, Sawyer? Just weeks ago, you were punching the crap out of the girl on the table."

My fists clench. "Get out."

She leaves without another word and shuts the door behind her. I look down at the boy whose tears fall steadily in a stream down his cheeks.

"Why did you come back here?"

He opens his eyes, but he doesn't look at me. For a moment, the tears stop as he keeps his focus on the ceiling. "They have my family. They said they would only let my family go if I did my job. I was afraid they would kill them, but now I'll never know."

I cross the room and pull a chair out from the desk. "What is your last name?"

"Hought, Liam Hought," he says with a quiver.

I type in the name "Hought," and the system *pings*. The Houghts are a family of three who were pushed through the process seven weeks ago in Ontario, Canada. I read through their file. The father, Joe, age forty-three; the mother, Anne-Marie, age forty-four; and the daughter, Haddie, age six were all diagnosed with a cancer gene. I look over my shoulder to the child who lies still, fearful of his future. He won't survive this phase—they never do. *Soon, he'll see his family.*

"Liam." I try to speak without emotion, but I can't. This used to be easy for me. "All of your family was detected with having a cancer gene. They've been pushed through the trials."

He finally looks at me and breaks down. Every part of his body thrashes against the table, and he sobs. I look away, but I can still hear him wailing. They aren't sobs of fear for his own life—he is past that now—but rather tears for his family. I walk to the computer and enter his data. As I input his height, age, and weight, his cries have softened to small whimper. When I finally finish, I brush the tears from my eyes and pull the vials from their container to load them. I am making sure each gun is loaded properly when I hear his voice. It is no louder than a small whisper.

"Will it hurt?"

I set down the vials and check his arm for a vein. "Yes, but only for a few minutes."

"I told them about you." He glares at me. "They know you're a traitor. Both of your friends will be on this table, just like me, and eventually, you will be too!" he spits at me.

My eyes glaze over from his words. I already know I will share his same fate. I prep his arm and look down at him. "Are you ready?"

"Didn't you hear me?" he yells. "You'll die!"

I can taste the tears on my lips when I speak, "Yes, I probably will."

He grits his teeth and closes his eyes. I wait for a response, but he doesn't give me one, so I inject the first vial. My heart empties as I watch the fluid run through his veins. I monitor his vitals as I press the second vial into his IV. This one is the numbing agent, but he isn't screaming from pain like the others have. *I'm impressed.* I wait longer to see if something will happen, if he will give me a reaction, but he doesn't. There is nothing more than an eerie, unsettling silence. After I dump the vial gun in the sink, I walk over to the monitors to check how the injections are affecting him, and I'm shocked. He's changing—adapting. I run to the door.

"Rathe!" I yell. "Rathe, where the hell are you?" I yell louder, hoping she will come running.

"What do you want, Sawyer? You kicked me out of—"

"Shut up! Go get my dad! Go! He is adapting! He is altering the virus! *Go!*"

She takes off down the hall in a full sprint, and I turn back to monitor the boy who could possibly hold the answers in his blood. He could be what helps me survive. I record as much as I can and double check it just to be safe. His vitals are calm. I look at the clock and feel like Rathe is taking too long. I place his chart against his bed and walk to the door. I have to go find my dad. I reach for the handle, but the door swings open. Royce walks in, rushing past me toward Liam.

"Wh-what are you doing?" she stammers.

"He's adapting, Royce. He's changing. He's—this has never happened before. I sent Rathe after my dad."

I don't mean to say "dad," but it just falls out that way. She turns suddenly and glares at me. Her eyes register anger or annoyance. Either way, it is a look I have never gotten from her before.

"What's wrong?" I ask.

"This has happened before, but your father never knew about it. He can't have another one like you. Being the only one is what's keeping you alive," Royce says, and for the first time, I get the sense that she truly does care for me.

"I didn't know…I thought the boy could help. I thought he could fix me."

"No, Henly. His signs of adaption are the final stamps on your death certificate." She loads a vial gun.

"What are you doing?" I ask, unable to move.

"Keeping you alive."

"You can't…don't!"

Before I can object further, she inserts the needle into the boy's IV, and I watch as he jolts against his restraints. I brush the dark hair from his eyes, trying to comfort him in any way I can. At this point, he doesn't feel anything. It will be just like he is sleeping. I turn when I hear the jostling of machines behind me.

"What are you doing?" I demand.

"Making this look like it never happened." She stops and looks at me. "Wipe your tears. You can cry later."

I cover my face with both hands and wipe underneath my eyes. I recover quickly and stand up straight when I hear footsteps. They are still a few meters away. I give Royce a look of gratitude before I go to the boy's chart and begin to record what should have happened. I begin to enter the new data, and Royce begins destroying the old data. I carefully adapt each entry that I had put special focus on to make it look like a coherent succession of my old thoughts. The door bursts open as I shout to Royce.

"We're losing him! Should I inject him with adrenaline?"

She looks over her shoulder and shakes her head. "We lost him."

"What happened?" my dad asks as he rushes into the room. He strips me of the chart and begins to go over the data. "Henly, what happened? Rathe said he was adapting." He scans the data. "It looks like he was, so what happened?"

"I don't know." I shrug my shoulders. "I went into the hallway to see if you were coming, and that's when I spotted Royce. She came in as he was crashing, and we tried everything to bring him back, but it didn't work."

I look up at him as he studies my face. I stare back at those green eyes that look so much like mine. I can't look away. I stand taller and reply, "Do you think I wanted him to die?" I begin. "He could've saved me."

My dad lowers the papers and looks over his shoulder at Royce. She meets his gaze, but doesn't say anything.

"You made me perfect, remember?" I say to my dad. He turns his attention back to me. "She didn't have to tell me. I can feel it. I'm dying, and you don't know how to stop it, do you?"

"Leave us," my father demands.

Royce pushes the chair in slowly and walks to the door. She motions for Rathe to join her, but Rathe's eyes are on me. I can't decide if she knows or if I am being paranoid. *Did Liam really tell them everything?*

"If there's anything you need, sir, I'll be on the other side of that door," she says to him.

I roll my eyes. She is such a teacher's pet. When she closes the door behind her, the sound of the machines fills the room instead of our voices. A part of me worries I have said too much. *What if he knows I'm myself again?* I've never spoken to him this way before. I swallow hard as he walks to the door and latches the lock.

He turns to me. "You should never reveal too much in front of strangers, Henly."

"Royce isn't a stranger, and doesn't Royce already know? She wouldn't confirm it, but her lack of denial said as much."

My father continues toward me. I think he might embrace me, but he doesn't. He walks past me to Liam's body. I follow his movements and watch as he dissects the boy. He cuts his shirt up from his naval to his chest and then spreads it open. He motions for me to stand across from him. I walk over and pick up the gloves he placed on Liam's chest. *He wants to do an autopsy now?* I don't object. The former version of myself would do this. She wouldn't care if the boy had just died or that he was too young to die. This was for science, and sometimes sacrifices need to be made in the name of science. She wouldn't have cared that he died for her own survival, but she does—I do. Before I know it, we are breaking into his chest cavity and extracting his heart, lungs, and liver. We look for things that could be a dead giveaway for fowl play, but I doubt we will find any. If Royce has done this before, I'm sure she has found a way to be discreet. When we are finished, we sew the boy back up and take his organs to be further analyzed.

"Don't speak to me like that in front of my subordinates again."

I look up at him. His eyes are full of fire. He stares at me like *I* am one of his subordinates. My eyes narrow as his voice reminds me of Ana's. I lean back and strip off the gloves, throwing them in the red bin behind me.

"Are we understood?" he shouts.

My back stiffens, not out of fear, but out of shock. I thought I still had his affections, but with the new failure lying on the table in front of us, his treatment of me says otherwise. I turn to face him and lean my body against the porcelain sink.

"Don't push me," I threaten.

He looks at me with one brow raised. "Don't forget who created you."

"How can I? I'm dying because of you!" I snap. "And don't you forget what I can do, what I can do to you." I grab the metal table and bend the corners of it in my hands, pulling it together and making it look like a balled up piece of paper.

My father stands across from me, trying to hide his emotions. He likes what I can do. The pupils of his eyes have dilated three times their normal size. He reaches for something in his coat pocket. I quicken my pace and grab for it before he does. It is a vial of some sort.

"What is this?" I question sarcastically. I hold him at an arm's reach, and he struggles to take the vial gun from my hand. He doesn't speak, so I do. "How long have you known?"

"Since your return. Do you take me for a fool?"

I feel the room spin slightly. That is not the question I wanted an answer to. I pause and look at him. *What do I do now?* I drag him to a chair and pull the strings from a few machines, tying him to it. After I make sure he is tied tightly, I take a few steps back and sit across from him.

"How long have you known?" I repeat.

"That you're a failed experiment?" he spits at me.

I lean back in my chair and wince at his words. I'm not dying to him. I'm just a failed experiment.

"Yeah, Dad."

"Some time now, but I wasn't sure if you would die wherever Vaughn and Royce took you or if you would come back, hoping I would save you."

"So, you won't save me?" I ask. "You won't save your own child?"

He leans back in his chair. "I can't save you. You were a trial, and you were successful, but that is it." He pauses and looks at the body behind me. "Royce has been doing this for some time now, and I wasn't sure if you were a part of it. When you called for me today, I thought you were going to keep doing the right thing, but then you helped Royce kill him. There will be others like you—better than you. You served your purpose, kiddo. It's time to move on. That's how it goes, and you of all people should know that."

I keep my grip on the vial gun. "What happens next?" I ask.

"We torture them to find out where this quarantine is and take the boy who is like you with us." He reads the shock on my face.

How does he know about Tucker?

He continues, "Kiddo, there's little I don't know. Of course I know about him. I know about Davis, and I know about your friends. The only thing I don't know is where they are."

I insert the vial into the gun and ready it. "You'll never know." I stand to inject my father.

"Hold on. Maybe I can save you, but I'll only know that if I have the boy."

I stare at him as he tries his best to manipulate me. When I was a child, he would use love to make me do things. He would say, "Henly, do it because you love me," or "If you love me, you'll do the right thing." But now, it isn't about his love. He is colder now. After years of watching me, he knows what will trigger a reaction. I would be lying if I didn't think about it, if I didn't consider bringing Tucker back to him so I could live, but I know him just as well as he knows me. I would be discarded, tossed to the side like last year's trend. If I could trust him, I would. What does that say about me? Ana's words come to my mind: "If you're not like me, then you're like him."

I set down the vial and wish for anger, something to push me over the edge, anything, but I feel nothing. I can't force myself to do this. I glance at my dad, who wears a sad look, but I can't bear to look at him for another minute. Turning away, I catch my reflection in a mirror. My expression matches his. It is the first time I have felt that I look like him. The distorted image is enough to send me over the edge.

"I'm not like you," I whisper.

I turn to face him, steadying the vial gun in my hand, and step toward him. He has no rebuttal when I approach, but he doesn't look at me. I feel the weight of his disappointment.

"I can't let you hurt them," I say. "I'm sorry."

He looks up, tears shinning in his eyes. "You're a disappointment, kiddo."

"I know." I nod in agreement and insert the needle, pressing the trigger.

The liquid is so quick to flow through him that he only stays conscious for a few seconds before he goes limp in the chair. I don't exactly know what was in the vial, but whatever it is will keep him unconscious for a bit. I unstrap him from the chair and let him fall from my arms, making sure he hits his head. I then walk to the door and slowly unlock it. I grab the bowl with Liam's organs and let them fall to the ground. They will be too contaminated to do anything with.

Kneeling next to my dad, I feel my anger flee. The only thing left is sadness. I loved him like a daughter should love her father. I believed in him whole-heartedly and wished he would feel compassion for me. I had hoped he would save me, but I was wrong. I was wrong about both parents.

I yell for Rathe, "Help! Rathe!"

She bursts through the door like a legionnaire fighting the brigade for her king. When she reaches me, she asks me what happened, and I tell her my version.

"We'd just finished closing Liam when he fell. His body gave out. He had the organs in his hands, and now they'll be useless!" I shout.

She looks at me, and I can't discern if she believes me or not. She yells for more guards, and they help carry my dad to one of the other surgeons on staff.

"Where did Royce go?" I ask her.

Rathe looks at me, but doesn't respond. She trails after my father's limp body. I stick around long enough to make it look like I'm picking up samples and cleaning, but once they're out of sight, I run to Vaughn's room. I knock until he comes to the door.

"He knows," I almost shout. "I can find Royce, but you need to find Dex!"

"What the hell happened? I leave you for a day—" he says, waving his hand as if he is waving off our imminent death.

For some reason, this makes me smile. "Keep up!"

I quickly tell him the whole story about what happened between my father and me. I tell him about the boy in Bowden, and how he confessed before we arrived. He asks me why Drew waited so long to act, and my only guess is that he was trying to play with me. He wanted to know as much as he could. Vaughn agrees we have to get out of here.

"All right, I'll find Dex. Do you know where Royce will be?"

I nod. *I'll find her.*

"Okay, we'll meet on the roof and then get the hell out of here," he instructs.

"I'll do my best to meet you, but if you guys see a chance to leave, go! I'm a goner anyway."

He stops in his tracks and looks at me. "I know

I'm a little slow, but what?"

I look down and then back at him. "My trial has expired."

"I thought he could help you." His eyes narrow, and he stares at me for such a long time that it makes me feel vulnerable.

I shake off his looks and scold him. "We don't have time. I will tell you everything later. I promise." I start running to find Royce. "Get Dex, please!"

CHAPTER 26

RENNER

My grip tightens around the journals as I make my way through the corridors. I only know of one place to go with all of this information and take the stairs up by two until I'm outside Slade's room. My fists collide with the door as I pound for him to wake, and when he answers, he is not enthusiastic about my appearance in the middle of the night. I push past him and into his room.

"Yes, do come in," he says sarcastically through a yawn.

"Slade, you have to reinstate me. Now."

"Now? In the middle of the night? No meeting or protocol?" He is annoyed.

I take a seat at the small dining table in his chambers and pull out the notebooks, placing them on the table in front of us. "She didn't tell us the whole story. I was in her room this morning and found another journal. This one tells a completely different story as to what happened to her while she was in Alaska."

I have piqued his curiosity. He sits across from me and quickly motions for me to give him the journals.

In one swift movement, I slide them across the table and wait as he reads a few passages.

"This would have been good information to have before she authorized her own mission to Alaska," Slade whispers, more to himself than to me.

"Why was the mission authorized?" I ask.

He looks up with amusement. "Thought the two of you were close friends? I guess not."

He lets the words sink in. He isn't the first to say it, and he won't be the last.

"Slade, my dad is alive."

Slade slowly sets the books on the table. "She said as much."

I look up, surprised. "So you knew?"

"Before she left, she came to see me and told me the extent of her mission back to Alaska. She explained she wanted to save as many lives as she could, and she wanted to bring back Andrew Sawyer and your father."

"She's not bringing anyone back," I reply. "She went back to Alaska to gather information on her sister, Davis, to figure out what Andrew wants with her."

Slade rubs the corners of his eyes in an attempt

to wipe the sleep away. "What on earth do you mean?"

"Davis is the virus. Ana has been giving Davis injections to keep the virus dormant. If and when their father finds them, he will use Davis like an atomic bomb." I feel bad throwing Davis out there like this, but I have come to realize there are no longer any lines of loyalty. I just need to do what has to be done for the greater good. *Fight the good fight. Help as many people as I can.* I want to protect every single life here, and if that means I have to expose Davis, then I will.

Slade walks over to the phone on his bedside table and dials four numbers, those of which I presume connect him to the other Board members. "Yes, sorry to wake you all, but we have a situation that needs attending to immediately. Yes, I'll standby."

Slade looks at me through the slits of his eyes. I know he is irritated; he has been played for a fool. After all, he was the one, with the help of Royce, who nudged the Board to vote in favor of Henly.

"Yes, thank you. We need to authorize an emergency reinstatement of Anson Renner."

From where I sit, I can hear the murmurs over the phone.

"He's brought me some very important

information that may change your mind." Slade looks over his shoulder and hands me the phone. "Would you be so kind as to share your discovery with the rest of the Board?"

I take the phone and tell them everything—my first mission out when I found all of the deviations, my suspicions of Davis, what I uncovered with the help of Quinn, the journals in Henly's room, the discovery of my father, and finally, my reasons for needing to be reinstated. The Board quickly agrees. And just like that, I'm back in. I hand the phone to Slade. He speaks for a few more minutes and then hangs up.

"I'm going after him," I announce.

"I expected that much. And what about Henly?" He sits across from me at his dining room table. "Can I trust you to do the right thing if it needs to be done?"

"I won't kill her, but I'll bring her back," I say with finality.

"We're going to secure Davis in a different facility. I will make some calls when the hour becomes more agreeable."

I nod in agreement. "I'll get a team prepped and be ready by sunrise."

"Renner, make sure you don't lead them back to us. We've been safe because Andrew and your father cannot pinpoint our precise location. If they locate even just one quarantine, then who knows what will come of us."

"I'll do my best," I respond.

"No, you do better than your best."

* * *

The team is ready, and all I have left to do is take care of a few last minute details. I'm walking around my room, packing and organizing things, when I hear a knock on my door.

"Come in."

I hear the door open and close, but there is no greeting. I turn to find Zoe staring at my bag on the floor.

"It's been a few days," she says, still staring at my pack.

"Yeah, things have been crazy."

"We haven't talked in a while. I thought I would come say…something before you went off to save her again."

"No, she can save herself. I'm going after my dad."

Her brows rise in shock. "He's alive?" She moves closer to me. "Are you okay? I mean, that is crazy," she says as she puts her arms around me.

I shrug off her embrace. "I will be when I find him and can make him answer for all the shit he's put us through."

Her eyes move around the room as if she were avoiding my gaze. Finally when she looks at me, she says what I've been trying to avoid. "Renner, look, the other night meant something to me, and I know it maybe didn't mean anything to you, but where do you stand? I need to know…" she tapers off.

At a loss for words, I take a minute to think about what is happening. I'm leaving in a few hours on a hunt for my father, and I don't know where it will take me. I look up at her, and her eyes are hopeful. "Look, Zoe, you and I are friends, and the other night, we…I mean, *I* crossed—"

"Okay, I get it," she blurts out, cutting me off.

"No, listen." I soften. "I just can't right now. I'm off to find my dad who I thought was dead. There's so much I have to get through in the next twenty-four hours, and I need to focus on that."

Her eyes well up and tears stream down her

cheeks, but she nods. I take her in my arms and offer her a million apologies, but it is not enough.

"We'll talk when I get back," I say.

She pulls away, her eyes still glossy, and for a moment, I wonder if I will ever be able to move on from Henly and learn to love someone else the way I love her. I want to make things better. I lean in and press my lips against hers. She clings to me, and I want to pretend everything is different, like our families are still alive and we still live across the street from each other. I wonder if in that world, she and I would have had a chance at being normal, at being together. But as I pull away, the realization hits: everything is how it should be. I can't force myself to love someone just because I'm lonely or because that person is in love with me. I can't force love to suffocate my pain. When I get back and my father is in custody, I'll tell her the truth.

"We'll talk when you get back," she whispers.

She kisses me one last time before whispering goodbye. I pull away from her and grab my pack. I head out the door and close it behind me.

I hurry down the hall to the medic unit to look for Quinn. I walk into her office and leave both of Henly's journals on her desk. I'm grabbing a pen to scribble a note when I notice the picture I took of us the other day is framed and sits on her desk next to the picture of her and Ellie. Having contributed to Ellie and Quinn's legacy makes me smile, like I'm a part of something bigger. Quickly, I scribble on the piece of paper that Davis will be transferred to another quarantine for safeguarding, Ana will most likely be going with her, and Slade will deal with this transfer at a more "agreeable hour." I leave her office and move into the medic unit.

A few Militaris soldiers stand guard over Tucker, including Tucker's brother, DJ. He must have opted out of coming with my team in order to protect his brother.

"No one but the medics can come in our out," I order to DJ.

"Yes, sir," he answers.

"If anything seems out of the ordinary, take Tucker down to the quarantine and keep him there until you are told otherwise."

"Will do, sir," he says as he looks behind me.

I follow his gaze to Quinn. She has a bag slung from her shoulder and searches the medic area for things to pack.

"What are you doing?" I ask.

"Coming with you," she states.

"Quinn—"

She holds her finger in the air as if to shush me. "Stop. I got your notes, and I have passed them on to someone I can trust. I am coming with you."

I place my hands in the air, showing her that I'm not protesting. "I was just going to tell you I left you a note in your office, but okay, come."

Her face looks smug, but then she smiles. "You can't be the only one who gets to have any fun."

We head for the stairs and reach the roof in a matter of minutes. As we are boarding our chopper, Slade bursts through the roof doors and approaches us.

"Change of plans. You're going to Alaska."

I look at him with confusion. "What?"

"Royce phoned in, and they know about Henly and where she's been. They don't have much time."

I look over my shoulder at Quinn and then back to Slade. "We don't have enough fuel for the choppers to make it all the way to Alaska."

Slade nods in agreement. He motions for us to look to his left, and we spot a carrier jet landing. I'm surprised he would go to such lengths to get Henly back after I had just proved she had fooled him.

"We're borrowing it from Bowden. Make sure it gets back in one piece!" he shouts as he walks away from us.

I watch as he pulls open the rooftop door, only to be pushed aside by Ana. She walks with authority, outfitted in gear meant only for rescue missions. *No way in hell is she coming with us.*

"Ana, what are you doing?"

She walks past me and toward the carrier, completely ignoring me.

"Ana, what are you doing?" Quinn repeats my question.

"I'm going after my daughter."

I stop, taken aback by her words. "What's in Alaska that you need?"

"Henly is. I can't configure the serum without her blood, so I'm going to get her."

There it is—the real reason why she is going after Henly.

"I have to figure out how to fix this before they relocate Davis.

I'm about to protest, but Quinn interjects. "Fine, maybe you'll actually help her this time." Her voice is direct, but not harsh. She is being honest.

I look at Ana, and before I can stop myself, I say, "All right, in and out. Sawyer and my father."

Her lips curl into a grin. "Excited to reunite with your father?" She pauses to take a step closer. "I wonder if he's thought about you once since you've been apart." She looks at me with judging eyes, a smirk lingering on her lips. "The lack of contact speaks volumes, don't you think?" She turns away from me and walks toward the jet. "At least he never mentioned anything to me."

I feel the veins in my neck pulse and my fingers clench into fists. Part of me feels angry, but the other part of me feels sick hearing her tell me a truth from which I have been trying to hide. I feel a mixture of shame and embarrassment, something I can't control. I didn't want to think that my father didn't want to find me, to reconcile. But now, said aloud, the truth sinks in more. She is right. He could have tried to make contact with me, but he didn't. I can see now why Henly lost it when she finally saw Ana again. Ana evokes anger. There's something about her that makes you want to hurt her as bad as she has hurt you. Though, I have yet to see that happen.

"Don't let it get to you," Quinn says.

"She's right." I look at Quinn and shrug. "One thing we can always count on is her honesty. We might as well get used to it."

Quinn shakes her head. "Maybe, but she has nothing to show for it except for two sick children, one of whom is dying."

My eyes widen. *Davis is dying?*

"Renner, let's go!" Johnson calls my attention before I have time to ask about Davis.

CHAPTER 27

HENLY

He knows, and it won't be long before he wakes up. I run through the first level, looking for Royce, but I can't find her. I feel my pulse strum louder and louder with every room I find empty. *Where is she?* I'm about to open the last door when the alarm blares. *That's it. That's all the time we have left.*

"Royce!" I shout her name as loudly as I can.

Her head pops out of the corner office. "Is that because of you?" she asks as she shoves papers into a briefcase.

I shrug my shoulders and smile. "The both of us. He knows that you've been killing the test subjects who adapt."

She stops in her tracks. "Did you dispose of the body so he can't test it?"

I shake my head. "No, I'll go do that. You need to meet Vaughn and Dex on the roof. I'll meet you there after I'm done."

"I called Slade." She turns to me and continues, "They're on their way. They'll land on the east side of the mountain."

"If I'm not there, just go, but make sure Dex gets on the plane."

She quickly gives me a hug. I'm not sure how to react. This is the most normal interaction I have had in days. I try not to overthink it and decide to embrace her back.

"I'll meet you at the plane, Henly," Royce says.

We part ways, and I head back to the lab.

The alarms are still blaring when I make it back to Liam. I push through the door and lock it behind me. His body lies lifeless on the table across the room. *He was so young, and because of me, his life is over.* I make my way over to him.

"I was supposed to save you, help you, but that's not what I do anymore. I haven't done that in a long time. I'm sorry for what I did, and I'm sorry for what I'm about to do," I whisper to him.

I look around the room and search for a way to get rid of his body. The only thing I can think to do is to burn it. I can't let my father have even the smallest bit of him. I walk to the storage cabinet and find bottles of ethanol and a box of matches. I walk back over to Liam and pour the alcohol all over him, saturating the sheet beneath him. I swipe a match and watch it burn almost to my fingertips before I throw it on him. The flames dance in hues of blue and orange as they attack his clothing. I stare at his body, and I realize I could stay here and perish with him. I too could become a lost experiment.

A noise takes my gaze to the window. As I stare out of it, the blue sky and the sprouting green trees calm me. I can't help but indulge in the idea of staying here with Liam. Davis would move on with the help of Dex. Renner would find some girl in the quarantine, someone who he could grow old with; they would have a family, a normal life. Vaughn would finally be free of this place and could explore the world. He and Royce would probably take on the next big research discovery, finding a cure. They would follow each other everywhere; they are a family after all. In the end, everyone would move on. They would be better off without me. *But what if my enhancements restrict me from dying? What if the fire merely scars my body, but isn't enough to kill me.* I can smell the fumes filling the room. I can hear someone pounding on the door. *I don't know what to do, but if by doing nothing, am I making my decision? Am I really going to do this?*

I keep my focus on the blue sky in front of me, searching for my answer, and then, there he is. Renner's eyes pierce through the window, and I gasp. Squeezing my eyes shut, I rub them with both hands. *He isn't here. My eyes are playing tricks on me.* But when I open my eyes again, he is still there. I can see him yelling something at me, and I realize I can't stay. I don't want to stay. I turn and say my goodbye to Liam and run to the window to unlatch it.

"What are you doing?" Renner demands. His question is loaded with accusations. He looks past me and into the room. He sees the burning body, the locked door, and the smoke filling the room.

I look behind me and then back at him. "I don't know," I whisper.

He pulls me through the window and closes it behind me. He and another soldier grab me by the arms and tries to pull me away. I watch through the window as Ana breaks through the door and into Liam's room. She scoffs at what I have done. *How typical of her to find a way to criticize even the way I dispose of a body.* She looks around and begins breaking the nozzles off the oxygen tanks. She then throws some vials into the flames and runs toward the window, but before she can make it to the latch, the door crashes open again.

"Ana!" the senator shouts.

I feel Renner's grip tighten. I look up at him through the water in my eyes, but he doesn't look at me. He is looking at his father, and I now see the similarities. They share the same dark hair and the same piercing eyes, though the senator's are a darker brown.

"Where is she?" My father comes barreling through the door behind the senator. His voice is angry, and his head is wrapped in gauze.

Ana laughs. "I see our daughter happened to you."

"Enough! Where is she?"

I watch as the senator looks up and spots me, or maybe he spots Renner because he freezes.

"Anson?" The senator says his son's name in shock. He shakes his head for a moment, but then walks away.

"It is going to blow any minute," I whisper.

"Ana!" Renner shouts. "Time to go."

I try to stand, but I can't tear my eyes away from my dad. He is beyond angry with me. He is angry at what I have done. I begin to panic. I feel myself become a child again, and all I want to do is hide. I want to hide from his anger, his disappointment. I turn away and bury my face into Renner's shoulder. Without hesitation, he wraps his arms around me and brings me to my feet. But then, I hear it—him.

"Henly, we made a deal, and you broke it! I said I'd try to save you!" he shouts.

I push Renner off of me and stare at my father across the room through the glass that separates us.

"I'm going to take everything from you and—" he starts to say.

"You will take nothing from my daughter, and soon you will have nothing," Ana interjects as she steps through the window and latches it behind her. There is a hint of happiness in her voice. She smiles and waves him one last farewell as she yells through the window, "Goodbye, Andrew! It was never fun!"

My dad narrows his eyes, and then I can see the true meaning of her words register on his face as the whole room erupts in smoke and flames. I can't bear to watch.

We make our way up the hill to where the chopper is waiting on the roof. I climb aboard, and instantly, I'm exhausted. My mind feels cloudy from the smoke, and I can't shake what I have just done, what I have just witnessed. I feel dizzy.

Within seconds, we are in the air. My eyes blur, and my head is heavy. A part of me still wishes I had stayed and burned in the explosion. If I had, there would not be any more threats to those I love. There would only be peace. I close my eyes and try to picture that world.

* * *

I wake with a startle when I hear a door being opened. I look around the room and find I'm back in Aurora. I lie still as Quinn checks my monitors and records my stats. I follow her gaze to the monitor that shows the unsteady beats of my heart. I notice her eyes are red as if she has been crying.

"What happened?" I whisper.

She looks over her files at me, but doesn't say a word. She just stares at me with a blank expression. Her eyes well up with tears, and I lose count of them as they fall down her cheeks. She takes a minute to compose herself, but still doesn't speak. I don't know whether to push for an answer or to console her. I try to sit up, but my arms give out. I'm exhausted. I take a deep breath and summon every ounce of energy within me to sit up. When I finally do, I look to Quinn for answers, but still, she is silent. Instead, she shifts her eyes to the door as Renner walks in. His face bears an unfamiliar look. His whole body hardens as he locks eyes with me.

"Quinn, I need a moment with Henly," he says. His voice is heavy and low.

Before she leaves, she turns back to take one more look at me. Her eyes pierce into mine, and I can't keep her gaze. I look away to the ground. *Why are they so angry with me? I left to help everyone here.*

"I'm sorr—" I try, but Renner doesn't let me finish.

"Do you know where your father would go if Alaska were not an option anymore?" he questions vaguely.

I shake my head. "There are some facilities we have heard about, but Royce should know more. The senator"—saying his name reminds me I never told Renner his father could still be alive, and now he knows I withheld that—"I mean, your dad has taken her to a variety of facilities." His body flinches at the word "dad."

"By the way, you should know Vaughn was injured while trying to get Dex."

"Is he okay? Where is he? Why didn't you tell me sooner?"

"Henly, stop," Renner demands. "He couldn't get to Dex. Your dad has him."

"What? No, what do you mean my dad has him? How's that even possible? You saw that fire. Dex was supposed to be with Vaughn. How did you let this happen?"

"*I* let this happen?" His voice is loud.

I close my eyes and try to calm down. "How did this happen? How is my dad still alive?"

"I don't know. He is a Sawyer, Henly. He can survive anything."

My father's words echo in my mind: *I'm going to take everything from you.* I feel it in my gut—the nausea that comes with the truth. I gag on knowing what my father will do to him. I can't let him hurt Dex the way he hurt me. *No, what if he hurts him worse than how he hurt me?* I realize Quinn's tears were for Dex. I stare at Renner who stands a few feet away from me, judging me and hating me for leaving him behind. I suddenly feel a force within me wake. I swing my feet around my bed and stand. I will not let him torture Dex.

"How long has he had him?" I force myself to

ask the question. "Has it been days? Weeks?"

"Two days," he replies.

"And you haven't gone looking for him?" I shout. "What the hell have you been doing?"

Renner's arms stiffen at his sides. "What do you think I've been doing while you have been asleep?" he demands. "I went back for him, but he was already gone. Your dad took him, and I need you to tell me where."

The harshness in his voice makes me take a few steps back. "I don't know," I reply flatly. "I never went to the other facilities, just the rallies."

"Right, where you would pick and choose people for surgery."

I look up in shock. "Yes," I say, feeling ashamed. "Then, I would fly home with them and experiment on them. I would do whatever I could to break them! Is that what you wanted to hear?" I say the words, and as they flee from me, they take all the energy out of me. I lose focus of the room and feel the ground beneath me shake. I lean back against the bed and grab onto it to secure myself. Renner doesn't move. He stares, analyzing me, waiting for me to tell him something I can't. "Sometimes they would fly the people in, but I never went to the other facilities." I feel the corner of my lip tug into a frown as the tears in my eyes become too much to contain. This is horrible. This type of regret and loss is a whole new thing. I may have lost Renner, but I still have a chance to find Dex. "Ask Royce. She'll know."

"I already did. I just wanted to make sure you didn't know anything."

I swallow his words. He says them as if trusting me were something impossible for him to do. I don't bother to offer my assistance because I know he won't take it. He won't have anything to do with me now. I look up at him through aqueous eyes.

"Davis will never forgive me..." I whisper.

Renner shakes his head. "No, she never will."

"Renner," I plead, and for the first time today, I see his eyes soften. "I have to go back. I have to save him from my dad. I have to save my best—" I choke on my words.

He stares at me and nods. He looks like he is about to say something, but an ear piercing howl roars and emergency lights flash red across the room. Renner's eyes remain on me. The sirens increase as the lights begin flashing more quickly. I cover my ears. The door flies open, and Vaughn and Johnson are shouting something I can't make out. The noise is too deafening, but then it stops. The only thing I hear now is Johnson and Renner's frantic conversation.

"How long?" Renner asks Johnson.

"What is happening?" I question, but neither of them answers me.

"Henly," Vaughn calls to me.

I push past Johnson and Renner and make my way into the hallway to meet Vaughn. He is banged up badly. His right arm hangs in a sling, and half his face is covered in gauze. I pull him toward me and keep him in an embrace. He hugs me with one arm, but then pushes me away.

"He's here." Vaughn's voice is full of worry.

"What?" I ask. *My father can't be here. He said he didn't know where the quarantines are.* My side tingles, and it finally sinks in—the surgery. *He put something in me. He's tracking me. He really is going to take everything from me.* I look back up to Vaughn in horror. "He tracked me! During my surgery, h-h-he—it is in my side! You need to cut it out! Cut it out! Now!"

I grab his arm, and he flinches. I turn to Renner. "You need to cut it out!"

"They're already here, Henly. There's no point," Renner says, his expression cold and clear.

He blames me. I set my jaw and push past him. If they aren't going to do it, then I will. I grab a scalpel from a cabinet in the far corner. I pull my gown aside and find the incision.

"Henly, stop!" Renner shouts.

"No! If you're not going to do it, then I will!" I shout at both him and Vaughn.

Without thinking too much, I push the blade against my skin and feel the scorching burn that erupts from my side. I lose sight of what I'm doing as my breath waivers. As soon as the stitches are gone, I set down the scalpel and brace myself against the wall with one arm. I look up at Renner, whose jaw is tightening into a hard line, but he steps closer to me.

"Johnson and Vaughn, grab her arm and make sure she doesn't fall," Renner says.

I let out a breath and brace myself against the two men. "It's close to my hip."

"How do you know?" Renner asks.

"I can feel it. It gives off a slight drumming. Hurry, *please*." I grit my teeth.

His features soften for a brief moment, but he

collects himself as he jams half of his hand into my incision. I try not to scream, but the pain is too much. Every second he continues to search, I lose sight of where I am more and more. It seems like it has been years when he finally yanks something free from my body. I feel Vaughn wipe a bit of sweat from my forehead as he helps me stand.

"We got to go, Renner. We're needed up top," Johnson announces, bringing me back to the present.

Renner throws the tracker to the ground and lifts his foot to smash it.

"Wait!" I pant, trying to regain my composure. "Use it. Have one of your men take it to Adam. We can use it to lure my dad away so we can ambush him," I say.

Vaughn steps forward to pick up the tracker from the ground and hands it to Renner. Without another word, Renner leaves.

I turn to Vaughn. "Take me to Ana."

He finds a wheelchair for me to sit in, and with one arm, he runs me down the hallway. He screams for Ana as we enter her office. Ana looks at me bewildered and confused.

"I need your help," I say. The words taste

bitter, but I say them anyway.

She nods. "What?" Her voice isn't as harsh as before.

"I need adrenaline. He's here, and he'll kill everyone."

Ana nods and turns to the shelf behind her. She inserts a syringe into a vial and pulls back the fluid. "When this runs its course on you, it may kill you," she states.

"I know," I say, exhaling.

"What? Henly, no," Vaughn interjects.

I turn to Vaughn. "I'm dying anyway. At least this way, I can do some good while I'm here."

He takes a step back. His eyes are wide. "You didn't find a cure?" he says to Ana.

She shakes her head. "Not yet."

"Then do it," he says.

Ana finds a vein in my arm and sinks the needle into me. Almost instantly, I feel like myself again—not my normal self, but my mutated self. I stand and am reminded of the sting in my side.

"Can you patch this?"

Quickly, she grabs gauze and some tape. She places the gauze over the incision and tapes it around my body.

"This will do for now. You won't even be able to feel it soon. Take these." She hands me two sets of pistols. "Stay armed."

I take them and hand two to Vaughn, keeping the other two for myself. I turn to leave, but linger by the door. "Tell Davis I'm sorry."

"I will not. You can tell her yourself."

I swallow hard and run down the narrow path. I can feel Vaughn on my heels.

"That was some Grade A mother-daughter time."

I look over my shoulder and laugh. He always knows how to make light of things.

"So, where are they?" he asks when we get to an elevator.

"Quarantine. That's where Tucker is, right?" I ask, but I already know the answer. He's the first person they would move down there. They probably thought he would be safe there, but he's not.

We take the elevator down to the Ave 6. It is the last level before the quarantines. When the doors open, it is chaos. Deviations run among screaming people. *They are already down here. They must have released the deviations.* I can't stop. I have to make sure my dad doesn't take Tucker, and more importantly, I need to end this. I need to kill my dad. Vaughn grabs my arm.

"They're gathering more test subjects!" he exclaims, his voice in disgust.

"I can't stop," I say to him.

"Go. I can't leave them to die."

I nod and race to the door that leads to the stairs below. The keypad that locks everything from here down is broken. I open the door and hurry down the stairs, until I'm outside the quarantine door. Before walking in, I ready my pistol, letting my finger hover over the trigger. I slowly push open the door. All the rooms are empty. I look down the hall both ways, but I find nothing. *They already took him.*

Then, I hear my father's voice. It carries down the corridor and leads me to the underground exit. I climb the back stairs and burst through the door, meeting the sunlight for the first time in days. It nearly blinds me, but I see my father as he begins to get into a Humvee.

"Dad!" I shout.

He turns and eyes me, but he doesn't run away.

He just smiles at me. "You can still come back with me, kiddo!" he yells.

I shake my head. "You're not going anywhere with him!" I yell to the men who load an unconscious Tucker into the vehicle.

My father laughs before he speaks. "You don't have a choice."

I raise my gun, ready to take the shot that will end his life, end his relentless torture. This moment takes me back to my simulation, the one where I found it so easy to kill Ana. But here I stand, face-to-face with the monster who has infected my entire world, and I hesitate. He is the one who has taken everything from me. It is only fitting that I be the one who takes everything from him.

"I will kill you if you move."

His back suddenly straightens. "It isn't that easy, is it?"

I follow his gaze to the senator. My heart falls when I see Dex barely conscious. The senator hands him to a pair of soldiers who carry him to my father.

"Let him go!" I demand.

"Oh no, kiddo. I made you a deal, and you broke it, and since I can no longer trust you..." he eludes as he points to Dex.

I shake my head violently. "You and I both know you need me." I pause, but decide to let the final piece fall. "I know what you're missing."

His taunting demeanor changes, and he becomes more serious. "You're bluffing."

"The last boy—I know what was different!" I say, the tears brimming my eyes. *I hate that I'm crying.*

"You're just lying to save him."

I shake my head. "Turns out Mom was right. I'm more like you. I can't help myself," I say with disgust.

"Tell me," he demands.

"No, not until you let go of Dex!"

My dad nods to another pair of soldiers, but before they have a chance to let him go, a loud boom shakes the ground beneath us. I look up at my dad. His eyes are furious, and he holds a needle in his hand.

"Dad, don't! Please!" I beg.

"See, kiddo, I don't need you to tell me because I'll find out with that boy," he says as he points over his shoulder.

"You need me!" I insist. "Dad!"

I look at Dex, and his eyes slowly open. His

brown eyes look darker, almost black, void of any and all emotion. *What has he done to him?* I feel my body break in more ways than I thought possible. My eyes narrow, and my hand clenches my gun tighter, aiming right for my father's head.

"I don't need you, not anymore," he sneers. He sinks the needle into Dex's neck. "A lesson for you. Remember, you're not above me! I told you I would take everything from you, and this is only the beginning, kiddo."

"No!" I shout.

He presses the liquid into his neck. Dex falls from my father's grasp to the ground. Without hesitation, I pull the trigger, but as the bullet races toward my dad, a soldier steps in front of him and takes it. I do this three more times, but each time I pull the trigger, I kill a different soldier. I keep shooting until the bullets in my first gun run out. I watch as my father runs toward the Humvee, the soldiers shielding him. Throwing my gun down, I take off in a dead sprint for him. A swarm of soldiers surround me. There are too many. I pull the second gun from behind me and land six execution shots, but by the time I'm finished with them, my father is already making his way down the road. I see his hand give me a salute from the truck window. I raise my gun, knowing I have only one chance left, and pull the trigger. I watch as it hits him in his upper arm. I'm more than ninety percent sure that I hit him just right so at least he will never be able to do surgery again.

"Henly…"

A lesson. His words echo. I hear Dex call me once more, but I can't turn to face him. I'm a coward. He calls for me again, but this time I can't ignore him. I turn to him and squeeze my eyes shut. *I can't do this.* He is in pain, yet still his voice is trying to calm me. *Me?* I finally open my eyes and walk toward him. I'm afraid of seeing him change—of what this means. It means I have failed again, and he is going to die.

"Dex…" My voice is pained and panicked.

"Hen…" he trails off. "It's okay."

"I'm sorry." I sob. "I have to get you to Ana."

He grits his teeth as his hands shake. "There isn't any time. I feel it. It's working."

I shake my head. "No, you have some time. It isn't that fast."

His hands find mine. "It is. I'm going to turn."

The fear in his voice hits me so hard that I

can't speak. I squeeze my eyes shut and lose my breath.

"Don't let me turn," he pleads, his voice quaking. "Don't let him control me to hurt you."

I shake my head, realizing what he is asking. "No! I won't. Ana can save you. She *will* save you. We just have to get you there," I say through my heartbreak.

"There's no cure," he whispers.

"Not yet, but I promise…I'll fix this," I try to convince him, but I feel deep down that I'm trying to convince myself.

"I don't want to be in those cells dying. That's no way to live!" he cries. I try to wipe the streams that fall from his eyes, but they just keep coming. "Please." His voice shakes.

"I can't. I won't. Anyone but you. Please, don't go, Dex. Please, stay with me. Please! I can't do this without you. Please," I whisper.

He looks up at the sky, his body shaking. "It is okay, Henly, really. I have family to see."

The fear behind his eyes makes me shudder even more. I can't save him. Every part of me feels like it's breaking into tiny sharp little fragments. The more I try to grab them, to piece together what is happening, the more they break and cut me. There's nothing I can do—no enhancements, fighting—nothing. Nothing I do can save him. What a helpless feeling to have no power of saving someone you love.

"But *I'm* your family," I whisper, my forehead pressing to his. "Don't go. Please, you're all I have."

"I know, and we'll see each other again," he whispers against my forehead, his lips quivering every time he speaks. "Tell Davis to keep fighting. You keep fighting." He pauses to look at me. "Please, just don't let me become a deviation."

I don't speak. I just nod in agreement.

His body goes completely still, and I shake him vigorously. "Dex! No! Please, wake up! You can't leave me! Please!"

But he doesn't wake up. I did this—I let him die. I pull away from him, staring at him in disbelief. I wait to see him change, but a part of me hopes he won't, that he will just pass on. Eternity seems to go by, but he is still motionless. *How can time be going this slow?* I turn away from him and let myself go. I scream, but find no relief. I raise my fist to punch the ground, but stop when I hear a low growl behind me. I turn back to see him ready to attack me.

"Dex!" I shout, but he is gone. "Dex! Dex!

Dex, it's me, Henly! Come on, Dex!" I say over and over again, trying to reason with him.

I give up. The tears blur my vision as he lunges at me. He throws me to the ground, his fingers closing around my neck. I stare into his vacant, brown eyes that used to hold so much more than the life my father has now given him. My hands find his, but his fingers tighten like a vise. Quickly, I feel the air burn out of me as I try to breath. I remember what Dex had said to me and repeat it over and over again in my mind: *Don't stop fighting.*

"I'm sorry," I force out.

I bring up my legs and kick him off, but it doesn't derail him for long.

"You will die, kiddo," Dex says.

For a moment, I'm taken aback. *He spoke. Deviations have never spoken before.* Dex's voice is dark and deep, and it sounds like something my father would say. *He's the only one who calls me "kiddo."*

Before I have time to think anymore, I launch myself at him and pin him to the ground. My eyes close as I bash his head against the pavement. I bash until he stops moving.

I kill him.

I push away from him and see the blood that streaks my hands. I fall to the ground and stare at my hands. *What have I done?* My hands are shaking and the world seems faded—darker. I turn over and gasp at what remains of Dex. My eyes widen in horror, and the air escapes my lungs. I get on my hands and knees and crawl to him. My hands clench his shirt and shake his body as if he could wake, but I made that impossible for him. The air around me is thin and nothing seems to be in focus, except his dead body that lies before me.

"I'm sorry, Dex. Please, I'm so sorry. I...I..." I can't finish. The cries gobble up my words, and all I can do is scream.

I'm a monster.

I lay my head on his chest and close my eyes, hoping I'll wake and all of this will only have been a dream, but I don't, and it isn't. I don't know how much time has passed when I feel a pair of arms tug at me. I look up and see faces all around me.

Renner kneels next to me. "Henly, he's gone."

"I did it," I say between cries.

Renner moves away from me, and I feel the rest of them follow suit.

"Oh, no," Vaughn whispers as he walks out

onto the pavement. "Henly, what did you do?"

Renner takes a few steps closer, his fingers wrapping around my arms. "He's gone."

"I know!" I shout. I wipe my eyes, but the tears keep falling beyond my control. "I did..." My voice fails me.

Renner pries me away from Dex and squares my shoulders to his. "Look at me. We have to go."

"No." I narrow my eyes at him. "I'm not leaving him again." I push him off of me.

"You already did," he says, which brings about a whole new wave of emotions.

"I didn't mean...I didn't want this." I babble at Renner.

"I'll take him," Vaughn says, looking at me.

"No!" I scream, "Don't touch him!"

Vaughn touches my arm, comforting me. "I'll make sure to get him cleaned up. Go."

Renner nods to him and grabs me by the hand to lead the way, but I pull my hand free. His jaw hardens, and he turns away from me. I follow his pace as we head back inside. By the time we get to the boardroom, my face is soaked. I try to clean my hands, wiping them on my jeans, but they're too stained and the red remains.

"Hey," he whispers, pulling me toward him. "You need to pull it together."

The harshness of his voice catches me off guard. I glare at him. "I need to pull it together," I say through gritted teeth. "Where's your dad?" I pull away from him and walk through the door.

"Sawyer. Renner," Royce announces.

I don't respond. I take a seat next to Ana because I know she won't ask me what is wrong or what I have done to merit the amount of blood on my hands. The image of Dex's lifeless body makes me cringe, and the tears erupt all over again. I try to hide it, but they fall too quickly. I flinch when I feel Renner's hand take my hand. I look up, and he mouths, "Sorry." The fresh tears fall steady from his eyes. He was Dex's friend too. I look away before I can feel his disappointment.

"We have been infiltrated. Davis was flown to a secret quarantine in the south, and Slade was killed during the attack. I'll take point," Royce says as she scans the crowd. She then gestures to me.

My eyes widen, and I swallow hard. I can't speak. "I did it. I killed him" plays on repeat in my mind. But if I say that, they will think I killed my father, not my best friend. I stand, swallowing it all away and try to say something other than what I feel.

"They found us through a tracker they put in me during surgery." I say flatly.

"I pulled the tracker out. Henly had no idea until it was too late," Renner adds in my defense.

I look up at Royce, water still falling from my eyes. "They have Tucker."

Royce presses her lips into a straight line, but after a few seconds, she speaks, "I know."

"I put the tracker on Tucker before they clocked me," Adam says, his voice serious. "I knew they would take him, so I made sure we would be able to find him. Renner's men are tracking him."

"Why do they want Tucker?" a voice in the crowd questions.

"He was like Henly—better than Henly actually," Hill speaks. I look for him in the crowd and find him sitting at the edge of the table. "He's not dying like Henly. He's different. He's what her father has been looking for."

"What?" Renner asks, looking at me now.

"I'm a failed experiment," I announce to everyone in the room, but mostly to him.

"You're dying?" He squares his shoulders to mine.

"Yes," Ana answers for me.

"Why didn't you say something to me? First my father and now this? What else are you keeping from me?" Renner asks, but only loud enough for me to hear. His jaw tightens as he slowly unclasps his hands from mine. I steal one last glance at him before the tears blur him from my vision. For a moment I could almost swear he had tears of his own. I could fall apart if I let myself, but now I'm forcing whatever I have left to go numb. I don't want to feel this—this aching pain that reaches into my soul, crushing me.

Hill continues, "They also took all of our Ave 1 and 2 residents."

I turn from Hill's gaze and stare at my mom, but she already knows what my father is doing. "He needs more test subjects, doesn't he?" I say. I don't know why I'm so shocked. This makes sense. He was running low on test subjects when I was there. I flinch at my thoughts; they sound just like his.

"So what now?" someone shouts.

The murmurs grow. I know what everyone else wants to hear, and I know I'm the only one who can say it. I may be dying, but before I am gone, I will make sure he is dead.

"I kill him," I say as I stand. "I find him, and then I kill him."

END OF BOOK II

ACKNOWLEDGMENTS

I just want to give a quick thanks to anyone and everyone who has read my first novel, *Deviations*. It's absolutely amazing when someone approaches me and asks me about the characters. *What is happening to Henly? Will Renner ever find her?* And the usual complaint, *the ending—why? How? It was the worst!* Even as I sit and laugh about your frustrations with my ending, it was truly my favorite part to write. And if you're reading this now, it means that you took a gamble on my second book—thank you! It is truly a humbling experience to know that my characters are liked and thought about.

A huge thank you to Anna Houghton and Lindsay Pagni, my two editors at Polished it. Thanks to their amazing edits and advice, I was able to overcome a lot of my own personal anxieties about finishing *Creations*. Even now, with new ideas and concepts coming into view, I am grateful to know that these two ladies at Polished it are more than an editing service—they're family. It's relieving to know that I can always count on them.

Thank you to my family and friends, Barrett, Cash, Jenni, Mom, Dad, Jessica, Abby, and so many others. Some I talk to daily, others I talk to occasionally, but it never matters because when I need them, they're ready to talk plot or hear me vent. These people have supported me and pushed me forward in all of my goals, professionally and personally. I'd be lost without them.

Finally, I want to thank the big guy upstairs, the one who often tells me I can do this, but in all reality, I know I couldn't without Him. Thank you for putting those hard trials in my way and blessing me with the good times in between. I am grateful for all the people you've placed in my path who have helped me achieve my goals today. Words cannot express how grateful I am for your ability to know what I need when I didn't even know it myself.

ABOUT THE AUTHOR

Crystal C. Johnson was born in a small town in Nevada where she found her love for stories. After she graduated from Brigham Young University-Idaho with a bachelor's in political science, she discovered her true passion for storytelling.

Her hobbies include breakfast, lunch, and dinner, but she entertains snacking as well. On any average day, her goal is to walk about a hundred steps; any more than that and, well, she'd be exhausted. Just kidding, she usually averages about two hundred steps a day—or does she? When she's not walking or eating, her favorite place in the whole world is being snug in her bed with a book.

She currently resides in Calgary with her husband and son where she is a part-time videographer and author. You can visit her online at crystalcervantesjohnson.com.

Thank you for reading *Creations*. If you enjoyed it, please take a moment to leave a review at your favorite retailer.

Be KIND!

Also, eat tacos! Because, why not!?

Made in the USA
Charleston, SC
09 March 2017